ROBERT HILFINGER

VICTOR

ISBN: 978-1-66780-194-0 (print)
ISBN: 978-1-66780-195-7 (eBook)

I dedicate this book to my wife, Maureen.

Section I

Chapter 1

Victor Drueding loved helicopters.

He considered himself one of the best helicopter mechanics in the country. This could not be verified, but he assumed it was true. Who could possibly be better?

Drueding was also an excellent helicopter pilot. He test-piloted all the choppers he worked on and would turn over to the owners, a safe and well-tuned machine. Often, he would wake up having dreamt of flying one of the many makes and models he had worked on over the years.

His real-life dream was that one day he would own one of these magnificent machines. But realistically, he knew he never would. His small paycheck barely paid the bills.

Far short of owning a helicopter, he counted himself lucky, when from time to time, he was able to buy an old shit box of a car. He and his wife, Peggy, would drive the car until its inevitable seizure and death. Then he would shop around for another shit box of a car.

At the age of thirty-six years, Victor considered himself a loser. A loser who was good with helicopters. At times, he thought it may have been better if he had been a good son, or a good husband, or possibly a good father. But in truth, he was none of these.

But he was a good chopper pilot.

As a youngster, Victor learned about helicopters by hanging around Whitman Field, the small airport that employed his father. His dad was Whitman's handyman, helicopter maintenance man, and janitor. It was a low-paying job, but it was at least a job. Victor's mother worked at the local Walmart, and between the two paychecks, the family was able to scrape by. Barely.

Victor would go to school from time to time, where he almost always found a reason to fight another student, or a teacher; it made no difference to him. From the womb, he was always bigger and stronger than anyone his own age, and when he reached the age of thirteen years, he was bigger and stronger than anyone in town.

When the boy did attend school, he was a terrible student, refusing to pay attention or engage in any meaningful way.

Homework was out of the question, and he generally just hated to read. However, under his shoddy bed could be found innumerable helicopter manuals, magazines, and his own personal journals covering the work that he had performed at the tiny airport.

Life was hard on young Victor. A life he did not enjoy. Except when he was helping his father tune a helicopter. It was the one thing in his world with which he was totally at peace. And fortunately, for the young boy, chopper repair work was frequently required at the little regional airport.

From his father's first lesson in helicopter maintenance, Victor caught on. He would listen, absorb, and apply the imparted knowledge properly and appropriately. His dad instructed him on the machine itself, and the aerodynamics of helicopter flight. Victor interpreted the information correctly and stored the knowledge and imagery securely in his memory bank.

Victor was well liked at Whitman Field, and his work ethic and attention to detail were respected. When he reached his late teens, he was asked to take over his father's job, when his dad died from lung cancer, the result of a four-pack-a-day habit. His mom died a year later. Victor figured she just gave up.

Victor continued his work as a mechanic, and at age twenty-three, in late 1993, married another offspring of a Whitman Field employee. The young couple moved into a small apartment building, one thousand yards from the end of runway number two. Victor and his wife, Peggy, conceived three babies in rapid succession and were well on their way to replicating their parents' lives—struggles and all.

And so their world progressed for a little more than twelve years.

Then, in January 2006, the knock came at their door.

Chapter 2

A knock at the door was usually not a good thing.

It came as Peggy and Victor were sitting at the kitchen table in their small apartment, both having taken the day off. They were reading the local newspaper and, at the same time, discussing the topic of most of their conversations—their children.

Two years prior, they had made the difficult decision to let their three little boys live with Peggy's mother, in Missouri. The boy's grandmother knew of Peg and her husband's financial and other troubles, and she made the offer to take the children.

It had been a heartbreaking decision for Peggy, but, in truth, a relief for her husband. The pressures of life were taking a toll on the big man, and, for the good of their children, Peggy let them go. She spoke to them regularly by phone and was constantly assured by her mother, of her children's well-being.

Peg hoped that she could convince Victor of making a huge life change and move to Missouri as well. They would live with her mother until they got on their feet financially and found their own place. For Victor's part, it was simply too much to process in his fragile state of mind. He had held only one job in his life, at the little airport down the road, and worried about his prospects to find another one, particularly in a strange place. Hell, he had serious doubts there would be any opportunities at all in a little cow town like Centerville, Missouri.

Until now, the morning had been peaceful, but the simple occurrence, like a knock at the door, was enough to send chills up their spines. They were two overly anxious people. Their usual cups of coffee sat in front of them, with coffee stains marking the San Diego Press newspaper, that was haphazardly spread over the table's surface.

Victor reluctantly went to the door.

A tall, skinny man with black hair sporting a dark suit stood before Victor. The man had an oversized smile, full of monstrous teeth, for his relatively petite frame and similarly skinny head. Victor's normal reaction to the infrequent and unwanted occasion someone actually came to the apartment, was to say, "What the hell do you want?"

His instinct today was to say, "What's up with those teeth?" But he squashed the urge to do so. Instead, he simply asked, "Can I help you?"

The man with the big teeth responded, "Actually, I think I can help you. My name is Eriq Steed. Any chance I can come in and talk with you?"

"About what?" Victor's intuitive distrust of all things human never gave way to even a remote notion of common courtesy, and his stern tone made his position known.

"Mr. Drueding, I have a proposition for you. One that may change you and your family's lives in a pretty dramatic way. Before you push me out into the parking lot, I will tell you that I'm talking about money, Mr. Drueding, a lot of money."

"Please come in, Mr. Steed," Peggy's voice was heard over the shoulder of her ever-the-paranoid husband. "You obviously know the magic word to enter our abode…'money'…and 'a lot of money' earns you the right to have a cup of coffee. Black or however?"

"Neither," responded Steed. "I've had my quota this morning. Any more coffee and my head starts to spin." He began to step forward, when he realized Victor had not budged and was fully blocking the doorway and his entrance into the apartment. The skinny man practically tripped.

Steed, upon regaining his balance, found himself staring face to face and into the menacing eyes of Victor Drueding. Then the visitor took a calculated risk of angering the big man in front of him, by saying "Did you happen to hear your wife, Mr. Drueding?" Steed smiled as he said this and, by doing so, drew Victor's total attention to the extraordinarily large pearly whites, framed by the equally odd narrow lips of Mr. Eriq Steed.

With his attention drawn away momentarily from his innate suspicion, Victor physically relented, backed up a step, and motioned for Steed to enter.

Steed did not hesitate and walked briskly past Victor and into the apartment.

Peggy pulled a chair out from the kitchen table and motioned for Steed to sit. He walked directly to the chair and sat down. She pointed toward the coffee pot in an effort to offer him another chance to comply, but he quickly put up his open right hand to suggest "no interest."

"Mr. and Mrs. Drueding, may I call you Victor and Peggy?"

"Be our guest, Eriq, and may we call you Eriq?" Peggy asked with a smile.

Steed flashed his oversized teeth once again and shook his head to the affirmative. As he did so, Victor could not help but feel a sense of distrust in the man. Besides the fact that Victor was never one to suffer fools gladly, smiley-faced people irritated him more than most.

"What's on your mind, Mr. Steed?", Drueding asked with an abruptness in his voice. Victor wanted this visit to be to the point and brief. The only company he could relax with were his wife, his three boys on the rare occasion, and any year, make, or model of an operational helicopter. Not necessarily in that order.

Steed's expression turned serious instantaneously as if he had flicked a facial switch.

"Victor, I'll get to the point. You, sir, have a talent the people I work for need and want. And if you are willing to sell this talent to them for a little less than one year's time, they will reward you handsomely. I guarantee you and your wife would be extremely happy with your remuneration."

"My what?" If anything irritated Victor more than smiley assholes, it was smiley assholes who used three-dollar words that no other idiot on earth would use.

"Your pay, caveman," Peggy interjected. "You have to excuse my husband, Eriq. Neither of us even graduated from high school, but I grew up along the way and found that reading the occasional book wasn't anything to be ashamed of. Unless the words are used in the sports pages of the *San Diego Press* or *Helicopter Aviation* magazine, our buddy here won't know what you're talking about."

"Screw both of you," Victor snapped.

Peggy instantly knew she had pushed the wrong button in front of a stranger and, realizing her mistake, knew her husband's reaction would not be pretty.

Victor continued, "Okay, here's the deal, pal. Tell me in plain English and in short fucking sentences, what you want me to do for exactly how much pay. Then I'll say 'yes' or 'no' and you can get your smiley ass back to your bosses. How's that sound?"

Peggy, who at once felt guilty for what she had said, and sorry for Victor's insult to their guest, looked at Mr. Steed to assess his reaction to her husband's verbal assault. Unexpectedly, she seemed to read into the face of the very thin man, an expression she wasn't expecting... enjoyment. His lips seemed to curl up ever so slightly, but enough to suggest a little macabre delight in her husband's anger.

She then turned toward her husband, who had already put his head down and had slipped into the world only he could inhabit from time to time. A world of self-doubt and anger, born of a lifetime void of self-confidence and joy. Peggy knew that she was responsible, this time, for his present anguish and felt culpable and sad for inflicting the hurt so unnecessarily.

She also knew, from experience, there was nothing she could say now that could help the situation.

"Mr. Steed," she said, "maybe we can talk about this another time."

"No," Victor spoke up, now in a softer, somewhat depressed tone. "Tell us what you came to say and that will be that. Do it quickly."

Chapter 3

Steed wasted no time.

With zero indication that he felt any discomfort or awkwardness, he proceeded as if he and the Druedings were old friends simply catching up.

"I work for a company that manufactures pharmaceutical products; in short, drugs. All the drugs are made in America. Many of the drugs are used every day by millions of people. Lifesaving drugs. You may see them in your medicine cabinet, and you definitely see them advertised on TV. This is a substantial company with a wonderful reputation."

"However?"

"Yes, Mr. Drueding. However. Very perceptive of you."

Peggy began to say something, indicating that she too, thought her husband's remark was insightful. She glanced over at him. His head was now upright, staring into the stranger's face across the table. She thought better of slicing into the atmosphere, that although thick, was at least civil, and she remained silent.

"However, Victor and Peggy, the FDA is an extremely conservative and careful agency, that sometimes translates to the unavailability of new lifesaving drugs for many years. They carefully test and retest, for good and obvious reasons. However, by the time a life-altering, or lifesaving, breakthrough drug becomes available, it is too late for a portion of the population."

"And this is where you come in?" Again, Victor reading ahead of the story.

"Yes, and this is where we come in. It's too difficult to do anything about it in the States, but there's a way to make these drugs available to many other parts of the world. We have a strategy in place to do just that. We intend to make available many of these potentially lifesaving drugs to certain foreign markets. We have a concrete plan, and we have most of the ingredients to implement our plan. But we are missing one critical ingredient...

...and that is why I'm here."

Steed stood up for dramatic effect. He circled around behind his chair and placed both hands on its metal backrest. Leaning somewhat forward, he looked intently at the couple across from him.

"A small group of concerned employees from our company are in strategic positions to collect, unnoticed, significant quantities of lifesaving drugs that are in various stages of testing. We have a network of clandestine distribution throughout Mexico, Central and parts of South America. Our central collection location is in Northwestern Mexico, on the outskirts of Tijuana. Everything is in place, with one exception."

Steed sized up the expressions across the table, seemed to be content with their level of attention, and continued.

"The one ingredient missing is the delivery system from our side of the Mexican border to the other. Then, a couple of months ago, we came up with what we think is the perfect solution. We have built a secure installation south of San Diego, where we currently keep a refurbished Alouette helicopter. Our plan is to periodically load the helicopter with these incredibly valuable drugs and fly the craft to a secure location on the northwestern Mexican coast. We will offload the inventory and fly the Alouette back to San Diego."

Steed paused for a moment, turned his focus directly at Victor, and proclaimed, "We need you to fly the helicopter, Mr. Drueding."

Steed peered directly into Drueding's eyes with greater intensity.

"You are the final piece to our strategy, Victor...you are the missing ingredient."

Chapter 4

Eriq Steed strolled into the tenth-floor corner office of a company named Community Betterment.

The company could have been named anything really, because Community Betterment was a ruse. It neither did own anything nor did it produce anything. It certainly didn't serve any community.

It did rent a handful of apartment units throughout the greater San Diego area.

One or two of the units were subleased from time to time, but often all five of them sat empty. They were really there for show, as evidence of a legitimate business…or in the event a safe house was needed.

Very few individuals knew what Community Betterment was really all about. That was exactly the way they wanted it. They paid their rent timely and made no fuss. The perfect tenant.

Community Betterment did, however, exist for two specific purposes: to provide a fancy address, imprinted on fancier still business cards, and to reflect a name that conveyed social concern.

Eriq Steed strolled into the fancy address.

"Hello, Mr. Steed," bellowed a finely attired middle-aged man.

"Why, hello Mr. Freeport, how are you this lovely morning?"

"I will be right as rain itself if you have good news for me."

"I do indeed, sir. Our friends took the bait; hook, line, and the slippery sinker. We have the last ingredients of our latest plan in place. We've had the couple ready to go, and now we've got the chopper pilot wrapped up. We are, as they say, 'locked and loaded.'"

"I can kind of see how you find the couples, but how the hell do you find naïve helicopter pilots all over the place, my man?"

Steed flashed his artificially white smile. "I find all of them at the 'college of the down and out'. They're just waiting for me. Hell, they are just waiting for anyone to come along and dangle a way out for them. And I love to dangle. The two I corralled yesterday even had a lovers' spat while I was doing my pitch. I'll tell ya, I love my job."

The distinguished-looking Mr. Raymond Freeport, his current alias, walked briskly in a straight line toward Mr. Eriq Steed, another alias, and put out his hand. "Eriq, you do know what this means, don't you?"

"I think I do, sir, but I wouldn't mind hearing you confirm it once again," Steed replied, still smiling.

"And I would love to do so, Mr. Steed. So with your indulgence, I will tell you once again."

As they stood a couple of feet from one another, they had the appearance of two little boys ready to burst apart with happiness.

Mr. Freeport crossed his arms and peered into Eriq Steed's eyes, as if preparing to share rare beads of wisdom. Then, mustering his best effort at speaking with false solemnity, quietly uttered, "If all continues to go well, my dear man, we'll wrap up our business together in ten months, and we will go our separate ways, very rich men. We may never see one another again, but I will always remember you fondly." He struggled not to laugh out loud.

"And I will remember you, sir. Whenever I go flying in my Alouette chopper, I will thank the man who gave it to me," replied Steed.

Mr. Freeport, frustrated with his less intelligent associate's inability to interpret his playfulness, snapped back to reality.

"Eriq, don't worry yourself. I promised that damn thing to you when this was over, and you'll have it. But really friend, you'll have enough dough to buy one yourself, if you felt you needed to."

"But I won't need to."

"No, you won't. Don't sweat it. I'll turn over ownership of the craft in ten months. Frankly, I can't fly it anyway, so why the hell would I want it. And you have such an emotional attachment to it, I couldn't think of a better home for it."

Steed did have an emotional attachment to the sleek and stealthy helicopter. For more reasons than he would ever divulge to Mr. Freeport.

Steed stared at the man who could make his dream of becoming rich and owning this particular helicopter, come true.

"Thank you, sir," he said, with uncharacteristic emotion, as his thin lips slightly quivered. He hugged the distinguished-looking man and then walked out of the office of Community Betterment.

Steed stood in the hallway, as Mr. Freeport shut the office door behind him. As the skinny man gazed down the empty corridor, a wide smile swept over his face. He had, once again, performed convincingly, as the dutiful and appreciative dote, for the benefit of his presumed boss. He wanted Freeport to believe the most important thing in the world to his younger associate was to own the slick and shiny aircraft. Steed knew that as long as Freeport was convinced of this, the older man would not concern himself with other nefarious intentions of the younger man.

Steed caught himself from laughing out loud, as he was only steps away from the office door that had just been closed behind him. He certainly didn't want the older man to hear him laughing out loud in the hallway. But he began to chuckle softly nonetheless. It couldn't be helped.

It cracked Steed up that Freeport could be convinced that a helicopter would be of such importance to his protégé. It irritated Steed that his supposed mentor would believe that Steed would obsess over the likes of a helicopter, even a classic beauty that was the Alouette.

"God," the skinny man thought, "I certainly have higher priorities than owning a piece of metal."

What Eriq Steed did care about was the hidden compartment behind the back seat, on the pilot side of the craft. What Eriq Steed did care about was the cash that he had been accumulating, in a leather briefcase, found within the same compartment.

The secret compartment was better than the most secure bank. And his supposed love of the chopper gave Steed the perfect cover to spend as much time with the helicopter as needed. The time he needed to siphon off cash revenue from the Mexican operation, and other endeavors, and neatly hide away the growing stash. The secret compartment was the perfect example of the expression "hiding in plain sight."

By Steed's accounting, by the end of this year's activities, he would have accumulated more than one million dollars in unnoticed bounty, all deposited in the helicopter. At the end of this year's mission, Freeport would pay Eriq his cut, an amount Steed was sure he would be cheated on. But he would act the obedient dote and fly away in the old, dated whirlybird…with his undeclared and unnoticed bonus.

Steed's total take from the three years of operations would be enough to satisfy the thin man with the abnormally large smile. He'd sell the helicopter at some point to add to his profits.

His life would be nicely financed for the foreseeable future.

Chapter 5

Peg and the three boys took the train to Missouri in early 2004. They moved into her mother's house on the outskirts of the small town of Centerville.

Although the term "outskirts" is a relative one, the "outskirts" in the small town of Centerville really meant that you must add another twenty minutes to your walk, if you were planning on going downtown.

Peg obsessively worried about the three boys when they were under her own roof. She knew she would worry herself sick when they were under her mother's roof, many states away.

Despite that reality, she knew without hesitation, that their boys had a better chance of growing up safely, healthy, and hopefully educated, if they lived with her somewhat-disciplinarian mother. Peg and

Victor agreed that Peg would visit her mom and sons as much as time allowed. She would split her time between San Diego and Missouri, knowing well that her husband needed her presence and support, absolutely as much as her boys did.

For Victor's part, he was so constantly wrought up over the infinite pressures of life, that the boys being away was at least one less daily burden. He loved his sons but did not have the capacity to deal with them…for now at least.

Peg's mode of transportation between San Diego and Centerville was the train, as they could not afford alternative means. They barely could afford the train. The trip was a full day's journey in each direction, and less than comfortable, at that, given the lower-class ticket she traveled on.

At the beginning, she didn't know how it would all work out, but she knew it would be an awkward arrangement at best. She did feel confident that Centerville was a wholesome environment, and that made all the difference to her. What she wasn't so sure about was the wholesomeness of her boys.

Her oldest, Dean, had already been regularly disciplined at the small elementary school he attended in San Diego. How he would act in the all-American surroundings of Centerville, Missouri, was yet to be known. She just prayed he would behave.

Peg was home in San Diego for Victor's maiden excursion from the helipad installation to the Mexican beach. It was mid-February 2006, a beautiful day hovering around seventy degrees and sunny. She sat nervously in the apartment awaiting her husband's return.

She had high hopes that this arrangement Victor was involved in could pay them the income they so desperately needed for the future of their family. That said, she had a pit in her belly ever since Mr. Steed left their apartment. There was so little they knew about the man himself and the whole operation in general.

But they could not help but feel that this was a once in a lifetime opportunity.

Chapter 6

Mid-February 2006

"How did your first day of work go?" Peg inquired, as Victor walked through the apartment door.

"It was the strangest day of my life," Victor replied.

"Then give me the scoop. All of it. Every last detail."

"Well, first I can say that I made two new best friends, Kevin and Elaine."

Peg didn't expect Victor to say anything about making friends as the answer to her question. Victor never cared to make friends. He really didn't have a taste for people in general. Even those he probably should have loved. So, to say he made "two new best friends" as the answer to her question was about as surprising to her as anything he could have said.

She looked at him puzzled for a long moment, then asked, "Who the hell are Kevin and Elaine?"

"They are the mules I fly to Mexico."

"You fly donkeys to Mexico?"

"Yeah, they are the donkeys I fly to Mexico. Then I fly them back to San Diego. They are the donkeys, and I'm the donkey pilot that flies the helicopter."

"You're really not being very specific, Mr. Mule Pilot. Any chance you can tell me plainly what happened today?"

Victor then proceeded to describe some of the day's events to his wife. Other details he left out as he didn't want to worry her.

He had flown the Alouette helicopter from Whitman Field, the small airport down the street from his and Peg's apartment, to a helipad complex in the hills of Otay County, southeast of San Diego.

Victor flew the helicopter low to the ground, "map of the earth," as he did not submit a flight plan. Nor did he have any intention of submitting flight plans for the many months ahead. He was hired for his expertise in flying fast and flying off the radar. Victor Drueding had no problem with this.

Fifteen minutes after departing Whitman Field, the surprisingly large helipad complex came into Victor's view. Built among the desert hills, the installation gave the impression of a very secure and clandestine property. It seemed to Victor to be a scene out of a mystery novel. A novel he was now a part of.

His craft descended toward the landing target in the exact middle of the installation. Victor pulled the chopper around in ever slower, concentric circles, and floated downward to the landing zone.

With the exception of the red circular landing mark, the entire vast floor plan of the inner sanctum was a light, bluish green, shimmering smooth cement surface. The usual swirling dirt, grass, and dust that typically spun up from helicopter rotor blades when landing, was missing. It struck Victor to be an overly sanitized environment and made him wonder about it, but only for a split second. He shook off the thought almost immediately, as he refocused on the landing.

He eased the helicopter down onto the center of the pad, with a familiar precision that always gave Victor a sense of pride that came from a well-executed touch down. Once the bird was stable, he cut the engines.

He sat at the controls for a couple of minutes and looked around the empty, expansive space outside. As he unlatched his shoulder straps, he noticed two figures walking toward the helicopter. He stepped out of the chopper, walked down the few steps leading off the pad and onto the bluish green floor of the complex.

The couple approached him with obvious interest.

"Hello, Sir, my name is Kevin, and this is my wife, Elaine. I guess we are all supposed to be on a 'first name only' basis." Kevin extended his right arm to Victor, for the obligatory handshake.

"Hi," the pilot replied. "My name is Victor." As he spoke, his head swiveled, taking in the panoramic view of the surreal environment he had just landed upon. "This is quite the place. What the hell is it?"

"Don't know. And don't think I want to know. Elaine and I would like to get the next ten months over with, without knowing any more than we have to."

"I know exactly what you mean," Victor agreed, as Elaine stepped into his direct vision, with her arm outstretched as well. "Nice to meet you, Ma'am," Victor said shaking her hand.

As the couple and Victor made idle chitchat, a black Lincoln Town Car pulled up alongside Kevin and Elaine's white Honda CR-V, parked outside the steel-walled enclosure. Behind the darkened, factory-tinted windows of the Lincoln sat three individuals. Willie, the driver, looked to his right and stared for a moment at the profile of the man next to him.

"Do you want us to come with you, boss?" Willie asked the very thin man in the front passenger seat.

"Not today, Willie," Steed replied, continuing to look straight ahead. "I'm just going to give them a quick 'once over' on the plan of action and let them go. I think we've learned that there is no substitution for just letting the day play out, and hope they know what the hell they're doing. Hell, so far, it's worked every time. You and Max stay here. I won't be long."

The short, fat man in the back seat, who went by the name Max, was quiet as a mouse as always.

Steed got out, carrying with him the familiar gray metal briefcase that he had carried on many prior visits to this very same location. As he began to close the car door, he paused, and peered back into the Lincoln. His stern expression turned abruptly into a broad, manufactured smile. A smile, that these men had learned from past experience, was not one of affection, but more of a muted threat.

"Don't go anywhere without me, boys, okay?"

The two men didn't know what he even meant by the instruction. Of course, they weren't going anywhere without him. But they had come to the understanding that whatever came out of Steed's mouth was to be received and translated as they hoped the very thin man intended.

In this instance, both Willie and Max simultaneously interpreted Steed's comment to be that of a flippant joke of some kind. At the same time, they both responded with very forced, muffled laughter.

"Of course we won't, boss," both replied, tripping over each other's words, making for a nervous, contrived sounding response.

Steed stopped smiling and glared at the two men, from one to the other. He slammed the door hard, as if to send an indecipherable message.

Steed hadn't said anything that made sense to either man. Yet, as they sat silently within the confines of the luxurious black automobile, a wave of fear bore through both men.

Victor and his two new associates were making idle conversation when the thin man came into their peripheral vision. All three turned at the same time toward the installation's entrance.

As Steed walked briskly toward them, he flashed his artificial smile. Even given the short time the threesome had spent with Eriq Steed, it was evident to each of them that his smile was the least genuine expression they had ever experienced. But given their circumstances, with the prospect of deriving significant financial benefit from the relationship with this scrawny man, all three responded with varied degrees of cordial reception.

Elaine was the first to speak. "Mr. Steed, it is so nice to see you again."

Steed's smile immediately dissipated. "Miss Elaine, first names only please. It is of upmost importance that you follow my instructions, and you mess up, right out of the gate." He stopped about ten feet from the trio, showing no intention of shaking hands or in any way indicating a sense of relaxed familiarity with the three of them. It was apparent by his behavior, language, and tone that he was conveying the unequivocal message that he was the boss.

If Victor, Kevin, and Elaine had for even a short amount of time begun to relax within the surreal environment they found themselves in, that feeling of relief was quickly gone.

Steed put the metal briefcase down on the ground beside him. Staring directly at Victor, he commenced his presentation.

"Pilot," he began, "We have gone over the route with you. Do not veer from the flight plan one degree. Keep it low to the ground, follow the route, and you'll arrive at the beach in thirty-five minutes. There will be a temporary landing platform set up on the beach. A red dot in the middle of it. You can't miss seeing it. Land there."

Steed's attention turned to the couple.

"You two," he said sternly, not even bothering with mock politeness. "Take this briefcase, and upon arrival at the beach, go with a man called Tomas. He will lead you to a building three minutes from the beach. Go there with him and show your credentials upon your arrival. People there will only accept the validity of this case and its contents, given these credentials. Once you're approved, they will take your briefcase and, in turn, will give you one. Take the briefcase they give you and hustle your ass back to the helicopter."

Again turning to Victor, Steed continued, "You fly this thing," pointing to the Alouette, "as fast as you can back here."

Steed paused for a moment, in what seemed to be for dramatic effect. Then, looking at all three of his underlings, and speaking in a softer, even more nauseating tone, said, "And do this once a month for the next nine months. And your financial reward will last a lifetime."

He shoved the metal briefcase a few feet toward them with the bottom of his right dress shoe. He would not show them the courtesy of handing it to one of them.

As he turned around to leave, he spoke over his shoulder. "I expect to see the three of you back here in no more than two hours from now. Be here. Go." He walked back toward the entrance of the installation.

Victor watched Steed in disbelief, half expecting him to turn around again and possibly say, "I'm kidding." But this did not happen. At the same time, he realized Steed was absolutely serious; Kevin and Elaine had come to the same conclusion. They turned and looked at Victor at the same moment he turned to look at them.

"Let's go," Victor said.

The couple was one step ahead of him, as Kevin had already run over and scooped up the briefcase.

The three of them boarded the helicopter, and in a little over three minutes, the bird lifted off. Within the Alouette sat three quiet and somewhat-stunned soldiers of a skinny man with artificially white teeth.

Chapter 7

Victor kept the aircraft low to the ground and flew a westward track from the installation. Ten minutes from takeoff, they were over water. Five minutes out over the Pacific, he turned southward and maintained a southern course for an additional fifteen minutes.

At thirty-two degrees latitude, the helicopter banked eastward, and the Mexican coastline came into view within minutes. When Victor spotted the lighthouse north of Rosarito Beach, he began scanning the beachfront for the landing area. A red dot on what appeared to be a landing zone came into his line of sight, and he knew the initial phase of their first mission was almost complete.

Kevin and Elaine sat in the seats behind the pilot. The anticipation of this first day on the job was nerve-racking enough, but the scene at the installation added a totally unexpected heightened pitch to their fragile collective psyche. They had already been anxious about the prospect of being caught and arrested for their actions concerning this questionable activity. And now, they were putting themselves at risk in not one, but two countries. They had never even been the slightest offenders of the law, and now they would be major offenders.

If they hadn't felt so boxed in, so lost in their lives, this day would never have come. But it had come, and they were here. Even so, up until moments ago, they had at least felt that the person who had approached them and suggested they become involved would be supportive. They had been convinced by Eriq Steed that this activity, at its core, was a humanitarian effort. The financial by-product was simply a benefit that came so timely for the young couple.

The added ingredient of doubt and fear toward the individuals they were involved with, and everything connected to this activity, weighed heavy upon them. Why would a man such as Steed, who they thought was committed to a humanitarian cause, act so callously toward them, especially at a moment when he must have known they were frightened enough to begin with.

Victor turned his head slightly toward the back seats and announced the beach landing zone was in sight. Kevin and Elaine propped themselves up and tried to obtain the view that the pilot had but were still only able to see the waters of the Pacific through the chopper's side windows.

The craft, flying very low to begin with, began to descend further. Within moments, the shoreline came into the couple's view as well, and all three inhabitants of the helicopter began to ready themselves for landing.

Victor, for his part, prepared the Alouette for a landing maneuver he had executed hundreds of times. Ocean wind and swirling sand would only sharpen his focus to the task, but he knew it would be a relatively standard touchdown, nonetheless.

For Kevin and Elaine's part, the prospect of leaving the relative safety of the helicopter, and accompanying a stranger named Tomas, to God knows where, heightened their paranoia and fear even more. They would both have backed out of this arrangement at this moment in time, if they thought they could. However, they were at the point of no return. They saw a group of men standing on the beach, awaiting their arrival, and backing out, now, was not an option. They would summon up the courage to get through the next moments of their lives and hope for the best.

Within minutes, the chopper was sitting on the portable helipad, and the doors of the helicopter opened.

Chapter 8

Apn
A pproximately forty minutes after their landing on the
beach north of Rosario, Victor and his two companions
lifted off once again, this time for the trip back to the
installation in the San Ysidro Mountains.

Upon takeoff, Kevin and Elaine breathed a large sigh of relief.
They held each other's hands in the back seat of the helicopter, both
thinking to themselves that they had just overcome a very large psychological hurdle.

Forty minutes earlier, upon landing and debarking the aircraft,
the couple, metal briefcase in hand, stood next to the Alouette. They
were met at the temporary helipad by two men, one of whom

introduced himself as Tomas. He was a short man with thick black hair, who spoke fluent English.

The couple were somewhat put at ease by the manner of the fellow, as he was polite, seemed to be in total control of the situation and made it known to them immediately that he knew the value of their time, promising to return them to the chopper in thirty minutes.

Three other men positioned themselves approximately sixty feet from the helicopter at various angles to the craft, setting up what seemed to be a protective perimeter. No guns were evident, but there was no doubt of their presence, visible or not.

Tomas and his companion led the couple off the beach and through a network of narrow, pebbled covered roads, to a small adobe constructed building. They entered through the front wooden doors, that seemed to be so old and worn, as not to offer much of a security, even when closed and locked. It was apparent to Kevin and Elaine that this location was primarily for its proximity to the beach and nothing more.

Two men waited within, sitting along the backside of what appeared to be a mahogany conference table. The men stood up, said hello to each of them, but did not offer to introduce themselves. A similar metal briefcase to the one the couple carried sat atop the conference table.

One of the two men motioned for the couple to sit. The other took the briefcase from Kevin, laid it on the table, and opened it. Tomas and his partner returned outside, presumably to stand guard, although the area they had just walked through seemed quite uninhabited.

The men checked the contents of the case against what seemed to be a paper manifest one of them held. They muttered a few words in Spanish that neither Kevin nor Elaine understood. No more than ten minutes after opening the briefcase, it was closed. One of the men pushed their case toward the seated couple, suggesting their satisfaction with the delivery.

Without any conversation, all four individuals stood up and shook hands. Kevin picked up the other briefcase, and he and Elaine left the small building. As they walked away down the narrow road, it dawned on Elaine that no request had been made to confirm their identities. She began to ask Tomas about this, but thinking back to the scene at the installation, thought better about it. She figured silence was a better alternative than saying the wrong thing.

Once airborne, the three sat quietly for the first portion of the trip, as the helicopter retraced its route. Ten minutes into the flight, Kevin leaned forward, having decided to ask Victor a question he had been itching to ask him on the trip down to the Mexican beach.

"Victor, what do you think about this guy, Steed?" Kevin actually had a plethora of questions to ask the pilot, but assumed simply opening the door with any question would convey where he was going.

"Don't know and don't really care," was the immediate response. "Just here to do a job." Actually, this was not quite the truth. Victor had the same initial concerns about Steed's words and actions earlier that day. He also had fought off his initial instinct to punch the little shit in the mouth, as the big man had never physically felt intimidated by anyone. But this was a job. And Victor would swallow his pride, to a point, to gain the promised reward at the end of the ten-month gig.

He also wasn't about to answer Kevin's question for another reason, one he would not share with the couple. This was Steed's chopper. And listening devices were a dime a dozen.

They landed back in the San Ysidro installation within the time-table Steed had alluded to. As the Alouette settled onto the helipad, Steed and the other two men appeared from the direction of the entranceway.

The three once again departed the aircraft and Kevin handed Steed the briefcase. Steed stepped back a few paces, knelt to the ground, and opened the case. He flipped his fingers through the contents and then closed the case back up.

He stood up, glanced from Victor, to the couple, and back to Victor. Then, to their surprise, he broke into one of his false good-natured smiles and said in as normal a voice as they had ever heard from him, "Good job, guys. Good job."

Steed reached into his inner sport coat pocket and pulled out three envelopes. As he handed each of the three an envelope, he said in an appreciative tone, "Hopefully, this holds you over for the next month. To show our gratitude."

He then turned around, motioned to his associates to follow, and walked toward the entranceway. Twenty feet away, he yelled over his shoulder, "You guys know how to lock up. See you next month. And pilot, take care of my helicopter."

Within a few minutes, Steed and the other two men returned to the Lincoln and drove away.

The remaining three stood silent, focused on the entranceway, once again feeling somewhat dumbfounded.

Then Victor broke the ice. "I should have kept this thing idling," he kiddingly announced, referring to the aircraft. "I didn't know we'd be leaving so quickly."

Victor was the caretaker of the Alouette for the next ten months and was babysitting the helicopter for that period of time. He would be flying it back to Whitman Field, down the street from his apartment. All maintenance and upkeep was in his hands.

"Well, as bad as the day started, I'm feeling a slight bit better," said Elaine, with an uptick of encouragement in her voice. Her husband moved close to her and put his arm around her.

Victor looked at them and was tempted to say, "Just be careful of that piece of shit," but again thought about the low cost of hearing devices. Instead, he gave the two a slight grin, put his right hand up to signify good-bye, and turned toward the chopper.

Minutes later, Victor was in the air and the couple pulled out of the parking lot in their white Honda.

Chapter 9

On the third Wednesday of every month for nine more months, Victor and his two companions made the same trip to the Mexican beach. Upon returning from each trip, Kevin and Elaine placed in Mr. Steed's hands a briefcase full of cash.

On the very next day, Steed would deliver the very same briefcase to his partner, Mr. Raymond Freeport, at the offices of Community Betterment, downtown San Diego.

But what Eriq Steed did, hours after receiving the case from the young couple, on the evening before delivering the case to Mr. Freeport the following day, was a secret known only to Mr. Steed.

The plan was as devious as it was perfect, thought Mr. Steed.

What no one but Steed knew about was the clandestine trip he would make on the evening of the third Wednesday of every month, following the helicopter's visit to Mexico. On these Wednesday evenings, around eleven o'clock, he would drive to Whitman Field, the airfield down the street from Victor Drueding's apartment, the airfield where the aircraft was kept.

As the very small airport facility closed at nine o'clock, Steed's visit was not only one of short duration but also one that went unnoticed. And that, after all, was the point.

Upon arrival at Whitman, Steed hurriedly made his way to the helicopter, sitting on the landing area reserved exclusively for the Alouette. He unlocked the pilot side door with the master key he carried and entered the craft.

Unlocking the secret compartment behind the back seat, with the very same key that unlocked the chopper door, Steed deposited ten bound stacks of one-hundred-dollar bills into the compartment.

As quickly as he reached the chopper, he returned to his car, and with absolutely no indication that he had been there to begin with, drove quietly into the night and directly back to his own apartment.

Steed thought himself nobody's fool.

Although his distinguished-looking boss, Mr. Freeport, considered himself the brilliant strategist, Steed knew better. In Steed's mind, it was the soldier on the ground who was the true leader. It was Steed himself on the front lines. He was the commander of operations. It was the skinny man himself, who created sufficient fear in those who served under him, that they would never betray him.

And it was Eriq Steed who carried out the dirty work when the time came.

Steed conceded the fact that Mr. Freeport devised the operation and funded it. It was Freeport who bought the helicopter and the helipad. It was Freeport who developed the Mexican connections. But Steed did not trust Freeport and Steed did not respect Freeport. And Steed would not rely on Freeport.

Freeport was an enigma who traveled in the shadows. He lived in a world of aliases and mock addresses. He feigned friendship as a means to an end. And, in the end, Steed knew Mr. Raymond Freeport would ultimately screw him. Maybe not altogether, but Freeport would never pay Steed what was totally owed to him. Freeport would ultimately have an excuse for undercompensating his younger associate.

However, Steed's nighttime visits to the helicopter ensured him the full payment he deserved. When payday finally did arrive, he knew he'd be cheated. But instead of challenging his boss, Steed would simply thank him and fly away in his newly acquired helicopter, and the stash hidden within it.

If by chance, Freeport discovered the truth, let him do something about it.

Let him just try.

Chapter 10

November 2006 – The last Mexican Flight

Victor Drueding finished his second cup of coffee and put down the newspaper that he was never actually reading anyway. He was using the newspaper this morning to hide his anxious face from his wife, who had been patiently looking at the backside of her husband's paper for the better part of two coffees.

Peg had come back from Missouri to be with her husband on this particular day; the one they had so impatiently waited for. This was pay day.

"There's no reason to be nervous, Victor, you've done this nine times already this year. You're an old pro at this."

"I'm a young, washed-up son of a bitch, who needs this to go well, or we are all screwed. And you know it." Victor folded the newspaper up neatly and placed it in the middle of the kitchen table, hoping that such a normal mechanical exercise would convince his nervous system to turn off from DEFCON 1. It didn't work.

"Fly the chopper to the Mexican beach. Leave the man and woman there and come back home. You can do it blindfolded." Peggy wanted to say just enough to keep her husband's spirits up and confidence high.

"I could go to prison, Peggy, and you know it. Hell, I could already be in prison if one of these trips had failed."

"And none of them did fail, so why are you tormenting yourself? Do you want me to do it? Do you want me to fly the friggin' bird to Mexico? Just tell me how to start the thing, and how to fly it, and where the beach is. No problem. And I won't be bitching about it like a little girl all day today. I would just 'man up' and get the stupid job done."

Victor finally cracked what could be construed as a grin. "You are very funny. Just know if they do catch me, the first thing I'm telling them is the name and address of my accomplice."

"Nice…you're my super hero."

They stared at each other for a brief moment, and then both started to laugh, but only for a couple of seconds. In truth, Peg's mind weighed as heavy as Victor's.

Peggy thought, "at least I got him to laugh, even for a brief moment."

For the first time all morning, Victor felt a bit of relief and began to take somewhat of a positive view toward the day ahead of him. He looked at his watch, and he knew he should be collecting his things for the short walk to Whitman's Field, only a thousand yards down the street.

He would complete a systems check on the helicopter and then make the twenty-minute flight to the company helipad in Otay County.

Victor hoped this would be the last time he would have to go through this exercise.

If all went well, the briefcase he would return with today would contain five hundred thousand dollars, his reward for a job well done, and his family's ticket to a new life. One far away from here.

"I'm glad you're here, Peg. But I want you and me to get out of here the minute I return. I don't want anybody rethinking the deal and come knocking at our door. In fact, I never want to see this door, table, or this crappy town ever again. When I come back, we are gone."

"I'm with you one hundred percent. Maybe you'll be my super hero after all."

With that, Victor collected a few items, kissed his wife, and left the apartment building. He waved at a few neighbors who were talking in the parking lot. They seemed surprised, but returned his kindness nevertheless. It was the first time they had ever been acknowledged by the big man. They could not have known that Victor was simply making mundane gestures, that he hoped would help calm his nerves.

If it meant waving to neighbors that he really didn't give a shit about, well, so be it. He hurried his gait as he walked toward Whitman Field. He just wanted to get this day over with.

Chapter 11

The Helipad Installation

arking just beyond the steel mesh fencing surrounding the building, Kevin and Elaine exited their white Honda. They walked through the fence's unlocked hinged gate and stood a few hundred feet from the installation.

A beautifully manicured Blackjack Bermuda grass lawn ran the entire length of the hundred-yard-long structure. The lawn always appeared to Kevin to have been mowed just moments prior to their previous arrivals, and he had the exact same thought today.

Directly in front of them, at the end of the mosaic brick walkway, they stared at the heliport's huge galvanized steel garage door, located exactly at the middle of the building, where one might generally expect to see a conventional entryway.

With the hand-held remote-control Max had given him, Kevin pressed the green button and the massive overhead rolling door began to whine as it slowly coiled upward.

As the garage door rose, the couple walked toward it. They watched in awe as the scene within the gigantic rectangular enclosure came into view. Within the four thirty-foot-high walls lay an expansive, ultra clean, and very level, aqua-colored cement floor. In the exact middle of the forty-five thousand square foot surface rose a circular, four-feet high, thirty-feet diameter, helipad.

A five-feet diameter fire engine red dot marked the exact center of the landing area. Steps leading up to the helipad's surface surrounded the entire raised circular disc.

For obvious reasons, there was no roof atop the large rectangular building, but nevertheless, it always gave one the impression of an ultra-secure environment. And for many reasons that did not meet the casual eye; it was secure beyond one's imagination.

Today was a special day for Kevin and Elaine. For the past year, the couple had made this visit on several occasions, and flown south to Mexico, to deliver the contents of similar briefcases to the one Kevin carried this beautiful morning.

Today, they were to be rewarded for their efforts.

The contents of previous briefcases were never actually made known to them. And this was quite fine by the young couple. They figured the less they knew, the better.

Steed had delivered the first briefcase to them for the initial trip to the Mexican beach. Thereafter, they collected the gray metal case at the office of Community Betterment, on Tuesday afternoons, for the following day's trip.

In contrast to other drives to the helipad, today, Kevin and Elaine were told the contents within the briefcase. One million dollars in cash.

A small fortune in appreciation for him and his wife's loyalty and the risk taken over the past ten months, and their promise never to speak of the past year's endeavors, or in any way reference the heliport, briefcase, or the company that had employed them.

This part of their life was to never have existed as far as the couple was concerned. Additionally, they would have to live the rest of their days in a lovely Mexican coastal village as part of the deal. Their life in the States would be a thing of the past, but Kevin and Elaine were excited and content to make this trade-off and transition. They would simply build their lives in Mexico.

As they approached the opened garage door, the sound of a helicopter broke the serene quiet of this perfectly still day. The helicopter settled onto the exact center of the fire engine red dot. As the chopper quieted, the pilot looked toward Kevin and Elaine and gave them an acknowledging wave and smile. The couple only knew him as Victor, but felt somewhat of a kinship with him, as Victor had piloted all of their flights into Mexico.

As Kevin and Elaine waved back to Victor, the pilot was idling the chopper's engine. It occurred to Kevin, that prior to today, he had never seen Victor smile, and prior to today, he himself had probably never smiled in this particular environment. Tension had always been the backdrop to these occasions. But not today.

Today was payoff day.

Coincidentally, Victor was of the same mind. Today was the end of his high-risk year, as it was for the couple. A briefcase was to be delivered to him as well, on this beautiful southern California morning. He was looking forward, to once and for all, leaving this installation and the people he worked for, and the life he was dead tired of living.

He would deliver the couple, one last time, to the Mexican beach. They would be left there to begin anew. He would then return the craft to the installation in the desert mountains one last time. Upon arrival,

Victor would be paid his share and be driven back to his apartment near Whitman Field.

He would walk away from this life and into what he desperately hoped to be a better one; clean slate and all.

As Kevin, Elaine, and Victor dreamt of what the future would bring, a black Lincoln pulled up outside the installation and parked beside the couple's white Honda. Three men sat within and behind the darkened, factory-tinted windows. The mood within the parked vehicle was excitement as well, but not for the same reason as the mood of the three within the building, as they stood and chatted on the raised circular disc of the helipad.

The muted conversation within the Lincoln was joined by the sound of cartridge clips being rammed into the semiautomatic pistols each of the men were carrying. This was not an exercise the men were inexperienced in. They had sat at this exact location, next to other parked cars, all of different makes and models, on other Wednesdays, during the past few years.

It was indeed payoff for those waiting beyond the Blackjack Bermuda grass lawn, past the galvanized steel garage door, and within the gigantic rectangular enclosure.

The three doors of the Lincoln sedan opened simultaneously, and three creatures without souls emerged. But only one harbored a smile. As he sprung up and out from the front passenger side door, Steed bounced energetically like a child on his way to see his grandparents.

The smile on his face was as natural and gleeful as he was capable of expressing. But his contentment was not born of human innocence and joy…

…he just loved to kill.

Chapter 12

The three men entered the installation.

In his left hand, Steed carried what appeared to be a rolled-up newspaper.

In his right hand, tucked out of sight, in his wind breaker coat pocket, he held the semiautomatic pistol that he planned to kill the young couple with. Willie and Max were assigned the task of killing the pilot. Both were expert marksmen. Both were deadly human beings. One or the other, or both, would easily take down Victor Drueding.

As the men strolled onto the smooth aqua-colored cement floor, Kevin and Elaine noticed them out of their peripheral vision. They had been yelling hello to Victor, but with the noise of the idling chopper blades, their voices were unheard.

As they turned to the three men, they both smiled and waved in acknowledgment to Mr. Steed and his associates. They both instinctively began to move in Steed's direction.

Victor had waved weakly to the couple, as he was primarily focused on completing his instrument check, before debarking the aircraft. Leaving the engine idling, and the blades revolving slowly, he finally opened the pilot-side door, and stepped down onto the helipad surface.

As was Steed's habit in previous years, he intended to initiate the bloodshed quickly. He was confident that his associates would take care of the pilot, so he concentrated on the man and woman.

As in the past, he drew his gun when he was approximately twenty feet from his prey. He stopped dead in his tracks, knelt down to one knee, taking a classic shooter's position.

At the same time, both Willie and Max hustled in separate forty-five-degree angles in an effort to flank the pilot. Once in position, they would shoot him from two directions and effectively take the helicopter out of the line of fire. Both men feared damaging the chopper and having to answer to their unforgiving boss.

Upon seeing Steed's weapon, Kevin and Elaine stopped moving toward the men. Each of their faces initially reflected confusion. As Steed raised his outstretched arms in their direction, with the barrel of what appeared to be a handgun pointed directly at them, the shocking realization of the moment paralyzed them. Both became frozen with abject fear.

Elaine turned toward her husband at the very moment Kevin's chest appeared to explode. As his body was thrown backward, his blood splashed upon his wife. Before she could scream, what felt like a sledgehammer slammed her right side, mid abdomen. Her body flew sideways in the same general direction as her husband's.

The rounds fired were rapid and deafening. The young couple, who thought that today would be the beginning of the rest of their lives, no longer heard sound. Nor would they ever hear anything again.

Their bodies lay motionless next to one another, in pools of dark red fluid.

Steed stopped shooting and pointed his hands and weapon downward, in order to size up his work. Still kneeling, a smile emerged on his calm, relaxed face. His blood pressure never elevated, and his breathing never changed.

He slowly stood with his eyes fixed squarely on the two bodies. If the slightest movement occurred, he would resume firing. But as in previous cases, his work was thorough and never required added effort.

As Victor moved away from the helicopter, but prior to descending the few steps down off of the elevated helipad itself, he noticed the movement of the men along the aqua-colored floor of the enclosure. He also noticed their weapons.

Victor stopped in his tracks in an effort to process what he was seeing. The scene before him should not have been any different than the scene that had played out with regularity over the past nine months. Except for the guns hanging from the hands of the men approaching him, the scene's template would have been the same.

Then, the gun blasts erupted.

Two bodies flew off the ground as blood splattered in every direction. Instinctively, Victor stepped backwards, until he was up against the pilot-side door of the chopper. He turned quickly and pulled the latch of the door, while expecting with all his internal radar, to feel his back ripped apart by the same gunfire.

Willie and Max moved as quickly as possible to Steed's instructed positions. When their boss so quickly shot the young couple, neither man had made it to their predetermined angles. And neither man could kill their assignment without doing collateral damage to the aircraft. Now, with the pilot having had the time to back up and re-enter the chopper, damage to the helicopter would have been inevitable.

Max gave up on the notion to fire. He would not entertain the thought of disappointing his deadly boss.

Willie did not have the same hesitation.

Chapter 13

Victor's body and mind were short-circuiting in so many ways. His head swirled in overdrive as his heart pounded out of his chest. He sat at the controls and was at a loss as to how to proceed. It was as if he had never flown the helicopter before. He couldn't remember the first thing to do.

He looked down to his left and through the air currents being kicked up by the copter blades, he could see one of the men. Through his mental fog, he couldn't determine which of the men he was looking at. But it really didn't matter who it was. What did matter was the gun the man was pointing in his direction.

He looked at the control panel and then shook his head violently, in an effort to toss off his confusion. Through his disorientation, the thought struck him hard; he must pull himself together if he were to have any chance of surviving the next few minutes.

One thought now crystalized as a final reality…his only hope…

...was to fly this eggbeater away.

Victor struggled to maintain focus. His heartbeat felt louder than the thumping of the chopper blades. The Alouette lifted off the helipad in a slow, heavy climb, easily allowing even short-range gunfire to take it down.

Victor assumed his flight would be of the briefest duration. He knew that a firearms assault on his aircraft would likely result in a deadly crash. But he would do what he could to escape and make his assailants take him down. He would not give up.

But the assault on the helicopter never came. As the chopper gained altitude, Victor allowed himself a glance downward. His vision, adjusting to the ground below, landed on an unbelievable sight...a broadly smiling Steed, glaring directly at the pilot's face. This astonishing reaction by the murdering menace, now clearly in Victor's view, added another element of confusion to the pilot's existing sense of fear.

As he began to return to the task at hand, Victor stopped suddenly and returned a hurried look downward, to verify what his eyes had just swept over. Just past the devil, holding the pistol, he clearly could see a nightmarish scene.

Three bodies lay at the feet of the skinny man.

Victor had witnessed the couple's fate, but it was apparent that at least another poor soul had completed their life's journey at the hands of Eriq Steed.

He brought his attention back to the primary objective. Victor would consider the mystery below at another time. At this moment, flying the helicopter up and away from the carnage below was his single goal.

Although, in short order, there would be other pressing concerns as well.

Chapter 14

Down on the ground, Steed stood erect, head angled upward toward the sky, watching the company's precious helicopter ascend slowly, banking somewhat toward the west, in what appeared to be an effort to find refuge within a single, white and puffy, cumulus cloud.

Steed laughed to himself, knowing fare well if he wanted to bring the chopper down, the thin, misty cloud would be of no consequence. He had plenty of fire power to do the job.

As he watched the pilot maneuver the chopper, Steed's thoughts regarding the aircraft shifted back and forth, as was the way of a schizophrenic maniac. He generally considered the helicopter as no more than a piece of steel. Now, as he watched in awe, he couldn't help but marvel at the grace and elegance of the machine he would one day own. The naked frame tailbone was a marvel of French design and a reflection of Steed's self-absorbed sense of good taste. It was more a piece of artwork than a helicopter, and in the near future, he would fly this beauty in pursuit of his unique personal interests. No, he would never harm the Alouette.

He would certainly not risk harming the bankroll hidden behind the back seat.

Upon realizing the very real possibility of Victor's escape, Steed's associate, Willie, forgot to concern himself with Steed's attachment to the helicopter. And Willie certainly was never aware of the fortune held within the craft.

When it became apparent that Victor's intention was to escape, Willie positioned himself in a stable firing stance, readying an assault on the skeletal-framed tail section of the aircraft. Out of the corner of Steed's left eye, he noticed Willie's position and knew his intent.

Steed began to yell for Willie to stop, but quickly realized that above the sound of the rising craft, nothing he screamed would be audible. His efforts would be totally ineffective.

Steed raised his pistol and rattled off a burst of gunfire that riddled Willie's body, ripping him open, from mid rib cage to his right ear. His corpse flew sideways and, for a moment, was entirely off the ground. When his body stopped rolling, his right outstretched arm overlapped the left leg of the lifeless Kevin.

Steed hustled directly to Willie's body to assess the certainty of his demise. Half a dozen feet away from the very damaged and bloody outstretched man, it was quite apparent that Willie was deceased.

At that very instant, Steed again looked up to the sky. This time he was met with the downward stare of the big man piloting the craft, and Steed smiled pleasantly back at him. Killing someone, even someone on his team, always gave Steed great pleasure, and a tremendous rush.

No, he would not kill the pilot at this moment, if it meant destroying the bird, and the money within. Steed had zero doubt that he still held all the cards. He was certain that within very short order, he or his minions, would catch up to the pilot and the helicopter.

He had no doubt that another opportunity to kill Victor Drueding would present itself very soon.

The thought made him smile all the more.

Section II

Chapter 15

As the helipad installation faded from view, Victor knew the immediate danger to him was miraculously avoided. He also knew that at least two innocent people lay dead on the helipad floor, having lost their lives to the skinny monster. His mind continued to swirl in a mix of confusion and fear. It all happened so fast and unexpectedly.

For five minutes, the chopper flew toward the Pacific, tracking the familiar route it had made over the past nine trips to the Mexican beach. Although Victor's pulse was still racing, his mind finally began to clear. He knew he had to settle his nerves and make decisions concerning his immediate situation.

He consciously drew a number of very deep breaths. As he came into view of the coast, Victor took in the serenity of the scene before him and, within moments, began to calm himself. For a few more minutes, he allowed himself to cruise without tortured thoughts and, by then, was a few miles out over the water.

As his mind settled, he again envisioned the horrific scene at the helipad. Replaying the images in his mind, his fear began to morph into anger. His anger built rapidly within him, as it tended to do on frequent occasions. The thought of turning the chopper around, and going back, became a serious consideration. He wanted badly to fight back.

But he had no weapon, and in all likelihood, the bad guys carried an arsenal. They could easily shoot him out of the sky or pick him off as he exited the helicopter.

In Victor's adjusted state of mind, however, he no longer was intimidated by the loathsome men he now knew were killers. His anger prompted him to return to the terrible scene and figure it out as he went.

However, as he banked the helicopter with the intention of backtracking, a consideration came to mind that overrode all other thoughts and plans. No, he was not afraid of the soulless characters back at the helipad. He was not consumed by the odds stacked against him. But what did create a cold wave that rippled through his body was the shock of a frightening reality…

…Eriq Steed knew where Victor Drueding lived.

And far, far worse, Victor knew something that truly frightened him…

Peg was home, awaiting Victor's return.

Chapter 16

Standing next to the helipad, watching the aircraft fade into the distance, Steed's mood shifted from mild amusement to rage. His initial thought was that this loner of a pilot would be easy prey to locate and take out. But as he stood there, eyes skyward, he realized that locating the craft, and its inhabitant, might be more difficult than he originally thought.

The pilot's escape was certainly the one possible outcome they had not considered. A shootout was considered. A helicopter crash was considered. Steed's associate's cowardice was considered. Foul weather was considered.

But…escape was never considered.

Steed and Max locked up the installation and sat for fifteen minutes in the Town Car. Max made the call to the cleaners and instructed them to come to the installation. The cleaners were staged at a point twenty minutes away and, as before, would arrive after the

Lincoln's departure. The cleaners were professional at their craft, and when they exited the helipad installation, the horrific scene would be nothing but a memory to those who had witnessed the bloodbath.

The bodies, blood, DNA, and fingerprints would be removed in absolute totality. The interior of the installation would be left as scrubbed and sanitized as any hospital operating room.

While Max was on the phone, Steed was deep in thought regarding the whereabouts of Victor Drueding. He figured by now the pilot would have calculated the range capacity of the chopper, given its available fuel. Range had never been an issue with the runs to the Mexican beach. The round-trip mileage was significantly under the chopper's maximum distance. But where would the pilot go today? Right now?

Steed considered the strategic aspect of any decision the pilot would make. Would he fly to the Mexican beach he was so familiar with? He may, but the pilot had to know Steed would alert his associates there of the situation. Would he fly back to Whitman Field? Possibly, but that would be too obvious. Additionally, Steed was aware that Victor's wife had moved to Missouri. So why would the pilot risk that option?

As Steed considered all possible destinations, he kept coming back to the craft's maximum range. He pulled out his laptop, and as Max drove away from the helipad installation, Steed began to make calculations. Given the available landing areas within range of his available fuel, where might the "soon-to-be-dead-piece-of-crap" fly Steed's precious helicopter? Where might the thief go?

Chapter 17

Victor's thoughts of revenge and retribution shifted immediately and totally. His focus was now a singular objective. He must act with urgency and with immediacy…to protect his wife.

He knew fuel would eventually be an issue, but not at this moment. There was plenty of fuel to fly to Whitman Field. Victor's concern was time. Not at all sure that Steed would think of Victor and Peg's home for now; he knew it would only be a matter of time.

If he flew low and fast, he could make it to Whitman Field in twenty minutes. Although Victor carried a cell phone, there was no reception from the helicopter, and if there had been, a conversation would have been impossible over the noise of the chopper blades. He had no alternative but to take the most direct route to Whitman Field, risking possible detection by the authorities. He would collect his wife as quickly as possible and fly away to destinations unknown.

The how, the why, and the where would have to be unanswered questions. The when was the only certainty in Victor's mind. The when was now.

He was committed to retrieve Peg; the hell with any consequences. If the airfield was to be the sight of an ambush, then so be it. If his apartment was to be an ambush, so be it. He hadn't the time to concern himself with the nuances of his actions. He would hope it would be the other guy, the killer, who would be indecisive, at least for the moment. Victor might have only the slightest crack of the closing window to act within, but he had to take the chance.

If the window were to close shut on him and his wife, before they could escape into the clouds, it would be the way it would just have to be.

"You can't live forever," thought Victor, as the earth's contour came into view. He pushed the helicopter harder than it was meant to be pushed. Its nose angled downward ever so slightly, as the machine sliced through the sky, faster than it had ever been flown.

Chapter 18

The aircraft flew at maximum speed in a direct line to Whitman field. Victor always had real concerns that local radar, airport or otherwise, would pick up the unmarked and uncharted helicopter.

To avoid detection, he rarely flew over an altitude of 300 feet and made sure to deviate the route to and from the helipad installation and Whitman field. The less the chopper was seen, the better. He would fly the direct route today, however. Victor had zero concern who spotted the craft or the attention it may have drawn. He had one objective and that was to get home as quickly as he could.

Thirty-eight minutes later, the helicopter nestled onto the landing area of the little airport down the street from Victor's home. As the chopper settled, the pilot saw old man Jake, the manager of the airfield, walking toward him. Jake Roach, the man who originally hired Victor's father, and then years later, Victor himself, was the big man's only friend.

The old man had a similar outlook on life and people, as did Victor, and his language was equally as salty. He had a raspy voice and a no-nonsense personality. He was the closest person to Victor, besides the big man's family. Victor would never admit to it, but he loved the old man.

As Victor hurriedly shut down the chopper and opened the pilot side door, he heard Jake yell out, "Thought you were getting back later today." Jake was standing just out of range of the quieting rotor blades, as they slowed with each revolution. Victor ignored the comment. He had not the time to chew the fat with his friend, but Jake was the only human being on earth who he would never offend or ignore in any manner.

"Jake," said Victor, with urgency in his voice, "Got to tell you something that's very important, but first I've got to get to my place and pick up my wife. We'll be back right away, and I'll tell you what I can then. Don't want to be rude, but gotta go."

Victor patted his friend on the arm, and said, "Be right back."

Victor hustled as fast as his bum left knee would allow and reached the apartment building in a little over ten minutes. He burst through the apartment door expecting to see his wife watching their small television in what they opted to call the living room, but what was more aptly described as a closet. Instead, he found her sitting at the kitchen table, with two luggage bags on the floor next to her.

"Why so soon?" Peg immediately asked.

"I'll tell you the whole story once we are on our way. What else do you have to pack?"

"Zero. You told me to be ready to go, and I'm ready to go. Didn't really think you meant the very second you walked through the door, but I'm good to go. Got you packed too, big guy. Ready to fly."

"You got that right. We're flying. The shit box stays here. Let's go."

Peg stood up as Victor picked up the bags. "What do you mean the shit box stays here. We're not walking, are we?"

"Tell you on the way, Peg. Kiss this place goodbye."

As Victor put down one of the suitcases to open the apartment door, Peg picked it up. She was well aware of the difficulty he had walking on some days, and today was one of those days. He didn't need to carry both bags. She walked by him and through the doorway of the apartment she would never see again. She took one last glance back into the space of the only home they had ever known as a married couple. A small lump formed in her throat, as Victor slammed the apartment door behind him.

Chapter 19

Jake sighted Victor and Peg, as he was washing down the chopper. Although Jake had no obligation to do any cleaning or maintenance, of any kind, on the craft, he was a man who had to stay busy. His curiosity piqued; Jake was not about to retreat to his small office in the airfield's tower, until he had heard from his large, younger protege. He placed the damp cloth he was using into a metal pail and walked a few feet away from the Alouette.

"My favorite girlfriend and the bum she married," he barked loudly to Peg, his unique raspy voice always a welcoming sound to Victor's wife. Jake tended to speak loudly these days as his hearing had suffered with age. As it weakened, his voice strengthened.

"The nicest person on the planet," Peg replied with a broad smile. She walked directly to the elderly man and gave him a big hug.

"Would join in on the love fest," said Victor, again with an urgency in his voice. "But I'm afraid a homicidal maniac is on his way to kill us. So, let me tell you the short version of the shitstorm I witnessed, and then Peg and I are going to get the hell out of here."

Victor proceeded to describe the high points of what led up to the tragic events of only an hour prior. With great anguish in his voice, he described quickly the murders and his escape.

Both Peg's and Jake's faces turned ashen gray. The joviality they embraced only moments before was a memory scraped away, replaced with a sense of horror.

"What now, son?" Jake queried, with a genuine father-like concern.

"We're taking the chopper and somehow making our way to Missouri. The shit box we call a car won't make it past the state line, and I want to build distance between us and that piece of shit as fast as possible. The chopper's the best bet. Figure it out as we go."

Jake thought for only a moment. He had an old body— old ears, eyes, hips, and everything really, connected to his skeletal frame. But he had a sharp mind that was now operating in overdrive.

"Here's the deal, people. I'll fill the bird with jet fuel now, all the way. On the house. Wait here for a couple of minutes, and I'll grab cash from the safe in the office. Shit, Victor, do you even have an idea how much damn jet fuel costs for that turbine?"

Victor stared at his friend with an embarrassed look on his face.

Recognizing the big man's discomfort, Jake changed his tone to one of optimism.

"Victor, we'll figure everything out. We first get the two of you to Missouri. You'll have to hopscotch your way from here to there, but I promise you, money won't get in the way. You can pay me back some day in the future when all this is just a bad memory."

Jake turned and moved as quickly as his seventy-something legs could travel. In a few minutes, he returned with a wad of cash and a bunch of maps.

Twenty minutes later, Peg and Jake hugged once again. This time with tears in Peg's eyes. She backed away from Jake to let her husband say goodbye.

Victor stood at arm's length from his mentor and slowly put his hand out to shake his friend's, in appreciation for everything the old man had ever done for him. Jake didn't move but, for a moment, simply stared at the man he met as a little boy.

Fighting back tears, Jake reached out and grabbed the much larger human being and hugged him. He felt two massive arms return the gesture. Nothing was said. Nothing needed to be said.

As the helicopter blades whirled loudly, working their way to flight speed, Jake stood next to the open cockpit door.

Holding a Rand McNally booklet opened to the southern region of Arizona, Jake repeated instructions he had gone over moments before. "Follow Interstate 8 and watch for the landmarks I mentioned. You should be over Dateland in less than three hours. The landing strip is easy to spot. I'll have it all arranged with Marty. Good guy, you'll like him."

Jake looked past Victor and yelled to Peg, who was bending over from the passenger seat to get a clear view of him. "Take care of this big lug. And he knows he better take care of you or he'll answer to me.

Don't worry, Peg. This will all be over soon, and we'll see each other again soon enough. Don't worry, honey."

Bending over, so the old man could see and hear her, Peg yelled, "Thanks for everything, Jake." Fighting her emotions, she sat upright, allowing another moment for the two men.

Jake stepped back and gave the "all clear" signal to the pilot. Through the closed plexiglass cockpit door, Victor gave a thumbs up to his friend. Jake smiled and waved his right arm in a semi-circular wave, indicating the message, "Now get out of here."

Victor smiled back as the helicopter lifted off the ground.

Chapter 20

Early the following morning, Eriq Steed had Max drop him off at the office of Community Betterment. He needed desperately to speak with Mr. Raymond Freeport. From the office, he phoned Freeport's private cell number and asked him to come downtown and that there was something important to discuss.

Although he had never felt a psychological dependence on Freeport, at this moment in time, he had an extraordinary urge to be with him. Steed's emotions were on edge, and he believed Freeport would lend a calming influence. Together, they could plan a clear and effective strategy to hunt down the son of a bitch who stole their helicopter.

Freeport was an elusive human being, connecting with Steed only when absolutely necessary and on a rigid predetermined timetable. Apart from periodic meetings, Freeport was a ghost. From the beginning of their relationship, the distinguished-looking man made it very clear, that the lesser information, and contact, all of the participants shared with one another, the better.

Steed heard back from Freeport by text, advising the anxious man that he would arrive at the office in twenty minutes. In the meantime, Steed paced and mumbled to himself, having lost the ability to settle. His consternation came from his replaying the events of the morning over and over again in his mind. "How had they allowed the oversized loser of a human being to get away?" "They should have shot up the chopper as it sat on the helipad. So what if the helicopter was destroyed?" These thoughts tortured the thin man.

They let a witness get away. The operation had always stayed clean and controlled. Once the final run to Mexico had taken place, the mules and the pilots were always eliminated. No witnesses. No problem.

Now a question mark loomed over their world. There was a missing witness and a missing helicopter. And a missing million dollars hiding in a secret compartment behind the back, pilot-side seat.

Chapter 21

Victor's first refueling location was Dateland, Arizona. The town of Dateland was located on Interstate 8, about sixty miles east of Yuma, Arizona. As much as possible, Victor circumvented settled areas to keep the craft unnoticed. He flew on the north side of Interstate 8 and at times on the south side, but always found his way back to what was effectively his "yellow brick road."

When they approached Dateland, they looked for a triangular pattern of three abandoned airstrips, situated just north of the Interstate.

Marty Goode, Jake's longtime friend, met the helicopter at the northern most point of the old airstrip. He drove a small tanker containing jet fuel, available to refill the Alouette. Goode and Jake Roach had been friends for years, brought together as aficionados of small aircraft and very small airfields. From time to time, they called on each other to assist friends of theirs. Mostly, these friends were pilots, just looking for a place to land. Once in a while, the requests were a little more complicated. This was one of those times.

Both Jake and Victor knew, that to reach Centerville, Victor and Peg would have to jump from airfield to airfield. Victor would need each airfield in order to refuel multiple times on route to Missouri. Introductions would have to be made along the way, along with payment and arrangements. Jake figured that just as his friend Marty was the manager of the Dateland airfield, Marty would have a friend at the next airfield, farther eastward. One phone call and requested favor would lead to another, and so on.

Managers knew other managers; that's the way the airfield community worked.

The helicopter touched down late in the afternoon. Marty waved at them as they approached the instructed location. High dry desert grass grew through the cracked and weathered surface of the long-ago-closed airstrip. Many decades before, pilots in-training landed mighty B25 bombers on the same airstrip; now only a helicopter could touch down safely.

Victor and Peg jumped down from the helicopter and shook the hand of the weather-beaten-looking man.

"Any friend of that ol' son of a bitch is a friend of mine," Marty proclaimed, in a loud introductory statement. "You're visiting the capital of date farming on one of the most beautiful days I can remember. But that's only because my memory's slipping, because the weather was the same yesterday, the day before, and the day before that. Be the same tomorrow."

He continued, and spoke for the next ten minutes, allowing absolutely no opportunity for a two-way conversation. Victor and Peg just stood and listened. The man either hadn't had much human contact in a while or was one strange old timer.

Finally, Marty took a breath, providing an opportunity for Victor to speak. But just as Victor uttered the first syllable, Marty stared directly into his eyes and sternly asked, "So, tell me why you're here."

Victor and Peg looked at one another, both caught off balance with Marty's simple question "tell me why you are here?"

The older man continued to stare at Victor and became as silent as he was talkative only moments before.

Victor had assumed he would land the helicopter, refuel, and be on his way. He never considered a question-and-answer session. Now, the man he was relying on was staring at him and awaiting some kind of response.

"We need fuel. My understanding was that Jake and you discussed all of this. We're here for fuel."

"Not good enough, what else?" Now Marty had become a man of few words. Victor's first thought was that he liked the man better when he was a jabber mouth.

"That's pretty much it. My wife and I have a way to go, but we need fuel to get there."

"Okay, if that's your story, you're on your own. There's a gas station down the street that a'way," as Marty pointed southbound toward Interstate 8. "Good luck, I hope they have jet fuel." He began to walk past them and toward the small tanker he had drove to the meeting.

"Hey, Marty, what's wrong," asked Victor, concerned now that he and Peg might be abandoned in this very lonesome place, with a helicopter about to run out of fuel. "What do you want to know?"

The old man turned around, and showing a genuine loss of patience, said, with a quiet resignation, "You have one last chance to tell me your story, son, or you ain't getting any gas from me, or anybody else you'll come in contact with. No more bullshit. What's the story?"

Chapter 22

Steed paced nervously, as he awaited Freeport's arrival. He recalled the normal scene that had always played out when seeing Mr. Freeport with the monthly briefcase.

The third Thursday afternoons of each of the past nine months were quite joyous occasions in the tenth-floor corner office. Steed would hand over to Mr. Freeport the metal briefcase containing a small fortune, and Mr. Freeport would react with the same faux surprise and words of puzzlement.

"Why, what have we here, Mr. Steed?"

"I found this ol' thing on the side of the road," Steed would reply. "Would you do me the favor of holding it for me for a short while?"

"It would be my pleasure, sir."

They would stand looking at one another for a few pregnant seconds longer, and then both would burst out laughing. Two categorically deranged and evil human beings attempting to humanize their destructive self-serving behavior with a form of oddball humor.

Today would be different.

Raymond Freeport entered the office and spotted the skinny man looking out a window behind what would normally be a receptionist's cubicle.

"Is that my friend Mr. Steed, or are my eyes deceiving me?"

Steed had been so consumed with nerves that he was staring into the distance and didn't notice the door opening. His concentration was broken by Freeport's voice and he was momentarily startled. He turned and greeted his boss with a muted acknowledgment.

Freeport noticed his associate's gloomy appearance.

"Why Mr. Steed, why so depressed looking? Did it take you more than one shot to take down your prey? Bullets aren't that expensive, my good man, so don't worry about it." He noticed clearly that Steed was not in the mood to laugh. "What can be so bad, my good man?"

Steed's head dropped, and as he stared at the paisley-patterned carpet, mumbled, "The pilot got away." He was hesitant to continue the story, not wanting to admit the helicopter was gone along with the son of a bitch. Every time Steed played the escape scene in his mind, his stomach turned, and his abdomen felt a squeezing sensation, as if his blood pressure was tormenting him.

"Eriq, I can barely hear you. Did you say, 'someone got away'?" Freeport's tone was one of instant concern. He did not clearly hear Steed's words but knew from Steed's body language that something was seriously wrong. "Eriq, repeat what you said."

Steed looked up at his boss and, with great anxiety in his expression and voice, repeated clearly this time, "The pilot got away. He flew away in the chopper."

Freeport picked up a small desk lamp, that would have been used by a receptionist, if Freeport indeed had one, and smashed it on the floor directly in front of Steed. Freeport's face instantly flushed a bright pinkish red, as he screamed at his younger associate. "What the hell did you just say? What the hell did you just say?"

Freeport took three angry steps toward Steed and, leaning forward, stared into the skinny man's face.

Chapter 23

Victor looked over at Peg, whose eyes read, "May as well tell him. What else can we do?" He turned to Marty and asked, "Long or short version?"

"Long, but do it quick and don't bore the shit out of me."

Both Victor and Peg had the same thought; that Marty had turned into a different man, totally unlike how he acted only moments before. But the reason why would have to go unanswered, at least for the time being. Far more important to the two of them was to gain Marty's trust and accomplish the purpose for their landing in this, the very warm capital of date growing.

Victor began his story. "Marty, I got involved in an operation that sold possible lifesaving drugs to Mexico and other southern countries. I was told these drugs had not yet been approved by the FDA, but had a strong demand in these markets. My job was to fly nine deliveries into Tijuana. A man and his wife came with me on all of the trips. I would stay with the chopper while they made the deliveries and received payment."

Victor took a breath as he began to relive the scene that would haunt him until the day he died.

"This morning was to be pay day for the couple and myself. At a helipad facility in the mountains southeast of San Diego, the three of us met the people we worked for, to receive our cut in the operation. Instead of payment, three men shot and killed the couple and wanted to kill me. I was standing near the helicopter, got in, and flew away. Why they didn't shoot the chopper down, I'll never know. I flew to Whitman Field, picked up my wife, and here we are. We just want to make it to Missouri, where our kids live with their grandmother, and figure it out from there. But we need your help to do that. And that's all there is."

Marty Goode's head was down while Victor spoke, seemingly gazing at the ground. When Victor finished, an uncomfortable silence fell over the three of them for a full minute.

Marty, lifting his head, and looking solemn, was next to speak.

"You didn't tell me about Jake filling your tank and him taking care of your fuel bill here. You also left out the ages of your three boys. You just said 'our kids.' Are you trying to bullshit me?" Marty glanced over at Peg with a hint of a grin.

Victor initially felt confused at Marty's reaction to his story. Then, when he noticed the older man's expression, it struck him that Mr. Goode had simply been testing him.

Marty's grin turned into a smile, and his dour behavior departed in an instant. "Just confirming what my buddy Jake told me. Said you were our kind of people and were in a little bit of trouble. Said we had to help you. I just had to find out for myself that you weren't bullshitters."

Peg immediately replied, "We do bullshit a little sometimes, but we do love Jake."

"Ha," proclaimed Marty, now smiling ear to ear. Now here's the deal. You're staying with me tonight. You obviously had a long and stressful day and don't need to be flying out again this afternoon. Plus, I told our buddy Jake that I would help you formulate a plan to make your way to Missouri. It would have been a helluva lot easier if your family lived in New Mexico. You kind of have a shit range in a chopper. But we'll figure it out at my place."

"I don't know," responded Victor, never one to cozy up to those he knew, let alone someone he just met. "Maybe we should just keep going."

Peg cut in, "I do know. And we're staying with you, Marty. Thank you very, very much." She glared at her husband with a *what the hell are you thinking* look? She turned back to the man who had just made the generous offer and said, "I need to sit back and relax for the rest of the day. It's been crazy. Thank you so much."

"Sounds good to you, Victor?" Marty asked, with a quizzical expression, not understanding why anyone having gone through what Victor had gone through earlier in the day would refuse some down time.

"Actually, it does sounds great, Marty. I'm sorry, I don't trust people too much. But I trust Jake, and regardless, you'll learn that I'm not the boss here anyway." Victor looked at his wife who was smirking.

"Damn straight, big man."

"Terrific," howled the older man, "Let's gas this flying machine up, then secure her, and get over to my house. Only a quarter of a mile from here. Chopper will be safe as can be, sitting right where it is. If you two imbibe, we'll have three frosties in our hands in twenty minutes. How's that sound?"

"Friggin' great," Peg replied, beginning to look more refreshed already.

"You're right, big guy," smiled Marty, "She's obviously the boss."

"No shit," responded Victor.

Chapter 24

Freeport's anger exploded. Protruding purple veins running up his neck begged to burst. Until now, the distinguished-looking man had always exhibited total composure while in Steed's presence, and the degree to which he was losing control shocked even the madman Steed himself.

As Freeport's self-control was decomposing while face to face with Steed, the skinny man became the recipient of projectile spittle along with a verbal thrashing. Steed had never experienced anything like this. Any other man who would ever dare to insult him, with even a fraction of such fury, would have been dead by now.

Finally, Freeport took a breath and made his way to a red leather overstuffed chair a few feet from the receptionist area. He sat down and made a conscious effort to settle himself. Steed continued to stand where he had been. He was almost afraid to move or talk or do anything except remain motionless. A few minutes passed and Freeport, looking somewhat more relaxed, looked at his younger associate once again. "Let me just make everything clear, Eriq. First, know you will not see one penny that I owe you until we take care of the pilot and retrieve the helicopter. He is a witness to what we've done and the chopper is evidence. Do you understand that?"

"I understand."

Freeport pointed to a desk chair against the wall. "Please take a seat, Eriq." Steed pulled the chair out from the wall and sat ten feet away from his boss.

Freeport continued. "Where is the couple?"

"Dead and disposed of forever."

"Good. Anything else of note besides the pilot and chopper gone?"

"Yeah. Had to kill Willie. One of our guys. Disposed of him too."

"I won't even ask about that. But okay. Three gone for good. The pilot got away. Who else was left with you?"

"Max. But he's okay."

"Lucky Max."

Freeport asked that Steed go over the events of the previous day, step by step, leaving nothing out. By the time Steed finished his detailed story, Freeport seemed to have formulated a plan. He interrupted Steed just as his underling blurted out, "And that's pretty much it. But I promise you, I'll get the bastard."

"Eriq, we are going to be okay." Freeport's voice had now quieted to an almost eerie calm, so much so that Steed's comment even made him grin slightly. "You're going to have to have a little patience, young man. I know we'll find him. I know we'll find the helicopter at the same time. But we have to hunt him down with brains and patience. When we find him, you can cut his heart out as far as I'm concerned. But first, Eriq, my boy, you have to put your faith in me and do what I tell you to do. That okay with you?"

Steed knew better than to suggest otherwise, but the fact was, his respect in Mr. Raymond Freeport had never been as strong as it was at this moment. Steed had witnessed only moments before that the man was indeed as crazy as he was. He was still boiling about the pilot, who he was confident would suffer mightily at his hand, but he was equally as confident, that the man standing in front of him would deliver the pilot and the Alouette to him.

"However you want to play it, Mr. Freeport. You're the boss."

They stood and faced one another. After a short moment, Freeport stepped toward Steed and stopped arm's length from the thin man. Staring him in the face once again, Freeport flashed an ominous smile, and in a restrained, yet threatening manner said, "Just remember that, Mr. Steed. I am the boss."

Freeport extended his right arm and took hold of Steed's sport coat lapel. Acting as if he was smoothing out a wrinkle by rubbing the lapel up and down between his forefinger and thumb, Freeport gazed further into Steed's nervous eyes.

"You don't want to disappoint me again, Mr. Steed. Remember that."

Chapter 25

Dateland was unusually warm for November, so the three sat on wicker chairs in Marty's air-conditioned porch, overlooking a vast field of date palms. The first ice-cold beers they consumed tasted like the finest brews Victor and Peg ever had. The second serving seemed like the second greatest suds they had ever had.

Marty reverted to the person they had first met and, for twenty minutes, rattled off the history of Dateland, Arizona. It didn't matter to the couple, as they were relaxed for the first time all day and were mesmerized by the desert scenery. Marty's chatter was the equivalent of white noise, almost soothing.

After a while, Marty wrapped up his monologue. He took a breather, and all sat quiet for an extended period of time. A peaceful quiet. Then Marty again began the conversation, this time related to Victor's and Peg's circumstances.

"When you two were flying here, Jake and I spoke at length. Given you're going to leapfrog your way to Missouri, we listed a number of very small air fields we know about, to refuel along the way. All low-profile places to keep you under the radar as much as possible. If you agree, he and I will make contact with these locations, arrange fuel, and a couple of spots to spend the night. You can stay in touch with Jake and confirm the plan each day. Jake and I will figure out paying for the fuel. Later, you can work out a repayment plan with Jake. You won't have to worry about it as you go. What do you think?

Peg was the first to reply. "I think you're wonderful, Mr. Goode. I can't believe what you're doing."

Then Victor broke in. "We'll pay you guys back, Marty, know that. We'll pay every penny back." The big man felt and acted embarrassed, as he had with Jake earlier in the day. The fact that these old men had to help them with money made him feel more the loser than he normally felt. As he was about to say one more thing, Marty put up his hand, to stop Victor from saying anything else.

The older man stood up and walked over to the large, younger man, who now had his head down. Marty stood over the big guy and put one hand on Victor's shoulder. "Don't you ever feel bad about things in my presence, son. Jake told me enough about you that I feel like I've known you for a long time. I only busted your chops out at the helicopter because I had never laid eyes on you before. But that will never happen again, I promise."

"Thanks, Marty," uttered the somber-sounding Victor, still looking downward.

"Okay then, let's have one more for the road, and you two hit the sack. The weather is supposed to be good for flying tomorrow, much like today. But again, the day after tomorrow will be the same, and the day after that. Weathermen don't make much money around here. You have to be a really bad one to blow the forecast."

Marty left the porch and returned with three frosted bottles. All three were asleep one hour later.

Chapter 26

Freeport and Steed met again Thursday morning in the office of Community Betterment. This time, the older man reached the office before the younger. Steed arrived late with great anxiety fearing the mood of his boss.

Fortunately for Steed, Mr. Freeport seemed to be his regular self, although Steed did not pretend to know what exactly that meant anymore. He had discovered the day before, that Freeport was not what he had always appeared to be. It was now clear to Steed that the distinguished-looking man had a heart of stone and was, in fact, a hard human being. There was one redeeming feature, however, about this realization. Steed now knew with certainty, that he was working with, and for, a harsh and cruel man. And Steed respected that.

A smiling Raymond Freeport welcomed Steed with a cup of coffee and a donut, a nicety he had never offered before. Steed, for his part, smiled as if to be smitten by his boss's most generous act of kindness. Two murderous swindlers fooling nobody.

"This is very kind of you, sir," gushed Steed.

"Think nothing of it, my boy. My way of apologizing for being such a brute yesterday."

Steed waved the comment away, as if he hadn't noticed the least bit of discourtesy the day before. As he did so, he thought to himself, "and you think a goddamned donut is adequate compensation, you cheap bastard."

"Eriq, let's sit over here and go over my thinking regarding our game plan." Holding their coffees and donuts, they moved to a small circular table and sat in chairs on opposing sides. Freeport proceeded to explain how he viewed the situation.

"Eriq, you said the pilot has family in Missouri, correct?"

"Yes, sir. His wife and whatever children he has. I think two or three."

"Alright. Let's assume he is heading to Missouri. A man with as little means as he has isn't heading off to his condo in Hawaii. Losers don't have many options, my boy, so let's suppose this piece of crap is going home."

"I think you're right. He's going home. I don't know where that is in Missouri, though."

"No matter. I'll find him, don't worry. He's scared. He knows he would be in a world of hurt if he goes to the cops. He can't be that dumb not to know he's been breaking the law for the better part of a year now. And even if he did go to the police, there are no bodies, no last names, no anything. The installation is now as clean as an operating room. The helicopter was already made unidentifiable in case of some unforeseen event. They can't trace it to anything. The only prints would be his and the couples. What would that tell anybody? No, Eriq, even he isn't that stupid to go to the cops."

Steed's attention was riveted to Freeport's smooth presentation and calmness, that was in such contrast to his initial reaction of only twenty-four hours before. But given that, Steed could only focus on one issue. "So what do we do?" he asked.

"Nothing." Freeport lifted his arms over his head as if to yawn, but really only for effect.

"Nothing, but Mr. Freeport, we can't let this jerk go. You really don't mean 'nothing', do you?"

Steed was now leaning forward and appeared as stressed as Freeport had ever seen him.

The older man released his risen arms and let them settle down, onto the table top. He smiled slightly, enjoying the passion at which his underling obviously wanted to act swiftly and violently.

"Don't worry, Eriq. I promise we will find this man, and you'll be able to dispatch him as you care to. But let's not run around like chickens with their heads cut off. He is on the move now. However he is able to reach Missouri, he will eventually get there, but it will take a little time. By car, by train, however. Let's just let him get there and settle. Give him some time to shake off the fear he's feeling. Give him time to let his guard down. And then we'll get him. And get him good."

"What about the chopper?"

"It will be around here someplace. At the little shit airport you mentioned that he kept it at. Or hidden in some field. Can't be too far away. He sure as hell didn't fly it to Missouri. If this maggot doesn't have a pot to piss in, he definitely doesn't have dough to pay the fuel costs. And anyway, who in their right mind would fly a helicopter halfway across the country. We'll find the aircraft's location; you can drag it out of him before you kill him. But even if you can't, who really cares. I know you wanted it, but it isn't a priority right now, is it?"

"No, I guess not", Steed replied, forcing himself to sound convincing. His blood began to boil again, as he thought of the helicopter sitting in some obscure field, covered in camouflage of some sort, keeping him from his nest egg within. He would surely find Victor Drueding, and as the oversized loser was begging for his life, he would extract the whereabouts of his whirlybird. Then he would inflict a final blow and end the life of the man responsible for the anxiety he was now experiencing.

Chapter 27

All three awakened at five in the morning. Airport people are early birds. Peg and Victor slept particularly deep as sleep had not come easily over the past week, anticipating the last helipad meeting and the promised payoff for Victor's efforts. Additionally, for months, the illegality of Victor's activity had weighed heavily on them, impacting their quality of slumber in general.

The fact that Peg and Victor felt safe and secure the night before, in this obscure town, and in Marty's home, contributed to their ability to doze off. The couple's murder weighed heavily on Victor's mind. Had he felt guilt, rest in general would have been impossible, but as he was as much the prey of these evil men, he felt sympathy and sadness at the couple's deaths, but not guilt. Victor and Peg's bodies surrendered to their circadian clocks, and both slept soundly.

Once up and about, Marty would not permit them to hurry out the door. The night before, they had finalized the flight plan for the new day, and Marty saw no need for their immediate departure. He banged around the kitchen and insisted they allow him to create breakfast magic. Translated, that meant bacon, eggs, and waffles; and in truth, that sounded very good to his guests.

They moved to the porch once again, as they took their time, and consumed a very hardy breakfast. Marty morphed into his talker self and regaled the couple with more tales of the history of Dateland. Victor and Peg found themselves enthralled with the story of the town's beginnings—in its role as a water stop for the railroad, to becoming the site of training camps for General Patton's troops in the Second World War. As with all towns, Dateland had its own story to tell and possessed a very unique personality. For sure, Marty Goode was part of that personality.

When the final waffle was consumed, and the coffee pot was filled and emptied for a third cycle, Marty completed the history lesson. It was time to head to the helicopter and begin the day's travels.

The plan on this warm and sunny Thursday was to make two stops; the first being Benson, Arizona, to refuel. Marty had a friend there and would make the arrangements with him after the couple was in the air.

The second stop would be Truth or Consequences, New Mexico. Another refuel, but they would spend the night as well. This would be enough flying for one day. Additionally, Victor would have the opportunity to check out the helicopter for any required maintenance. The airfield was run by an old flame of Marty's, Maggie Crotty.

In Marty's opinion, Maggie was one of the best single engine flyers in the country. They had crop dusted fields together a long time ago up north. Marty even seemed to have a little catch in his throat, when speaking about her. This was apparent to Peg, who was now interested in meeting Maggie for more than refueling reasons. Victor didn't notice.

At eight thirty, the couple sat in the cockpit of the chopper. Marty stood next to the open pilot-side door, and rambled on, as if to purposely delay their lift off. Peg and Victor both noticed, but felt they owed the old timer a few more moments of patience.

Finally, Marty backed away, and Victor started the blades moving. Minutes later, having waved goodbye to their new friend, they hovered over a grove of date palms. Peg held the map in her lap, and Victor pointed the Alouette eastward.

Chapter 28

November 2006

Dot Collins lived on Railroad Street on the outskirts of Centerville, Missouri. She was divorced in 1990 and moved to Centerville after her marriage broke up. Her ex-husband, who passed away in 1995, had been an aircraft mechanic at Whitman Airfield, just outside of San Diego.

When she left her husband, Dot took her grown-up son to Missouri, while her nineteen-year-old daughter, Peggy, stayed behind, to live with her dad. Peggy had become somewhat of a mechanic herself and would work from time to time at the little airfield. It was at Whitman Field that Peggy met Victor Drueding, and eventually, the two were married.

Dot owned a small ranch-styled house on a large piece of property. Everyone in Centerville seemed to have a large piece of real estate, as there was land to spare. From her days in high school, Dot had always had a job. Her entire working life found her selling apparel of one sort or another, at any number of department stores. She was a very knowledgeable saleswoman and loved to chat customers up. Never on the receiving end of a large paycheck, nonetheless, she found herself to be a very effective saver.

Once settled and employed in Centerville, it did not take her long to purchase her little home. Periodically, her daughter Peggy would visit with her three boys, and it was always an enjoyable time. So in 2004, when Dot floated the idea that the kids move in with her for a while, she was thrilled when her daughter complied. Dot's hope was that the children would enjoy Centerville, and that her daughter and son-in-law would soon follow.

What Dot could not have known, in November of 2006, was that her daughter and son-in-law were, in fact, on their way to Centerville. And she surely would never have guessed that they were flying there... by helicopter.

If Dot had one problematic issue regarding Peg's boys, it was their behavior. Although all three acted fine while in her company, Dot had heard to the contrary from their school, and from more than one neighbor. The bulk of the concerning reports had to do with the eldest boy, Dean.

It was November of 2006 and Dean was almost fourteen years old. Dean, who should have been in the ninth grade, was only in the seventh. Along the way, the boy was held back two grades. This was a generous alternative to what school officials really wanted, which was to expel the boy.

Peg's hope was that under her mother's roof, her sons would be subject to the discipline and structure that she and her husband were woefully lacking in. Dean and his brothers did find discipline under their grandmother's roof, but unfortunately, once out the door, it was another story.

Dean ran with two other thirteen-year-old boys, 'Worm' Crawl and 'Kane' Shuger. Nicknames were not very imaginative in Centerville, Missouri. All three cast silhouettes of stringy scarecrows, not one extra pound of flesh among them.

Unfortunately for each boy, their two buddies were not particularly good influences, regardless of how you shuffled the order.

Kane came from a very respectable family—his father a Centerville lawyer, his mother a volunteer at the town hospital and local shelter. What seemed like a proper family was in truth missing one key ingredient that their son desperately needed. His parents' time. Both parents were rarely around. The outward image of the perfect home was in fact, a barren, lonely place.

Worm was from a broken home, where his parents still lived under the same roof, but hated one another. His father was abusive, both to him and his mother. As best he could, Worm stayed away from home.

With the passage of time, the three boys were increasingly losing their moral compass and risking their very futures with behavior that was becoming more dangerous by the day.

Under ordinary circumstances, the Drueding parents, en route to Centerville, would have been a good thing. Their boys, especially their oldest, needed them badly.

The arrival of Dean's parents would have been just what the doctor ordered...

...if it wasn't for the murderers hunting them.

Chapter 29

The helicopter touched down in Benson, Arizona, forty-five miles east-southeast of Tucson, a little over two hours after leaving Dateland. The town was located just south of I-10 allowing Victor and Peg to easily keep a constant landmark, the highway, in sight. The Rand McNally Road Atlas, given them by Jake, served their needs handily. They may as well have been driving a car.

A young fellow who had been contacted by Marty was waiting at the airstrip with a small fuel truck. They debarked the craft, and the lad began to fill the tank. The two took the opportunity to use the services available at the small field and purchase a couple bottles of water and a few snacks.

After a needed break, they jumped back into the helicopter and continued on.

Following I-10 for a little over two hours, they arrived at the town of Las Cruces, New Mexico, and turned north, continuing on over I-25. A half hour later, they arrived at the southernmost portion of the town of Truth or Consequences. They were instructed to hug the western side of the town and look for an unusual landmark that marked the location of the small airfield where they were to land.

The landmark, a bright orange, neon-colored water tower was the ground feature guiding them to their objective. They saw the unusually bright structure from very far away and both laughed at the sight.

"That is the ugliest thing I have ever seen," chuckled Victor.

"So much for environmental purity," replied his wife, flabbergasted at the sight. "It's such a beautiful part of the country. Who the hell thought of that?"

"Someone trying to assist lost souls like us to find their way," Victor said solemnly, changing his tone as he considered the reality of their situation once again.

"Heaven help me, my husband is becoming a profoundly wise man. You are absolutely right, my hubby. God bless the son of a bitch who thought of painting that thing. It's lovely."

There was a short period of silence, and then at the exact same time, they burst out laughing. And these days, anytime they spontaneously erupted in laughter, was a physical and mental relief the man and his wife desperately needed.

Chapter 30

The town of Truth or Consequences was both a refueling stop and a planned overnight stay. As Victor was positioning the chopper for landing, he thought to himself, "We've been very fortunate having met the likes of Marty Goode. Would they be so lucky this time around?" he wondered.

In truth, Peg was having the same thoughts. Their story was not one they were comfortable telling people, especially strangers. She feared that telling their story could lead to an unfortunate outcome for her and her husband.

As they descended, they saw a woman, dressed in what appeared to be light blue work overalls. She was waving furiously in their direction. Her shoulder length, grayish white hair was flipping from one direction to the other, with each exaggerated wave. Victor halted the choppers' descent, and hovered. The woman was pointing with her extended right arm, toward a black painted circle, about thirty yards in front of her. She was directing them to land in the circle.

A minute later, the helicopter touched down. As Victor was checking off his instruments, Peg found herself giving a royal wave to the woman, not exactly sure how enthusiastic she should act. The woman in the overalls spotted the wave, and responded with a broad, handsome smile. She lifted her right hand and returned the royal wave.

Then Maggie Crotty began to laugh.

Chapter 31

Dean, Worm, and Kane met in front of Brown's Bike Shop. The cool November air had a biting edge to it; typical November weather in the beautiful little town of Centerville. Dean and Worm drew deeply from their Winston cigarettes and puffed perfectly formed oval rings of smoke, as they rocked back and forth in unison. On this early Saturday morning, the downtown street was practically void of humanity. Nonetheless, the boy's heads swiveled from one direction to another, always on guard for the authorities to appear, or something ominous to happen.

His spent cigarette flicked to the ground, Kane leaned back against the wall and let his chin hang down. Plunging his hands deep into his baggy blue jeans' pockets, his body seemed lifeless. His body language belied the fact that barely ninety minutes earlier, he was being served breakfast by his mother and hugged by his father, as he headed out the door. However, this was the only time of day he ever saw his parents.

The casual observer could easily believe that Kane's silhouette, reflected against the bike shop wall, belonged to an indigent, a poor homeless street urchin. Kane's family was certainly not poor, and he was by no means homeless. In some ways, however, Kane was, in fact, an indigent. He was a young boy in need. In need of his parent's time and involvement.

Worm was the classic nervous Nellie. The young man was never relaxed, whether in the streets, or within the walls of his dysfunctional home. Worm's life was one perched on an emotional ledge. His parents fought whenever they were near one another. The house was shelter for the boy, but little else; unless you counted a constant source of anxiety. He found a modicum of calm with his friends, cigarettes, and more recently, alcohol.

Dean was the ringleader of his motley gang. He was the idea man. The other two relied on Dean to make plans, to schedule their lives. There was only one rule. No boredom. Today, there would be no boredom. Today, the three boys would attempt to execute Dean's most daring idea to date.

They would rob a house.

Chapter 32

The Alouette quieted and Victor and Peg exited the craft. Maggie Crotty welcomed them both with a big hug and a loud, "Howdy, welcome to Truth or Consequences. I love meeting new people and you come highly recommended from my good friend, Marty."

"Well, we're thrilled to be here," answered Peg, herself smiling widely in response to the enthusiastic greeting by this older, yet very attractive woman. "Marty said some very nice things about you as well."

"I bet he did, the ol' rattlesnake." Maggie gave them a wink, obviously not one to shy away from an indication that she and Marty had known one another rather well.

"Listen, my shit box of a car is right there. Let's say we shoot over to my shack and get you guys settled in. I can run back here, fill this thing up with fuel, while you two freshen up. I have pizzas coming over in about an hour and a half, and we have plenty of refreshments. Okay by you?"

Victor, who hadn't said a word until now, raised his eyebrows, shrugged his shoulders, and simply said, "Sounds great." He knew the woman in front of him had everything in control, and it probably wasn't a good idea to give a contrary opinion, even if he had one. The fact was, he didn't have one.

Maggie's car was an old Chevy of some kind. There obviously had been a massive amount of homegrown body work done to the auto, probably due to prior accidents and overall rough treatment. The make, model, and year would be all but impossible to determine. It was a four-door sedan, with a blue door, two maroon doors, and a door of an undecipherable color.

The car's starter took about thirty seconds of whining to start the engine, but once it got running, it seemed to perform well enough. No one would be insane enough to trust it on an open highway, but Maggie gave the impression that her long-distance traveling days were well behind her.

A few minutes after leaving the airfield, the patchwork vehicle pulled into a gravel driveway next to a small wooden house. The habitat really could be described in very much the same way as Maggie's car. The brown-painted shingles were peeling on all sides and the roof was badly in need of replacement. Maggie made no mention regarding any of her home's shortcomings and carried on with the same upbeat and happy attitude that seemed to define the woman's spirit.

"Let me show you guys where you're going to crash tonight," Maggie said, as they climbed the creaky wooden planks leading up to the front door. "You have the bedroom in the back. Not a big space, but a very comfortable double bed. Bathroom is down the hall. All set up with towels and everything. I'll be back in about thirty minutes once the bird is fueled. All okay?"

Again, Victor merely looked resigned to any and all instructions the woman threw in their direction. "We're good, Maggie," he replied, as he glanced at Peg, who was obviously enjoying the unique personality that was Maggie Crotty.

"We couldn't be better, Maggie. You are too good a host," Peg chimed in, her spirits lifted simply by being in the company of this unusual woman.

Maggie walked briskly to the car of many colors, and after the starter strained for a period of time, the engine roared to life once again. Gravel shot up from the back tires, as Maggie accelerated clearly too aggressively for the feeble condition of the car. She sped out of the driveway and turned back in the direction of the airfield.

As Victor looked at his wife once again, his lips curled up slightly, and declared, "I wonder why the car is in the shape it's in?"

"Oh, shut up you. She is the nicest person in the world. I love her already."

A little over thirty minutes later, they heard the sound of a car, followed by the crackle of spitting gravel once again. Victor, sitting on a living room couch, while glancing through the Rand McNally Atlas, looked up and smiled. Reading a local magazine, while reclining on an overstuffed lounge chair, Peg looked at Victor, and quietly said, "Shut up."

"I didn't say anything."

"Just shut up."

"The bird's belly is full, Victor," stated Maggie, referring to the helicopter. "You've got full range ahead of you, but I suggest we do a full mechanical check before you guys head out again. What do you think?"

"We were planning on leaving in the morning, Maggie. I don't see how we can..."

"Forget tomorrow morning. Be safe. Take the day off from flying, and I'll help you tune the thing up."

Victor looked to his wife, who obviously liked the idea. "A little relaxation would be good for the both of us," Peg said to her husband. "Maggie's also right about being safe. Why not take a close look at the aircraft?"

Maggie chimed in again, "Great, it's a deal. Right, Victor? By the way, I'm the best helicopter mechanic in this entire region, so we can both check the thing out. It'll be a blast."

Victor knew he was defeated before he began, so resigned to the inevitable, he shook his head in the affirmative and said, "Sounds like a plan."

Both women let out a happy yelp, and Maggie continued, "The pizza is on its way. What's your pleasure for drinks? Beer, coke, or beer?"

Victor hadn't been finding much of anything funny of late, but Maggie broke through the barrier, and he let out a genuine chuckle. "Beer sounds perfect."

Two large pizzas and a few beers later, the three of them found almost everything funny, and laughed with ease. At one point, Victor asked Maggie if she had any idea who painted the water tower the ugly neon color. "No clue," she responded, "but it got you here, didn't it?"

Victor smiled. "You did it, didn't you?"

"You're an asshole," Maggie responded.

And the laughter continued.

They sat around for the next few hours, finding each other's company totally enjoyable. When they finally turned in, they had found the evening one of the most relaxing they had experienced in a long, long time.

Chapter 33

Centerville

Robbing a house requires planning. At least successfully robbing a house does. Dean had planned the robbery for nearly two weeks.

The target of Dean's planning was the house of Charlie Mann, a seventy-two-year-old wounded veteran of the Vietnam War. Charlie lived down the dead-end side street that ran alongside Brown's Bike Shop. Unfortunately for Charlie, Dean and his friends had noticed him limping by them the same time every morning, on the days they hung out in front of the bike shop. This was the case on Saturday mornings; this was the case on weekday mornings. To notice Charlie's habit on a weekday morning meant the boys were skipping school, but that was a regular occurrence for these three youngsters.

Dean figured that an old soldier like Mr. Mann would have stored away a great variety of army memorabilia. An old man like him probably wouldn't even miss paraphernalia that Dean and his friends would dig the hell out of. It seemed only fair that some forgotten junk to Mr. Mann would be used and enjoyed by young potential soldiers like Dean and his friends.

When Dean hatched the scheme, he began reconnaissance immediately. One morning two weeks prior, he strolled down the dead end, in order to size up Charlie's house. It was apparent from Dean's observation, that Charlie lived in a convenient hidden location on the right, at the of the road. The older man left the house exactly on schedule. As soon as Dean confirmed this, he pivoted and walked directly back to the bike shop, awaiting his friends.

Once all were present, the three retraced Dean's steps, to investigate the targeted house once again. Kane and Worm had no interest in further investigation, but Dean convinced them they must be aware of their surroundings, in order to have the desired outcome. If one element of this operation was critical, it was to pull off this house invasion undetected.

Dean observed that the faded red brick house had a broken-down front porch, visible to neighbors and passersby. Entry from the front was dismissed. However, a high, untrimmed hedge lined the right side of the property, and to the left, a deep, dense grove of pine trees; allowing total privacy from the back. They would enter from there. A perfect set up, thought Dean.

That is, if one was so prone to rob the place. And Dean was so prone.

The day of reckoning had arrived. The three boys knew the plan was to move quickly once Mr. Mann hobbled by. The three hustled down the dead-end road and made their way into the pines just beyond Charlie Mann's house. In case any neighbors noticed them, it would appear as if the boys were heading into the woods, to explore, as boys tended to do.

Once within the visual protection of the pine grove, the boys stopped. Worm was to remain exactly where he was, out of sight from Mann's neighbors, but in full view of the road as it led back up the street. If Mr. Mann was to unexpectedly return, Worm would spot him, alert his partners, and all three would have the benefit of Mann's slow gait, to escape unnoticed.

Dean and Kane moved through the woods until they were parallel to Mann's backyard. They ran into the open space behind the house and toward the back door. The plan was to try the door and, if locked, move quickly to the windows. Centerville was not lock happy, as the crime level was exceptionally low relative to the state of Missouri, and for the matter, the country at large.

Dean hoped that they would find easy entry, and the best-case scenario presented itself. The back door was unlocked.

They entered the house.

Chapter 34

Having slept soundly, Victor and Peg awakened refreshed and energized. Their slumber was interrupted by the racket of clashing pots and pans, as Maggie banged around in the kitchen preparing a hardy breakfast. If she seemed unconcerned by the disturbance she was causing, it was because she wasn't. Maggie didn't have much regard for the value of sleep and showed very little sympathy for anyone who did. There was simply too much life to live and too few hours to live it.

Early birds themselves, Victor and Peg were happy to have a good restorative sleep for two consecutive nights, rejuvenating their bodies so desperately needed. Both rose with renewed energy and clear heads. The smell of bacon and eggs were an added and appreciated incentive to rise and engage the new day.

An impressive buffet of scrambled eggs, bacon, blueberry muffins, mixed fruit, orange juice, and coffee was compiled by the high-energy woman of the house. All three helped themselves to a hearty quantity of the mouthwatering offerings. They enjoyed almost an hour and a half of each other's company, poking fun at one another, while consuming every last morsel of food and drink.

At one point, Maggie, at her entertaining best, said, "I have the perfect career for you, Victor, given your flying and mechanical skills."

Victor, expecting a joke of some kind, responded, "Stealing small aircraft?"

Peg burst out laughing, particularly happy to hear her overly sensitive husband actually make a self-depreciating comment.

"No, you crazy thing. I'm being serious," Maggie came back. "I've been thinking about this for a long time. First, I thought I'd be a good candidate for the job description, but I stopped enjoying regular travel a long time ago. But if you don't mind being away for a couple, three nights every now and then, there's a real need for a 'same day delivery service' aimed at the small airfield market."

Peg noticed her husband's body language indicating a shift to his mood. He dipped his head downward and stared at the linoleum covered kitchen floor. He didn't respond to Maggie's comment regarding a possible job opportunity. He merely went quiet.

Whether Maggie noticed this or not, she wasn't particularly interested in stroking other people's egos or sensitivities. "Hey, big man, I'm being serious. There's a real potential here for a terrific job, and I can help you out. I've thought this through a million times."

Victor, head still hanging downward, finally spoke up. "Maggie, I appreciate you thinking of me, but I'm not sure you actually know the situation I'm in."

"Well, tell me then. What's the deal? And by the way, I told you guys that Marty gave me the 'heads up' on a few background facts. Doesn't mean you've got to stick your head in the sand. Gonna have to make a living somehow, right? Probably going to have to take some risks, right? The bad guys aren't going to rat you out, right?"

"Maggie, I stole this helicopter. I don't own it. And I don't plan on always flying under the radar, looking over my shoulder all day long, making sure a gun isn't pointed at me. I'm in a lot of shit, in case you didn't know, and I'm not sure what tomorrow's gonna bring, let alone plan my new career path."

"Then, go to the cops, Victor. Tell them the whole story. You messed up, but you kind of got drawn into it. You sure as hell didn't kill anyone. Hell, they would probably cut you a deal, just to catch that thin-lipped, saber-toothed, murdering bastard. Did you ever think of that?"

"I don't want to think about any of that right now, Maggie. We've had a rough week. I just want to get to Centerville and take a breather. We'll decide what the hell to do then. Hell, those killers might be hunting us down as we speak. I just don't know." Victor kept his eyes on his wife, who he knew didn't deserve any of this, and her involvement made him feel even worse.

Maggie stepped up to the big man and put her right hand on his shoulder. "I won't keep talking about it, my new friend, but I just want to say one last thing. Is that okay?"

Victor looked up at the gray-haired lady and said softly, "Go ahead, Maggie." He wouldn't have been so accommodating, but this woman had been more than a generous host, and he found himself drawn to her straightforward personality. He wouldn't consider insulting her or denying her anything at this point.

"Victor, let me tell you a story about the town you're in. It's called Truth or Consequences. We changed the name when I was a teenager, and I thought it was the stupidest thing I'd ever heard of. The town had a perfectly good name, and the wackos changed it to the name of a game show on the radio. That's what I thought. The wackos, by the way, included my mother and father. They loved the idea and wholeheart-edly supported it. I thought, 'we'll be the laughing stock of the whole country.'"

Peg spoke up, 'What was the name before?'

"Hot Springs. Great name. Made sense. And we change it to a game show. My friends and I figured we would move out of this place as soon as we possibly could, so we wouldn't have to go through life being laughed at."

As she spoke, Maggie poured herself another cup of coffee and sat back down at the kitchen table.

"But the funny thing is, none of us moved away. In fact, as time went by, we all grew fond of the new name. After a while, we wouldn't have changed the name for anything in the world." She paused for a moment, thinking of how to explain the reason she was going into all of this, without sounding phony, or simply ridiculous.

"Do you want to know why? And please say 'yes' so I don't feel like an idiot." She smiled at both of them.

"Yes," Peg blurted out, but not because she was being polite. She was genuinely interested in the unusual story line.

"Good. I'll tell you then, since you two are pressuring me to do so." Maggie laughed, knowing that she was often her own best audi-ence. "Let me tell you."

Maggie continued. "The original name change to Truth or Consequences was a fun thing. It brought an energy and life to the town it had never quite known before. It also brought Ralph Edwards to the town the first of May, every year, for the next fifty years. But that's beside the point."

Victor looked puzzled and acted as though he'd never heard of Ralph Edwards and had no idea what Maggie was talking about. Peg, unlike Victor, knew a little bit about the game show and its host, Ralph

Edwards, and got a kick out of Maggie's sense of humor. "Go on, Mag. I'll explain to Victor later."

Maggie grinned at the big man. "It wasn't that funny anyway, Victor, but let me get back to my point. The name was just a funny topic for a while. It gave the town something everyone could talk about and relate to. Kind of brought us together. Then, a funny and unexpected thing happened."

She paused for a sip of coffee and to catch her breath.

"People began to view the new name of the town as a directive, a way to live. Truth or Consequences. When you think about it, all life decisions are based on these two basic options. Live in truth and face the truth, or live the consequences. People began to make decisions based on this. Incredibly, our little town became more caring for one another, more giving of ourselves to others. Now, we love the name. And we love our town even more."

Maggie looked intently at Victor, her expression now having turned serious. She reached out and took Victor's hand, that was resting on the kitchen table. "Victor," she said softly, "you and Peg have your whole lives in front of you. You may have made a mistake or two, but from where I sit, that's exactly what most people have done."

She turned from Victor to Peg, and back to Victor again. "Get your butts to Centerville. Take a breather. But once you catch your breath, think about our little town's name. Act on the truth. Don't worry about it. You may even have to face some consequences. But life will go on. You have a good soul, Victor. I can tell from our short time together. I have faith in you. I have faith in both of you. And that's all I have to say. Please don't hate me."

All three sat in silence for a few minutes. Peg didn't feel it was her time to say anything. She felt it was her husband's right to react as he wished. If he wished to at all.

Finally, Victor glanced somberly from one woman to the other, as he considered how to respond to Maggie's monologue.

Gazing at Maggie, he said, "I know who Ralph Edwards is. How big a dummy do you think I am?" He grinned slightly, gave her a subtle wink, and asked, "Is there any more coffee, or did you drink it all?"

Maggie leaned over and put her arms around the big man.

"Anything you want, my new buddy. Anything you want."

Chapter 35

Dean and Kane worked quickly. Dean had given Kane a brown grocery bag with instructions to take only what easily fit into the bag. Once filled, that was it. No more. Dean's thinking was that if they walked down the street with grocery bags in their arms, no one would be suspicious. He had given Worm a couple of bottles of soda to carry, to give the same impression.

Dean further instructed Kane to strictly follow the game plan. Kane was to stay on the main floor and take only small war items that might not be missed immediately. Keep it neat and leave the house looking as untouched as possible.

Dean took the upstairs, focusing on the bedroom. He would be even more vigilant in leaving the area appearing unruffled. His hope was, even if the old man were to notice something out of place, he would probably blame it on his aging memory. Or at least that is what Dean hoped.

As Dean scoured through dresser drawers and closets, he heard clanging of articles being moved and dropped, down in the living room. At one point, he yelled to Kane, "A little more careful, pal, we don't want to wake the neighbors." Kane responded, "Whatever you say, mother."

Dean often wondered why these clowns were the two people on the planet he hung with; Tweedledum and Tweedledee. But for better or worse, this was his posse. A posse that would do anything Dean wished, and this did give their leader a sense of power.

When Dean filled his grocery bag, he moved down to the living room and saw that Kane's bag was practically filled as well. "Let's go, man. That's enough. Let's get out of here clean and unnoticed."

"Good to go," said Kane.

They walked out the back door and straight into the pine grove once again. Worm was intensely looking down the street for any possible sighting of Mr. Mann. "Clear," he whispered.

"Okay, boys. Here's the deal. Worm, you swing those bottles like you don't have a care in the world." Looking at Kane, Dean continued, "Put your free arm around my neck and keep smiling, but don't say anything until we're at Brown's. No need drawing attention with noisy conversation. Once at the bike shop, we can make all the noise we want, all while holding the bags and soda in clear sight. But we keep moving, until we get to your house. Got it?"

Tweedledum and Tweedledee responded at the same time. "Yes, sir."

The three boys took Charley Mann's property to Kane's house. His parents would be out, as always and wouldn't be home for hours. They would have plenty of space and privacy. Dean and Kane appeared to be carrying groceries. Following Dean's instructions, Worm swung two large bottles of soda to complete the imagery. They were just three boys returning from the grocery store.

Once in Kane's perfectly all-American home, they made their way downstairs to the semifinished basement. According to Kane, his parents primarily visited the basement to do laundry. Once in a blue moon, his dad would descend the stairs to take late night phone calls, so not to bother his sleeping family.

The boys fell backwards on the two opposing couches, then slid down to the navy, woven, area rug. They sat crossed-legged across from one another, in preparation to exhibit and divide the bounty. Dean and Kane placed the grocery bags in front of them, and for a prolonged moment, the three quietly stared at the bags containing their ill-gotten haul.

For a brief moment, Dean felt a pang of guilt surge through him, but no sooner the sensation struck, he shook it off. "Hell," he thought, "it's just a bunch of old army stuff. The old man won't even miss it."

"Here's how we do this," said Dean. "We take one thing out of a bag at a time and figure out who'll take it. We split this stuff up evenly. Worm was the lookout, but he gets the same amount of shit as we do," saying this as he looked directly into Kane's eyes. Both Dean and Worm knew that Kane was the most selfish of the three, which seemed weird to them, as Kane was, without a doubt, the most privileged of the three.

"Okay, okay," replied Kane, understanding clearly that Dean's words held the subliminal message that Kane should not screw around. "Got it, now can we dig in?"

Dean put up his right index finger, signaling a pause for one second longer. Then, he slowly dug into the brown bag closest to him, pulling out the first piece, drawing an "ahhh" from the others. Dean held in his hand a dark green, woolen beret.

"Wow," exclaimed Worm, who hadn't seen any of the loot until this moment and was totally unaware of the nature of the spoils. "Old man Mann was really a soldier."

"Soldier?" said Dean, "This shit might be Green Beret. He may have been a killer."

"I got dibs," cried out Kane, as he reached for the beret.

Dean yanked it back quickly from Kane's outstretched hand and said, "No friggin' way, pal. We flip for this." He dug into his pocket and pulled out a quarter. Two flips later, he reluctantly handed the beret over to Kane, the winner of the coin toss between him and his compatriots.

Kane set the beret on his head and proclaimed, "Now I'm the badass," as he smiled broadly.

Dean was about to pull out another object from the bag, then stopped and swiped his right backhanded fist across Kane's left arm. "You wear that in public and we are all screwed, got it? We gotta keep this shit secret." He looked from Kane to Worm and back to Kane. "Secret, boys. Got it? This is serious crap, guys. Clear?"

"Okay, okay okay," the other two swore over and over again. At that moment, another uncomfortable sensation overcame Dean. When he planned to rob this well-known figure in Centerville, he failed to consider the mindlessness and carelessness of his friends. Any bragging, or worse, showing off the goods, would put them all at risk.

Almost reluctantly now, Dean pulled out an old army canteen; a little rusty, but very cool. Pieces were placed on the rug one after another; a jackknife, a nonworking flashlight, what looked to be a hunting knife, a compass, an empty ID wallet, and a multitude of army paraphernalia. They knew before they entered the house, the old man would not have any money to speak of and money wasn't their intention to begin with. They wanted the army stuff and figured he had enough of it that he wouldn't even notice some of it missing. Plus, the old guy's mind was probably starting to slip anyway.

When the grocery bags were emptied, they began handling the goods, and each sized up what they wanted. As there were additional military headwear, shirts, and jerseys, Dean reminded his friends, once again, they could not wear anything in public.

They negotiated on who got what, and flipped a coin, when there was no consensus. An hour after they had arrived at Kane's home, the distribution of Charley Mann's memories was complete. The boys felt no regret at the actions they had taken. Quite to the contrary.

Back in the streets, Dean and Worm made their way to their respective homes, carrying grocery bags under their arms. Kane stayed behind, in his own home, to size up his share of the bounty. Dean's route to his grandmother's house allowed him to pass by Brown's Bike Shop and take a peek down the dead-end road. He half expected to see police cars and camera crews, in their initial phase of solving the crime of the century. There were no cars at all, and in fact, no signs of life. Dean felt a bit of relief.

As he continued on, the bag squeezed under his left armpit, Dean's right hand felt the outline of the contents of his jacket's right pocket. One item he had come across at Mann's house, and taken, he did not share with the other boys. He wasn't sure what it was; all he knew was it looked too cool to pass up. He found it in the back of a bedroom drawer and stuffed the rectangular box into his jacket pocket. It did not find its way into one of the grocery bags. No coins were being flipped over this piece.

He would figure out what it was at a later time. But for now, it would be a secret within a secret.

As he walked along, a sense of pride overcame Dean. Never had he felt quite the leader as he felt at this moment in time. And he was more than that. He was a planner, a plotter. He imagined the adventure, then saw it through. And he brought his followers along for the experience of a lifetime.

Was this a sign? Was this what he was meant to do? Time would tell, he thought. Time would tell. He smiled as he walked briskly along.

Chapter 36

Maggie and Victor worked on the helicopter in the early afternoon, while Peg relaxed back at the house. The visitors had only been in Truth or Consequences for a little over a day, and Maggie had made them feel totally at home. Peg found herself picking up around the house as if it were her own. It was a very good and warm feeling that she had never welcomed more. Both she and her husband needed all the human kindness they could get, and Maggie's graciousness and generosity had given them exactly that.

At the airfield, Victor found that Maggie had not been exaggerating about her knowledge and interest in all aircraft, including helicopters. She spoke to him about the old days when she and Marty moved around the mid-west, crop dusting on contract. They were young and both capable of spraying fertilizer and fungicide from both single engine airplanes or choppers. Whatever the farmer had available, they were happy to accommodate.

It was a great time in her life, but unfortunately, it was the life for the young. As she grew older and began to look for something more established in her life, Marty and she began to drift apart from one another. He was not at all interested in giving up the wanderlust life, and when she moved back to her hometown, he continued the gypsy lifestyle. They remained friends, however, and have stayed in touch to this day.

"How do you like this machine, Victor?"

"I love it, Maggie. It flies like a dream. Again, too bad it's not mine. But then again, I'm not sure anybody owns it."

"What do you mean by that?"

"No identification numbers. All professionally erased. I've looked all over the chopper. There's not a number or letter on it. I suppose if you murder people, it's a good idea not to have IDs of any kind, whether it's your chopper, your car, or your name. My guess is that they're all ghosts."

"Do you think the ghosts are coming for you?"

"Not sure, but I saw what they did, so I wouldn't be surprised. I'll just be on guard and hope they can't find us."

"I know this sounds like empty bullshit, big guy, and I doubt you would ever take me up on it; but if you ever need anything, please call me, okay?"

"Maggie, if I called you, it wouldn't be fair to the bad guys. But I'll keep your offer in mind. You're something else. Thanks, Maggie."

"Don't thank me. I would love a shot at those pieces of crap. And I mean shot, if you know what I mean?" She reached into the large right pocket of her cargo pants, drew out a twenty-five-caliber revolver, and gave Victor a knowing grin.

"I think I know what you mean, Maggie. And like I said, it wouldn't be fair to those assholes."

Victor and Maggie returned to the house with the makings of a hamburger and hot dog cookout. They had stopped at the local convenience store on their way back and picked up the main ingredients, including salad, desert, and most importantly, beer.

Peg had finished cleaning the house, watering the plants, squeezing in a nap, and met them at the door. Maggie smiled at Peg. "The chopper is all set and raring to go. It'll fly itself, now that we massaged the hell out of it. More importantly, we have the fixings for a dinner fit for those that don't know better. I don't know about you, but I'm starving."

Maggie made her way directly to the gas grill in the backyard and lit it up. Within minutes, the smell of dogs and burgers wafted through the dry air.

They sat around a wrought iron table in the middle of the sunburnt lawn, laughing as they ate, while consuming multiple beers. Maggie, ever the curious and courteous host, asked her two guests about their family. "Your kids live in Missouri, is that right?"

"The three boys live with my mother in Centerville, Missouri. We moved them out there in February of 2004. Just thought it would be the best place for them for the time being, and now I'm extremely glad we did. This whole awful situation would have been even a bigger nightmare if we had the kids with us."

"And your mom's okay with the kids?" Maggie asked, as if wondering how anyone would take three kids that they didn't bring into this world themselves. Having never had much of a maternal instinct, Maggie was in awe of such generous souls.

"My mother suggested it. She loves them being there. Gives her a purpose in her life and companionship she really needed since my parents' divorce. They're not the easiest boys in the world, but she seems to enjoy them nonetheless. And it was a good thing for us as well." Peg quickly glanced at Victor but did not want to look obvious in doing so.

Maggie was more interested in their family dynamic the more she heard. "So how often do you see them?"

Peg continued answering Maggie's questions, as Victor showed little interest in the subject matter. "I go every few months. Take the train. I wished it were more often, but now, obviously, I'll make up for time lost."

Maggie, not one to be shy about inquiring into other people's business, turned her attention to Victor, and asked, "How about you, big guy? How often have you been able to see the boys?"

"Saw them a little over a year ago. Been tough for me to get out there."

There was an uncomfortable silence among the three of them, and then Peg spoke up again. "Oh, hell, Victor, why not just tell Maggie the truth. She'll understand. Why beat around the bush?" Victor, obviously reluctant to talk about any family business at all, was particularly hesitant to speak on this subject. However, he had uncharacteristically developed a familial attachment to the owner of the home and kitchen, he now sat in, and nodded to Peg, as if to say "go ahead."

"Maggie, I'll give you the short version, if you don't mind."

"Not at all, Peg. I'm honored you guys are willing to tell me your story at all. That said, I'm all ears." She smiled sheepishly, and continued, "Plus, you know, not that much shit happens in Truth or Consequences." She nodded to Peg, indicating that she go on.

"Okay then. The short version. Like I said before, I took the boys to Centerville in February of 2004. I returned to San Diego shortly thereafter. Victor and I returned to Centerville late summer that same year. Victor got into a fight on Main Street when some guy cracked a joke about his size. Got arrested after giving the police a difficult time, and I bailed him out. Wasn't the best first impression to give the authorities in that sleepy little town. We returned to San Diego as soon as the judge allowed us to."

Maggie and Peg both looked at Victor, who had his head back, held up by his interlocked fingers, and staring at the ceiling. Nothing was said, and Peg continued.

"Well, we decided a little over a year later, after the new school year began, to give it another try. We both went back to Centerville. After holed up in my mother's house for a few days, we came to the decision that Victor would go to Dean's school the evening of the Sports Assembly. My hope was, by my guy here showing some positive involvement in his boy's athletic life, he would begin to resurrect his own image in our future home.

Peg paused for a moment and once again looked toward her husband, who returned her glance with an expression of resigned acceptance, as if he himself wondered how she would complete the story of that evening. Peg then turned toward Maggie, who seemed totally immersed and invested in the account of the Drueding family in Centerville.

"Well, Maggie, my newfound friend and the most perfect hostess Victor and I have ever encountered, things didn't quite turn out the way we hoped." Peg actually turned a slight grin, as if to convey that she had become slightly amused, given the passage of time, with the events of that evening now so long ago.

"Victor went to the school with all of the best intentions. He walked, as I needed the one available car we had. That turned out to be a bad decision. My extra-large hubby has always had quirky knees, and hips for that matter, and a long walk that evening didn't make those collection of joints feel any better. By the time he arrived at the school, he was not only hurting, but he was late for the meeting."

Peg took a sip from the bottle of beer that had been sitting in front of her, unattended, since her story began. She exhaled, with the satisfied sound that comes from the taste of an ice-cold brew.

"Once in school, a woman who was supposed to welcome parents, chided him for being late, and then gave him reluctant directions to the meeting. He hustled down the hall, asked another parent for further directions, and didn't like his response either. One thing led to another, and my husband unfortunately got into a fight with the man in the hallway. Cops came. He ended up down at the jailhouse. And all in all, our plans to resurrect Victor's reputation went to shit."

"Well, is that all?" Maggie somewhat humorously asked, trying to lighten the moment.

"Actually, not really, Maggie. Victor happened to also pick on the father of one of the most popular families of the Centerville community. And not only this man and his wife are highly regarded in Centerville, but they have a young son, who is somewhat of a baseball phenomenon in town."

Maggie looked somewhat puzzled. "Why is the kid such a big deal in this story?"

Both Peg and Victor reacted with muted grins. Peg turned to Maggie and in a very solemn and serious tone, said, "Maggie, baseball is everything in Centerville, Missouri."

Maggie then asked, "What should Victor have done, Peg?"

"Regardless of how my husband was treated, Maggie, I wish he had done nothing and simply said one thing."

"What thing should he have said?"

"'Hey, how you doin'?' Nobody ever got into trouble with those few simple words. No matter what's said to you. No matter how pissed you get. Just take a breath. Keep your temper in check, and say 'Hey, how you doin'?' Isn't that better than wanting to beat the shit out of someone whenever you're in a bad mood?"

Maggie didn't respond right away.

Peg's eyebrows lifted, as if to ask "Well?"

"Thinking about it," was all Maggie said.

Chapter 37

The following morning was a perfectly clear and brisk Saturday. Once again, Maggie whipped up a hardy breakfast, but this time she did so with a heavy heart.

Her houseguests would be flying away in a couple of hours, and she missed them already. They had only stayed two nights, but she felt she had known them all her life. The fact was, it was a mutual feeling by the departing couple.

They sat around the kitchen table once again, sharing stories of bygone years; opportunities taken, and opportunities lost. They laughed easily among themselves and poked fun at one another with a light touch. This was not time to begin heavy conversation or philosophical nonsense. In essence, they were saying goodbye, while trying to act as though they were not.

By eight o'clock, they were at the airfield and the helicopter blades were beginning to spin. It would be a long day for Victor and

Peg, as they would be making three stops—two to refuel and the final one for the night. If all went well, they would make it to Garden City, Kansas before the sun went down.

Victor hugged Maggie for a prolonged period of time, especially for him. Maggie spoke nonstop all the while, which was fine with him, as he had no words. He would miss her, and the woman knew it.

As Victor sat at the controls, it was Peg's turn, and it was practically excruciating. They would have had much to say, if they were able to stop crying. Finally, they pushed back from one another and just nodded their heads knowingly.

As Peg turned to approach the helicopter, she heard Maggie saying something to her. Peg turned and indicated she could not hear over the noise of the engine and blades. Maggie summoned as much sound as she could muster and yelled, "I'll be seeing you." Then she backed away from the increasing swirl of the dirt and dust.

Peg shook her head in the affirmative, raced around to her side of the craft, and boarded.

The Alouette lifted and hovered fifty feet off the ground. Victor smiled down at Maggie and mouthed "thank you." He then rotated the chopper 180 degrees, so his wife could see the beautiful woman below. Peg waved her right hand and wiped her eyes with her left.

Looking up, Maggie gave Peg the royal wave and smiled.

The helicopter turned northbound and disappeared into the distant sky.

Chapter 38

The chopper landed in Garden City, Kansas just before dusk, Saturday evening. It had been an extremely long day with fuel stops in Santa Rosa, New Mexico and Trinidad, Colorado. There was somewhat of a payment glitch in Santa Rosa, requiring Victor to place a phone call to Jake, back at Whitman Field. Once Jake resolved the problem with the field manager, they were refueled and on their way once again.

Fortunately for Victor and Peg, their bodies had been fully rested, courtesy of Maggie's hospitality, allowing them to hold up over the course of an unusually long day. They arrived in Garden City feeling somewhat tired, but in good shape. Also, the closer they were to Centerville, the more upbeat were their spirits. If all were to go well, they would arrive at their new address the following night.

They were met at the landing zone by a very young-looking man. Upon introductions, they learned his name was Bucky Lynch. Bucky looked far too young to be working at all, let alone around the aircraft. When shaking the boy's hand, Victor could not help but ask him his age.

"Thirteen, sir, but don't worry, I don't work on the birds here, and I certainly don't fly any of them…yet."

"So, what do you do?" asked the big man, thinking back to when he helped his father at Whitman Field, beginning when he was even younger than the boy in front of him.

"Mainly clean up and all the crappy jobs my dad and his co-workers don't want to do. But I do refuel helicopters, if that's what you're asking."

"So, you work for your father? What does he do?"

"Everything. His friends call him an airplane junkie. Knows everything about them, and choppers to boot. He's teaching me when he has the time, and I already love it. I can't wait to fly."

"Fly what?"

"Whatever leaves the ground, sir. You name it, I'm gonna fly it."

"Good man. If I had any hesitation about you filling up the chopper, I don't know. Fill 'er up and change the oil."

"Change the oil?"

Both Victor and Peg grinned at the boy, and then Victor said, "Forget the oil, just fill it up. Thanks. By the way, where's your dad?"

Bucky pointed toward a small building about one hundred yards away, past a field dotted with small single- and twin-engine airplanes, all parked for the night. "His office is in there," advised the boy.

Victor went over the nuances of the chopper's fuel tanks with the boy. This was Victor's habit, whether the helicopter was to be serviced by a young pup such as Bucky, or a crusty old chopper veteran who would always find Victor's reminders irritating.

Victor didn't care. If you were a conscientious pilot, you were involved in every detail of your aircraft.

The couple began the short trek to the small airfield offices.

They would have knocked on the door, but Pete Lynch saw the two of them approaching and opened the door the moment they reached it.

"I'm Pete, guys, and I figure you just met my son. I've been expecting you. Come on in."

Victor introduced Peg and himself to Pete and immediately said how impressive his young son was.

"Well, thanks, Victor. Yeah, I think the boy has already found his passion and his future. I just hope he can make a living out of it. It sure as hell didn't make me rich, but working with him is a blast."

Pete shook Victor's hand and then turned to Peg. "Peg, do you need anything? There are facilities in that building over there," pointing to another small building only fifty feet away. "I was speaking to your friend, Jake, earlier, so I know you've had a long day."

"I'm good for now," Peg said, "but thanks."

Pete turned again to Victor. "Victor, we can go over things if you want in a little while, but first I suggest we check you two into our little motel just down the road. You guys can freshen up, and then we can grab a bite at a little joint across the street. By the way, Jake wanted me to tell you that the bill for your layover here is covered. Everything. You must be a hell of a guy." Pete smiled in a lighthearted way and made both Victor and Peg feel very comfortable and relaxed with the new surroundings.

"Sounds great," said Peg, thinking how lucky they were to keep meeting such nice people along the way. "Thanks, Pete. And believe me, we won't keep you up very late tonight."

Pete again opened the door for his visitors, and they made their way to his well-worn Jeep.

An hour later, Victor, Peg, Pete, and Bucky were dining on steak tips and potatoes. As Pete never suggested ordering beers or any other alcoholic beverages, Victor and Peg followed suit, and both sipped on diet cokes.

It was obvious that Pete didn't have a clue about the couple's situation and that was definitely fine with Victor and Peg. By now, they were mentally exhausted from conversations surrounding their predicament and found discussing more normal subjects a relief and a pleasure.

"So, Bucky," asked Peg, "You are going to be a pilot phenomenon, is that about right?" She smiled widely as she asked the overstated complimentary question.

Bucky began to blush a little and looked to his father for help in answering the stranger's query. His dad grinned at his son and nodded for him to go ahead and answer for himself.

"I don't know about that, Ma'am. I'm a long way from even becoming a pilot, but I certainly intend to, and I hope someday I'm a real good one."

Pete spoke up, enhancing his son's response. "That's all he wants. All he thinks about. And all he plans to do. He'll be a great pilot someday, but I wouldn't mind if for now, he blends in a few other things that his friends do. You've still gotta be a kid. It doesn't last that long."

Bucky smiled sheepishly and looking upward toward the ceiling, said, "I know, I know. I gotta play baseball and football with the guys, and I do, sort of."

Both Victor and Peg were amused at the father–son banter, and both felt a bit jealous that this wasn't the relationship they had with their children. But nevertheless, it was good to see and experience.

They enjoyed each other's company for the next hour and a half, talking about the airfield, the town of Garden City, and Bucky's school life. It was no problem for Victor and Peg to steer the conversation in any direction that did not include their life and circumstances. Then, Peg uncontrollably yawned, sending the unintended signal, that the evening was coming to a close.

The four stood, spoke briefly about the timetable for departure the next day, and then began to say their goodbyes. As the motel was across the street, Pete and his son would be leaving them at the restaurant's front door.

When it was the young boy's turn to say "see ya," he uncharacteristically brought up an unexpected topic. Having heard their destination was Centerville and the fact it was their home, he asked, "Mr. and Mrs. Drueding, do you follow Youth League Baseball in Missouri at all?"

Victor and Peg looked at one another, knowing the answer, but hoping the other would reply. Peg did. "Not really, Bucky. Do you have friends playing there?"

"No, not at all, but all we hear about here is how good this kid from Centerville is. All we ever hear about is Centerville, Centerville, Centerville; never hear beans about Youth League Baseball in Kansas, because the sports pages are all about Missouri now, and this kid. Do you know him? What's his name, Stan something?"

Bucky's father chimed in. "Johnson, son. His name is Stan Johnson, and there's another kid who is supposed to be great too. And Bucky's right, the boys play in your new hometown. It'll make Missouri baseball fun for you guys, if you're into that stuff."

"Not so much," said Peg. "Of course, we know about him, and the team, but we're not big into baseball. Our kids are a little into it, but we're not the most athletic family around." As she was speaking, her thoughts were actually, *Yeah, we know the little shit; my husband got into a fight with his father, what do you think about that?*

Victor stayed silent, not believing what he was hearing. Then it struck him that once in Missouri, he was going to hear this crap everywhere he went. *Great*, he thought. *Maybe we'd be better off flying back to San Diego. We just can't win.*

The next morning, after thanking Pete and Bucky for the assist and good company, Victor and Peg took off once again, with the hope of landing in Centerville by the end of the day.

Late in the afternoon, after refueling stops in McPherson, Kansas and Rich Hill, Missouri, Victor and Peg found themselves in the final leg of their journey home. The trip that seemed to take forever had lasted less than one week. Now, with every mile, they transitioned from recognizing the occasional town, lake, and other landmarks, to identifying most of their aerial surroundings. Centerville was not their actual home, but they had visited Peg's mom frequently enough over the years, to have a familiar connection to the region. Both felt a growing sense of comfort and security as they closed in on their destination.

Early evening, they landed at Pavilion Field, which conveniently was located in the outskirts of Centerville, not far at all from Dot's house. Earlier in the day, Victor had notified the manager of the field of their projected arrival time. They had been directed where to place the helicopter and did so with no problem. As the manager would be gone upon their arrival, Victor would meet with him the following day, to discuss various issues.

At seven o'clock Sunday evening, a knock came on Dot Collin's front door. Within the house could be heard the hollering of three young boys wrestling, mixed with the high-volume sound of a television set. The boy's grandmother was the only one who heard the knock over the mayhem existing in her living room.

"Boys," she yelled. "Quiet for a half a second, and somebody answer the door."

Dean, who was kneeling over one of his younger brothers, and twisting his ear hard enough to make the younger boy beg loudly for mercy, rolled off him, and rose up from the carpet. *Who the hell is at the door at this hour on a Saturday night?* He thought to himself, with a slight bit of trepidation rising through him. Dean had a number of reasons to carry some level of apprehension whenever anything unexpectedly occurred in his life. He unenthusiastically made his way to the door.

He unlocked and opened the door slowly. He peered into the eyes of the visitors before him, and the thirteen-year-old's jaw dropped. This was by no means the standard reaction of a young boy who was staring into the smiling faces…of his parents.

Section III

Chapter 39

Monday was a most unusual day for the Drueding family. It had been a while since they all had awakened under the same roof, and never had it been such a total surprise for the majority of the family.

The three boys had somewhat different reactions to their parent's arrival. The younger two were happy to have their mother back in their lives on a regular basis. Dean, the oldest of the three, thought differently. He knew the presence of his parents meant less freedom, as his folks would not be as easy to fool as his grandmother.

Peg's mother, Dot, although caught totally off guard herself, was like a child on Christmas morning; the arrival of her daughter and her son-in-law was a gift of immeasurable value. The added knowledge that her daughter was home for good kept a constant smile on her face. Dot called her workplace and took the day off; additionally, she notified the schools that the boys would be absent as well.

The three adults sat around the kitchen table and discussed life going forward. Neither Victor nor Peg were forthright with Dot about the reason for their unexpected appearance, other than they wanted to surprise her. The emotional high Dot was experiencing overrode any logical questions she may have otherwise had. It mattered not to her at this moment, as she relished the euphoria.

Dean was not experiencing anything close to euphoria. He had effectively carved out a comfortable life for himself while living under his grandmother's roof. He came and went as he pleased. Among his questionable friends, he enjoyed an identity of independence and power. Many of his other peers saw Dean as a bully, but this was a mantle he was happy and willing to carry. Now, with the dynamic at home in flux, a sliver of vulnerability crept back into his life. He was not happy about this, and he was damned if anyone, parents included, were going to change his world.

Victor returned to the Pavilion Air Field the next morning and discussed the storage of the helicopter with the manager of the field. He wished to protect the craft and shield it from curious eyes. Victor knew there were two small hangers on the property and negotiated securing affordable space within one of the hangers. He hoped the bad guys would decide not to hunt him down, but he felt hiding the chopper, in any event, was a smart move for the time being.

Peg and her mother enjoyed the day together, with one big hug fest. In the morning, they moved from room to room, chatting, smiling, and hugging each other. In the afternoon, they went food shopping and hugged once in an aisle; and again, at the house, while putting the food away. Mother and daughter had been in each other's company many times over the years, but this was different. Peg was home, and home for good.

Late in the afternoon, as the initial excitement and glow of the family reunion started to fade, normalcy began to creep in. The boys were outside shooting hoops at a rim set up on the side of the house. With every shot, the side wall banged and vibrated, causing Peg to inquire as to the wisdom of this particular placement of the backboard. Her mother laughed and informed Peg that the boys were only this close to the house at all, because of the presence of their parents. "I'm shocked they even were able to find the basketball, that's how infrequently they play," she said.

As the two women were placing the dinner setting on the table, the phone rang. Dot grabbed the phone and, after a brief exchange of courtesies with the caller, told Victor the call was for him. Victor had a look of surprise, as the possible field of candidates on the other end of the line was obviously a narrow one. One or two of the possibilities were nightmares.

Luckily, it was Jake. Victor asked if he could call him back after dinner. Jake, stunned by his protege's newfound table manners, shockingly responded, "Fine, Sally, but don't make it too late."

Once dinner was over and the sun was setting, the boys were instructed to remain in the house for the evening, presumably to do homework. Once secluded in their rooms, each found some other form of entertainment, as the term "homework" was not, and never was, in their vernacular.

Dean, for his part, sat on his bed, once again sifting through the bounty from the war veteran's heist. When Dean's only concern was his grandmother, hiding these small treasures was no problem at all. Dean knew with certainty that she had no prying tendencies at all.

Today was a new day. Dean must now find legitimate hiding places, as his mother was as good as any CIA agent when it came to uncovering what was not to be found. But Dean was up to the task, especially when it came to his most prized possession. Although as yet he still didn't know what it was, the medal within the rectangular box did seem important. Dean figured it must have had great value as well. He would hide this item with the greatest care.

Finding himself alone in the living room, Victor phoned Jake back. Jake asked if Victor had permission from the girls to speak to him, as he "didn't want the boy to get into any trouble." "Funny," replied Victor, "What's up?"

"Something that may not be anything, my boy, or something that may be something."

"Jake, I always know exactly what you're saying, you know that? No wait, what I mean is that I have no friggin' idea what you're talking about, ol' timer." Victor waited a few seconds and then chuckled at his own response. He loved the old guy, and Jake was the only human being on the planet he teased. They had that kind of relationship.

"Are you done, asshole," replied his mentor. "And if you're not, no problem here, as this call is on your nickel, wise guy."

This made Victor laugh all the more, "Okay, okay, Jake. I'm sorry, my friend. What's up for real?"

"Victor, this could be serious shit, my boy. So, listen carefully. Not sure this is anything, but a black Lincoln Town Car drove through here the other day, then again, this morning. They didn't stop, and I couldn't see through the darkened windshield. You said they drove a black Lincoln and I thought you should know. If it's them, they're looking for the chopper. What do you think?"

"I don't think, Jake. I know. It's them."

"I didn't want to call you when I first saw the car, because I figured you needed a day to settle in and get some rest. However, when I saw the damn car again today, I had to call. But it may not be them, Victor." Jake's tone was serious now, as he was very concerned about the man on the other end of the line.

There was a prolonged silence. Finally, Jake spoke up again. "Do you think it's them, Victor?"

Again, silence. Then, a whisper from the biggest man Jake had ever known, softly passed through the receiver. A barely audible response.

"It's them, Jake. They're coming."

Chapter 40

As was his daily habit for many years, Charlie Mann spent a few hours visiting the local VFW club. Every day, he and a dozen other vets would meet in the club room, drink coffee, have a snack of some sort or another, and solve the world's problems. On occasion, their own problems would creep into the conversation, and those were the most beneficial discussions.

War veterans, especially those having experienced long-term battle, carried more than their share of mental scarring. Sessions with shrinks helped, but there was no substitution for sharing your problems, often of the most sensitive nature, with your comrades.

Corporal Mann returned from Vietnam in 1970 after his fourth tour of duty. During his last tour, he was shot in the knee and suffered a combat ending injury. The wounded knee was the outward, most visible damage, inflicted upon the Corporal. After a series of surgeries, and what seemed like a lifetime of physical therapy, Charlie learned to walk with his compromised knee. A permanent limp became part of his personal profile, and the disability made him unsuited for a variety of employment opportunities he was otherwise qualified for.

In Vietnam, Charlie was strong, courageous, and respected. He was known to never issue an order that he would not carry out personally. He placed himself in harm's way on innumerable occasions, often in protection of his men. And they loved him for it. When the bullet entered his body on the battlefield, and he was carried off, his thoughts were immediately those of his comrades. He knew instantaneously that his war was over, and he would be leaving his men behind.

Charlie returned to the States and was honorably discharged. Due to the sensibilities of the time, his country was not the "welcoming home" environment that returning soldiers would hope for. The war was unpopular as were the soldiers fighting it. He was regarded as simply a man with a limp, who barely had a high school education. He settled in Centerville, Missouri. His grandparents had lived there all of their lives, and it seemed as inviting a place as he could expect to find.

Still, the work was scarce for a man like Charlie. He awoke early every morning, combed the newspaper for possible jobs, and made hopeful phone calls. Once in a while, he was hired for part-time employment, and he scraped by, with his disability check and the occasional pay check.

With the assistance of a VA loan, he bought an extremely modest house, down the street from Brown's Bike Shop. The location came in quite handy actually, because from time to time, Arnie Brown, the proprietor, would give Charlie a used bicycle. Weather permitting, Charlie would use the bike to get around. Otherwise, he walked. At times, the bicycle would be difficult as well, and he would walk anyway, with a discernible limp.

Returning from the VFW, he would enter his home and begin switching on lights that would stay on until he retired for the night. Charlie had the habit of taking a late afternoon nap, so rather than awaken to a dark house, he opted to pay the electric company a little bit more each month and keep the lights on.

The VFW was an important part of Charlie's life. In fact, it was an essential part of Charlie's well-being. He was the happiest when he shared time with his brethren veterans. They had a way of uplifting his spirits, and he did his best to uplift theirs. These men were better than shrinks.

Charlie was somewhat set apart from his friends at the fraternal club, as he had held longer active service than the rest and was awarded a distinguished commendation. Never one to flaunt this fact, it seemed to be mentioned by someone, at some point of his visit, every day.

The old soldier would leave the VFW every afternoon with his chest slightly more expanded than when he arrived. While making his twenty-minute excursion home, he would replay in his head conversations of the day. When he arrived at his modest house, as he did on this day, and after flipping on most of the lights, he had one more habit to satisfy, before he laid his tired body down on the couch.

Charlie went into his bedroom, directly off the kitchen, and made his way to the chest of drawers. Pulling out the second drawer from the top, he reached in, as he had done hundreds of times, to the back of the drawer. Pushing aside folded-up socks, his opened right hand felt its way around. The object of his maneuvering was sure to come into contact with a finger or two.

The object was not there. Charlie chuckled to himself, as he pulled on the third drawer, figuring his fading mind couldn't remember into which drawer he had put it. "I'm definitely one old bastard," he thought to himself. The neatly folded underwear in the third drawer was a remnant behavior left over from the army, one habit he would never kick. Working both hands now, he gently flipped over one pair of underpants to another, finding nothing once again.

His heart rate began to climb ever so slightly as he moved to the bottom drawer, then to the top. He tried the second drawer once again, now pushing the socks around haphazardly, with two rolled-up pairs jumping up and out of the drawer and onto the floor. Uncharacteristically, Charlie didn't bother to pick them up.

His pulse racing now, he stood erect and looked around the room. His eyes settled on a bureau top that held the antique hunting knife he was given by a private in Nam, as a *thank you* for getting him home alive. No knife. He moved to a small bookcase that was the depository for a number of other, less important, but relevant memories. Canteen, gone. An old army hat, gone.

Feeling nauseous, he moved to his closet. The door, as always, was ajar. He had not closed it since childhood, for fear of sheltering the bogeyman. He slowly pulled the door open, praying he would find one of his most precious belongings. The hook on the inside upper door was bare, holding nothing. He stepped back to the bed and sat down, feeling faint. His green beret had hung from that hook since the day he moved into the house. Occasionally, Charlie would take it off the hook and place it on his head. He would step in front of the mirror, see his reflection, and feel pride. One day long ago, he was somebody.

His shoulders slumped over. He put his hands to his face, and let his emotions release. They had taken everything that meant anything to him. His beret was gone. His knife, the symbol of a soldier's gratitude, was gone. Other memories, with little or no value to anyone, but himself, were gone.

All terrible enough, but survivable, if it wasn't for the object in the second drawer. It was his pride. It was his legacy. It told the world that Corporal Charlie Mann was a worthwhile human being. And now, his Purple Heart, was gone.

Chapter 41

Eriq Steed wanted to find the pilot so badly, it was eating him up inside. He wanted to kill the bastard more than he ever wanted to kill anyone. Mr. Freeport's strategy of patience, a measured approach to finding and then attending to the pilot, was torture to Steed.

Freeport's plan was to hire an outside entity, a private investigator if you will, to locate the thief who stole his helicopter. Freeport was in no hurry. In fact, he knew time was on his side. The pilot was sure to let his guard down after a couple of months, becoming confident with time, that he was not being hunted. Then Mr. Raymond Freeport would strike.

Steed's instincts were to rush headlong after the pilot, and possibly allowing mistakes to be made. But Freeport would not allow any more mistakes by his unhinged underling. He kept a tight leash on the skinny man, promising Steed he would have his opportunity to kill

Drueding. But it would be on Freeport's timetable, and on a date and time of Freeport's choosing.

Soon after the helipad incident, Freeport instructed Steed to visit Whitman Field at odd hours of pre-selected days and simply survey the grounds. In the unlikely event, the helicopter appeared back at Whitman, they would spot it. Freeport never actually believed that the man who stole the chopper would be so obvious and stupid to return to the small airfield, but in the interest of "covering all their bases," they would not presume anything.

The boss made it perfectly clear to Steed that he was not to exit his vehicle when visiting the field and was to speak to no one about anything. He was only to observe. If by unexpected luck, he was to discover the missing helicopter, he was to notify Freeport. Only then, would Steed be given further instructions.

After two weeks, Freeport instructed Steed to stop visiting the airfield altogether. Additionally, Freeport made it clear to Steed, that his presence was not required at the offices of Community Betterment. The less he laid eyes on the skinny man, the better. Unfortunately, for Freeport, Steed had a key and would let himself into the Community Betterment location whenever he thought Freeport might appear there. Freeport regretted the day he gave an office key to Mr. Eriq Steed.

Freeport's plan was simple. He would handle the investigation into the whereabouts of one missing helicopter and one missing, soon-to-be-dead, large pilot. Steed was to wait patiently for further instructions. However, patience was not a virtue of Eriq Steed's. He phoned Mr. Freeport daily, for weeks, asking for updates. Steed also visited the office with regularity.

Given his underling's proclivities, Freeport rarely stopped by Community Betterment and only visited to continue the process of closing operations down. He had never actually spent quality or quantitative time there, as the address was primarily for show, but there were utilities and other mundane services to discontinue. Detail was an important element in the life of this successful criminal.

Knowing his charge was overly anxious and unpredictable, Freeport deliberately moved quickly and at odd hours, to accomplish whatever tasks requiring him to visit the office. This irritated Freeport, but the inconvenience was better than having to spend face time with the erratic Steed.

For his part, Steed had three obsessive motives contributing to his hyper impatience and was consumed with each obsession. His thirst for revenge was one overhanging motive; that the oversized piece of crap had the audacity to escape, making Steed look incompetent, was in and of itself, enough to enrage the skinny man.

The money Freeport owed Steed was a second driving factor in Steed's anxiousness. Freeport made it clear that these ntil the pilot was found and dealt with. This angered Steed, as it was never part of the deal. He was owed the money funds would not be released u now but had no choice but to suck this aggravation up. At least, for now.

Without question, however, the single most important motive was the chopper, and the fortune hidden within. The secret ingredient in all of Steed's work and sacrifice was sitting in a clandestine compartment behind the rear passenger seat, this fact alone, gave him a craving motivation, to find the pilot and the aircraft.

Raymond Freeport had the capacity to reel his temper in and let his intellect take over. He had always been able to think through, plan out, and eventually solve the inevitable problems that confronted him. In this case, he was convinced that moving slowly and carefully in his efforts to find the pilot was absolutely to his advantage. Let his prey settle in, probably in Missouri where he had family, and Freeport would strike when least expected.

He was systematic and exacting, and his approach had always served him well. However, he had never had to build into the equation, the unpredictable and often times illogical behavior of the likes of Mr. Steed. Until now.

Freeport believed that having a ruthless killer, such as Steed, was a nice asset to have in your toolbox. As long as control was not an issue. At present, however, Freeport harbored concerns regarding control. As weeks turned into months, the situation worsened; Steed's constant efforts to contact Freeport concerned the older man more and more. Freeport's apprehension began to peak.

Freeport knew well the mind of a psychopath and the unpredictable dangers it posed. One had to keep that person busy, well used, and content. Otherwise, as with a hammer or saw, unfocused use could result in serious harm. Freeport would not let this occur. If need be, he would deal with Mr. Steed in a very definitive way.

He would not allow the skinny crazy man to ruin the brilliant work that he had accomplished up until now. And he would do whatever it took to remedy the situation.

Chapter 42

January 2007

The holidays came and went in the Drueding/Collins household, but they weren't quite the joyous occasion they should have been, given the true family reunion that had occurred. Victor could not shake off the possibility of receiving deadly visitors and never fully relaxed. Even on Christmas Day, he felt the chances of an attack would be a real possibility.

For Peg's part, she read Victor like an open book and sensed his anxiety. She attempted to put on an optimistic face and professed to her husband that she had no concerns regarding their security. However, she too was living a fearful existence. *How difficult would it be to find us?* she thought. She slept poorly and worried about the well-being of their children.

The two younger boys seemed fine, and apparently unaware of anything out of the ordinary with their mother and father. To them, their parents seemed to be acting normally. The fact was, as they had not been in the company of their folks for such a long time, they had no basis to compare their behavior now, with their normal behavior. The boys were simply happy to have their parents home.

Their older brother, Dean, however, found little happiness in the new family dynamic. His grandmother had been of no consequence when it came to his lifestyle. He enjoyed that reality. Now, the worst-case scenario had occurred. Mom and Dad were very much of consequence. Dean's world was turned upside down. And he did not like it.

Poor Dot Collins. The ecstasy she experienced upon laying eyes on her daughter and her son-in-law, standing unexpectedly at her front door, had long since dissipated. She didn't know why things did not feel right but knew something was definitely wrong. She did not understand the reason why, but a sadness grew within her.

March 2007

By early March, nerves were frayed. Dot had helped her daughter find part-time employment at the department store, while Victor practically lived in front of the television set. Victor and Peg began to drink more than usual, and financially were just getting by. They clearly realized that their salvation was living rent free, due to an older, very hard-working woman, doing what she could to keep the family together. There was no escaping the reality that Dot Collins was the family glue. This was both a source of gratitude and frustration.

One morning, after Dot had left for work, Victor and Peg sat quietly in the tiny kitchen, sipping coffees, eating toast and peanut butter, and harboring hangovers. Peg's prolonged silence meant only one thing to Victor—his wife was mad about something. However, he had no intention of inquiring the reason why, as he knew better, from experience. He wasn't in the mood to talk anyway. Victor's plan was to let time take care of whatever it was that was bothering her.

He wasn't that lucky.

Twenty minutes into the conversational void, Peggy blinked, and began the day's communication with the last topic Victor wanted to hear.

"Are you going to look for work today, Vic? We can barely afford this crappy cup of coffee we're drinking on my pathetic paycheck. And it's getting to be a little unfair to my mom, don't you think?"

"Are we going to start with this shit right now?" Victor answered in a low, tired, and irritated voice. "I thought I was keeping a low profile for the time being?"

"For the time being, yeah, but it's been over two months now. I don't think the bad guys are going to find us, or maybe they just don't give a crap about us anymore. They don't know where we are, and it's a big damn country. The helicopter is out of sight. When do we just get on with our lives?"

"You know, it's the other thing too, Peg. People here hate me. What chance will I have finding something. Maybe we're better off going somewhere else, where I'll get a fair shake."

"Somewhere else?" Peg loudly responded. "The only reason we stay above water is my mother. We have a house here and we have food on the table for us and our kids. Let's build from there. Get out and prove to the assholes in this town that you're just as good as they are."

"Doing what?"

"Go to the airfield. Tell them you're willing to do anything. See what happens."

"I'll go and see what I can do, Peg." Victor capitulated in an emotionless and equally deflated manner. He knew that they had to get back to living, but between the traumatic experience they had escaped from, to the small town that had grown wary of both him and his boys, he felt trapped in a vortex of helplessness. But Victor also knew that he had to do something to crawl out from under the mess he was largely responsible for.

His head down, he left the house, heading toward the airfield, only a short distance away.

Chapter 43

March 15, 2007

The Ides of March was a good day for Raymond Freeport. The Private Investigator he had hired two months prior called him mid-morning with the news he had so anxiously been waiting to hear.

"I found your friends, Mr. Freeport."

"Excellent, Harry. And where might they be?"

"In a Norman Rockwell setting in the middle of Missouri."

"I've always wanted to visit that beautiful part of the world. Where exactly?"

"Centerville."

"Thank you, Harry. You can give me all the details later. I haven't seen these friends of mine for a lifetime, and when I show up, it will be the biggest surprise of their lives."

"It's good to have friends like you, sir. I'll speak to you later. It's been a pleasure working for you."

"The pleasure is all mine, my friend. Thank you."

Mr. Freeport hung up the phone, leaned back in his overstuffed Manhattan leather armchair, and savored the news he had just been given. His private investigator, Harry Croteau, had indeed done his job. Although his services didn't come cheap, Freeport was happy to pay the man's price.

He had hired Croteau given the PI's spotless reputation for following instructions to the letter. Freeport gave one simple, yet very important order, to Private Investigator Harry Croteau—speak to no one who may have a direct relationship of any kind with the man Freeport was looking for. He advised Croteau not to take any risks whatsoever, that could spoil the surprise. If this meant the search might take a little longer than normal to bear fruit, then so be it.

Freeport informed the private investigator that he was seeking to find an old friend and his family, who seemed to have fallen off the planet. Further, he told the PI that he planned to give his friend a great deal of money, to repay a friendship that had helped Freeport through a very rough patch many decades ago.

He failed to tell the private investigator that once in possession of the whereabouts of this old friend and his family, Freeport planned to pay them a visit. But not to give anyone money.

Raymond Freeport grabbed a legal pad from the desk drawer and a ball point pen from his inside sport coat pocket. Freeport was a man of discipline, constantly updating his life's master plan. The current phase of his master plan had only a few line items left to accomplish. He planned to personally see each objective to fruition. He scribbled notes updating details surrounding each of the three line-items.

Once his remaining plans were completed, Freeport would disappear from the world he had been living in, change his name once again, and live out his days enjoying the fruits of his past labors. The money he had amassed over the years would easily see to his comfort and happiness. And although unneeded, he would yet again add to his wealth.

He wrote down the final objectives of the remaining phase to his plan:

1. Eliminate Victor Drueding and his family.

2. Retrieve the helicopter that holds the small fortune Eriq Steed has stolen from him.

3. Inform Eriq Steed that his boss had known of his deception from the first day, then…kill Eriq Steed.

Chapter 44

Victor was given a job at Pavilion Field. He was initially assigned menial tasks at the airfield. The pay was minimal and the hours few, but it gave the big man at least something to look forward to. After only working part time for two weeks, as an assistant to the master mechanic and manager, Teddy Thompson, Victor's talent became apparent.

Teddy not only appreciated Victor's passion in his work but also realized, in short order, that Victor was in fact a superior mechanic. Another manager may have felt threatened by the talented Mr. Drueding, but Thompson was delighted to have such an asset to assist him in building the reputation of the facility.

The first few days of work, Victor would leave his mother-in-law's house and walk down the road to Pavilion Field, with a reluctant step and low level of energy. His heart was not into a part time, entry level position, that was without a doubt, beneath him. However, by the end of the second week, after receiving constant accolades from his boss, Victor sprang from his bed in the morning and returned home with animated tales of the day.

Upon returning to Dot's house one evening, toward the end of March, Victor found his wife standing just inside the front door, harboring the biggest smile he had ever seen on the face of his favorite girl. Standing just to Peg's right, and leaning against her daughter, was Dot, also smiling, almost giddy.

Victor stopped just inside the door, looked from one woman to the other, and found himself grinning as well. What he was witnessing had a contagious effect. Expecting something to be said at some point by one of the two women, and receiving nothing, he finally asked, "So what's going on?"

Mother and daughter gave each other a quick glance, then moved apart, giving Victor a view to what was behind them. Sitting on the couch, smiling widely herself, was Maggie Crotty. "Hi, big guy, didn't expect to see me, did you?"

Victor looked stunned for a moment, finding the scene in front of him out of context. It had been four months since he last laid eyes on the woman; a memory that now seemed like a dream. Once reality sunk in, he walked directly to the gray-haired woman with his large, bear like arms, opened wide.

"Are you kidding me, this couldn't be a better surprise," his voice uncharacteristically raised, to emphasize his genuine happiness to see her. His upper body totally encompassed the visitor, as they hugged enthusiastically. "My wife obviously knows how to keep secrets from me," he laughed.

"You don't know the half of it, Victor, my friend. I know all the secrets and I'm not tellin.'" Maggie pushed the large man away from her. "Let me take a look at you. Looking good. This metropolis must be settling well with you, huh?"

"Only the last couple of weeks, Mag. Now that I'm not hanging around being useless. But I'm sure you know more about my life by now than I do." He looked back at his still smiling wife and winked. Victor, in fact, was actually feeling better about his world and prospects, than he had in many, many months. The unexpected appearance of this wonderful woman, was another piece of positive karma, that for unexplained reasons were impacting his life.

The four sat around the living room for the next two hours, having a few drinks and enjoying each other's company. For Dot's benefit, they recapped their first meeting in Truth or Consequences. As much as Victor was thrilled to see his newfound friend, Peg was the happiest she had been in recent memory, knowing that for the next couple of weeks, she would have this buoyant woman to share time with.

Peg was already planning in her mind, all the things she and Maggie would do. She gladly included her mother, but realistically knew Dot could only participate in the occasional event. It would be hard enough for Peg to keep up with this tornado of a houseguest. Her mother would never have a chance keeping pace with the inexhaustible human being that was Maggie Crotty. But Peg was psyched to give it a try.

For her part, Maggie knew when she first met Victor and Peg, that they were her kind of people. She too longed to share time with another passionate aircraft mechanic and a girlfriend.

Life at Dot Collin's house had a very different vibe than it had only days before. The boys even seemed to be somewhat happier as Victor's mood lightened over that same period of time. Peg finally sensed hope that the corner may have been turned for the Drueding family. She began to feel, in her heart, that the life and prospects for her family had the makings of a new beginning.

Chapter 45

By the end of March 2007, Eriq Steed was becoming physically and mentally impacted by the lack of progress in locating Victor Drueding and the helicopter. The very thin man lost even more weight and found he was developing various rashes, due probably, to his nervous condition.

His obsession for the opportunity to deploy his rage against the pilot, created immense frustration, affecting every part of his life. Sleep was never restorative, and accomplishing everyday activities was confounded by a growing depression.

Steed clearly knew the remedy for his condition. Whether by pistol, knife, or his bare hands, he was certain that terminating the life of Victor Dreading and retrieving his chopper would be the elixir and cure to his maladies.

Mr. Raymond Freeport had made it perfectly clear to Steed that his presence was not required or needed at the offices of Community Betterment. Nonetheless, Eriq would show up with regularity, sometimes catching Mr. Freeport shuffling papers or moving furniture. Steed was always primed to talk, but they would only speak briefly. The older man repeatedly found a reason to leave, having some important place to be. This left Steed with the strong impression that Freeport was ducking him, which was so clearly the case.

Steed had faith, however, that it was only a matter of time, and Freeport would have good news for him. He was certain that when that news came, Freeport would celebrate with Steed, and they would plan the assault on the pilot together as a team.

They would execute their plan expeditiously and eliminate the large, but insignificant, ant that had been such an unfortunate irritant. Raymond would then happily reward Eriq, the financial bounty that was long overdue. And their celebration would continue. Steed dreamt of this moment practically every night.

Steed again stopped by the Community Betterment office on Friday morning the 30th of March. Taking the elevator to the tenth floor, he walked briskly down the hall, toward the corner office. As he approached the office door, he noticed it was uncharacteristically left ajar. Mr. Freeport had a couple of identifiable traits. One, he always dressed and acted the very distinguished gentleman; two, he was very fastidious in every action and detail. He would never leave an office door open.

Steed entered the office and called out for Mr. Freeport. Silence. He walked further into the interior of the office and scanned the periphery for any sign of activity. There was none. Only then did it strike Steed that the offices were bare, except for the building-owned furniture. He moved around with anxiousness and quickness, from one room to the other; his head on a swivel as he darted back and forth.

"Mr. Freeport?" he loudly cried. No response. Again, he called the boss's name without a response. He looked desperately for a piece of paper, a note of some kind, that would detail the whereabouts of Mr. Freeport. "Certainly, my mentor would leave me all the details concerning this development," thought Steed. But no note was to be found.

Eriq moved back into the hallway, looking for any sign of life. He called out for anyone to respond to him. Silence. Running down the hall, he pushed against other office doors on this tenth and top floor of the downtown building. "Can anyone hear me?" he now yelled at the top of his lungs.

A door opened only feet away from Steed. A short, slender young woman appeared and asked, "Can I help you?"

Steed turned in a startled fashion and then moved directly to the woman, standing awkwardly close to her. "Do you know where Mr. Freeport might be?" he aggressively asked, his eyes bulging out from above his emaciated cheekbones.

The young woman looked frightened, immediately regretting her leaving the security of her office. "Sir, I don't know who Mr. Freeport even is," she replied in a weak and shaky voice. As she answered, an older, white-haired man appeared from the same office and moved to her side.

"I think I know who you're talking about," the white-haired man said. "If it's the guy in the corner office, I'm pretty sure he moved out the day before yesterday. There was a lot of activity and what appeared to be men from a moving company were taking boxes to the elevator. I think he is gone."

Now Steed appeared frantic. "Where, where, where did he go?" He shifted his position to a stance uncomfortably close to the older man.

The white-haired man, now realizing the person in front of him was less than stable, stepped one pace backward, away from Steed, and then answered, "Sir, I wouldn't know. We wouldn't know. We didn't even know the guy. He kept to himself always. The most we got out of him was the occasional *Hello*. Besides that, nothing. Sorry, but we can't help you." He motioned for the young girl to return to the office, as he kept Steed's attention.

The older man continued. "Sir, the building management office is on the first floor. They might be able to tell you something. That's probably your best bet."

Steed didn't say anymore to the man or woman. He turned and walked back to the corner office, slamming the door behind him. The older man followed the young woman into their office, closing and securely locking the door behind them.

Pacing back and forth in the practically empty offices of Community Betterment, Eriq Steed attempted to calm himself down. As was his habit, he mumbled to himself as he paced. He must interpret what was going on correctly, he thought. "Don't rush to conclusions," he decided at one interval, and then the next moment, he was convinced Mr. Raymond Freeport "was totally screwing him." His swirling thoughts went back and forth for a half an hour.

Finally, Steed sat down on the top of a low-level bookcase, void of books or any other decor for that matter. He stared at the street traffic ten stories below. He sat quietly for fifteen minutes, which was a lifetime of tranquility for the skinny man. For the first time since he arrived, his mind settled.

As his eyes were fixated on the street below, Steed came to a decision regarding the position he found himself in. Freeport, he knew for sure, had left the office for good. He knew the distinguished-looking man would not be returning. Steed's hope was that circumstances were such that Freeport had not as yet been in a position to contact Steed, in order to advise him of the office closure, and of the current state of pursuit.

He would give Mr. Freeport the benefit of the doubt and await his phone call, email, or text. Steed hoped with all his heart that he would hear from his boss within the next day or two. In the unfortunate event Steed did not hear from Mr. Freeport, Eriq would accept the harsh reality that the man he admired and trusted had betrayed him.

"But he would wait. Mr. Freeport would call. Wouldn't he? Sure, he would call."

Chapter 46

April 5, Thursday 10 a.m.

The boys were at school. Presumably. It was never an absolute certainty that Dean was definitely in school. He had no choice but to leave for school, that was a certainty. However, the connection between leaving for school, and actually attending school, was a fragile one. It seemed to Dot that even the truant officer had lost interest in whether Dean attended or not. She figured that the officer's return on effort was simply not worth it to him.

One certainty did exist. Dot was, without a doubt, at work. The woman was reliable as a Swiss watch. Her pride was an all-encompassing element of her character. Her house was impeccably clean and orderly. Her clothes, although inexpensive, were of high quality and fashionable. And she was always at her job with time to spare. A manager's dream.

Victor had been out of the house for hours. The new job was a great boost to his morale. Up at five and out of the house by five forty-five, Victor had become a much happier man. His life felt more worthwhile as his productivity grew. The man's behavior toward others was more engaging with each and every day.

On this particular morning, with the sun shining bright, and a clear, cool crispness in the air, Peg was thrilled with the current pattern of their lives. Her mom and husband were at jobs they loved, and where they were appreciated. Her boys were hopefully at school.

She found herself watering the plants, doing a wash, and generally picking and poking around the house. All the while, she unconsciously whistled and hummed, her body's rhythm in sync with music from the kitchen radio, wafting through the home.

She was fluffing up pillows from the living room couch, when she heard a light knock at the door. Her first thought was that her husband had returned, having forgotten something, including his front door key.

"Just a moment, will be right there," she yelled out. Placing the pillow she had been slapping into fullness back on the couch, she skipped the few steps over to the door. Without hesitation or checking on who it might be, she briskly turned the knob and opened the door. On the other side of the threshold was an unfamiliar face. A pleasant face, but one that seemed somewhat out of place in their little agricultural town. The man she found herself smiling at and greeting had a distinguished look to him, somewhat unusual for this part of the country.

"Why, hello, sir. Can I help you?"

The well-dressed-looking gentleman smiled back and replied in a comfortable voice, "I hope so, ma'am. I'm looking for someone and am not sure this is the correct house. By any chance, are you Mrs. Drueding?"

"Yes I am, sir. And who might you be?"

"My name is Freeport. But I'm actually looking for a Mr. Drueding. I was told he's a top mechanic, and I need someone to look at my car."

Peg laughed and thought to herself, "Victor would not have been recommended from anyone in this town, for anything, more than two weeks ago. Now people are hearing good things about him from the airfield. How things can change." "My husband, Victor, is at work right now, and won't be home until five or so. But in any event, I think you'd be better off with an auto mechanic. He's more of an aircraft kind of guy. Someone downtown should be able to help you, I'm sure." She looked past the man and out into the street, to ascertain if the man's car was parked there. Unable to see an unfamiliar auto, she asked, "Do you have transportation?"

"I do, Mrs. Drueding, but I have one other thing to ask, if you don't mind?"

"Ask away."

The distinguished-looking man continued to smile, but this time it struck Peg that his facial expression changed; no longer friendly, but a bit ominous. He took one long step toward her and, with his body's forward motion, caused her to step backward into the living room. Once inside, he reached back and grabbed the inside doorknob, slamming the door behind him.

Peg's pulse increased, as her sense of unease quickly turned to intimidation. She summoned the inner fortitude to sound confidently indignant, saying in a defiant tone, "What the hell is this all about?"

The man stood squarely in front of the tightly closed door and simply looked amused. His sinister demeanor frightened the woman. Her nerves began to overwhelm her. She tried to think of appropriate action, but was losing her composure to do so.

"What this is about, my dear Mrs. Drueding, is that I need to know one thing from you. And let me clue you in on something, my dear. I ask things once, not twice, not three times. And I'm going to ask something of you...once. And I suggest you answer with haste. Got it?"

Peg's fear was evident, as her body now shook uncontrollably. Her knees felt weak, and the moisture dissipated from her mouth. "What do you want to know?" her raspy voice uttered.

Before the stranger answered, he pulled a small handgun from his sport coat pocket and aimed it directly at her abdomen.

Standing only feet away from his victim, Raymond Freeport raised his voice and practically shouted in Peg's face. "I know your mother and kids are gone for the day. And now you've told me your piece of shit of a husband is gone. So, it's just you and me, sister. My question is this: where is the damn helicopter your husband stole from me?"

Peg had no idea who this man was, but never considered he had something to do with the helicopter or the events in San Diego. She had met the skinny man with the big teeth, but this was not him. She did know, however, that the helicopter was down the street, in a Pavilion Airfield warehouse. And her husband was there as well. To tell this man the whereabouts of the chopper would also lead him to Victor. She hesitated as she tried to think of what to do or say.

"I'm not sure what you want, Mr. Freeport."

"Not the right answer, Mrs. Drueding." He fired the small caliber pistol, shooting her in the right side of her lower abdomen. The blast was not much louder than a small firecracker and one that would barely escape the confines of the house.

Peg recoiled at the shock delivered to her body but did not fall over. She saw the fire from the muzzle of the gun and heard the loud pop but did not feel the entry wound until a few seconds later. She found herself looking downward at the same time the pain within her abdomen erupted. The oversized sweatshirt she wore doing housework began to blot red, and then accelerated in its absorption of her escaping blood. Within seconds, weakness overcame her, and she collapsed to the floor.

Freeport moved to her immediately. "Oh, hold on, honey. You're not allowed to die yet. You have some information for me first." He bent over her, as she lay on her side groaning and turned her on her back. He straddled her, placed the revolver on the floor next to them, and then put his hands around her throat.

Peg's eyes bulged out, and although aware of her plight, her senses had dulled with the loss of blood. Freeport let his grip lighten for a moment, allowing her to speak. Her world was fading with every second, but she had no intention of offering another word to this monster.

"Speak to me, Peg," he screamed into her face. "Where is my chopper?"

"Up your ass, you piece of crap," came another female's voice, confusing the man on his knees. When Freeport looked up, he saw a woman with grayish-white hair standing ten feet away, just inside the opening to the kitchen. She held another small caliber handgun pointed in his direction. "Let her go. Now!" Maggie yelled at the man.

"Nobody else is supposed to be here. Who the hell are you?"

"Wrong answer, asshole." Maggie moved two steps in the direction of the puzzled-looking man, who had not released his grasp on Peg's neck. Another pop, and a bullet struck Freeport's forehead. The bullet entered, but did not exit, as there was not enough firepower to do more than crack through the frontal bone.

His eyes registered the ultimate shock of the moment, but incredibly his body harbored enough strength to allow him to rise up. As he did so, Maggie took yet another step toward him and fired again, this time pointing her weapon at his midsection. A pinprick dot of red appeared in the middle of his chest. His body hovered vertically for a few seconds, as his expression seemed to convey anger. But what the murderer was thinking, one will never know. Finally, his body fell to one side, landing squarely on the coffee table, exploding it into pieces.

Chapter 47

The big man was working on a vintage, single engine piper cub, when he saw Teddy Thompson running toward him. Having been tinkering with the small, half-century old airplane for a couple of hours, Victor was about to take a short break anyway. From his vantage point in the small hangar at the side of the primary runway, Victor had a full view of the airfield through the large opening of the hanger door. He was wiping oil off his hands with a small rag when he noticed the manager of the airfield jogging in his direction.

"What's your hurry, Teddy?" Victor called out before his boss reached him. Nobody generally ran for any reason at the small airfield. Actually, the fact was, that the knees of most of the employees were beyond running condition. Age was the primary reason, but in Victor's case, the sheer workload his knees had supported over the years and was the main contributing factor.

Teddy, huffing and puffing now, bent over and placed his hands on his thighs, as he fought to catch his breath. "Victor, just got a call from a woman at your house. Peg...something's wrong with Peg. Sounded like she's hurt." He paused to take a breath as he labored to speak. "You gotta' go home...now."

Victor's eyes opened wide, as his heart began to race. He threw the rag to the ground and started in the direction of the house. "Victor, here, we'll take the cart." Thompson pointed to a golf cart that was used when anyone at the field was tired of walking. It happened to be situated in the small hangar near the entranceway.

Victor instinctively jumped into the driver side of the cart, as Thompson swung himself onto the passenger seat. The body of the cart moaned at once, under the weight of the two men. Most golfers were not the size of Thompson and probably none the size of Victor Drueding. Nonetheless, the machine started up immediately, and when Victor hit the pedal, the little machine pulled away with impressive pick up. Someone or another, each and every year, tinkered with the golf cart, so it had added acceleration from that of a standard country club model.

Even though the cart moved as quickly as any golf cart could, Victor considered getting out and running to the house, as he knew a normal human would outpace this recreational form of transportation. But he also was well aware of his physical condition, and he certainly could not afford breaking down himself, while attempting to run.

They made their way along a path, turning onto a narrow road leading to Dot's house. At the same time, the house came into view, they spotted an arriving ambulance. A police car was parked on the street, and the front door of the house was opened wide. Victor's pulse raced faster and harder. A fear gripped him greater than what he experienced at the helipad.

When they were twenty yards from the front walk, Victor slammed on the brakes and jumped out. The small vehicle began to roll forward once again, until Thompson shuffled over to the driver's side and took control. He parked the cart next to a tree on the side lawn, jumped out, and followed Victor, who now was entering the opened front door.

It was a little after eleven o'clock in the morning when Victor entered the living room and saw his wife on the floor. Two EMTs were feverishly working on Peg who was lying on her back, a pool of blood surrounding her midsection. A young policeman met Victor just inside the door and placed himself between the big man and his wife.

"Sir, I know you want to go to her, but they need room right now. Please stay here for a moment."

Victor, who was consumed with Peg's condition, peered over the young cop and, without actually hearing the young officer's words, knew they didn't need him in the way. He turned to the policeman and asked frantically, "What happened to her?"

It was then Victor noticed the smashed coffee table, and the body half hidden among the broken wood. "Who's that?" he loudly and anxiously asked. A distraught, yet familiar female voice, responded to his question. "Victor," Maggie answered, her voice quivering. "That guy shot Peg. I was in the kitchen, next to the radio, and I didn't know he was even in the house until I heard the shot. Then I rushed in…but was too late." Her voice trailed off.

Maggie was standing in the corner now, her shirt and cargo pants covered with blood. Once the ambulance attendants arrived and took over Maggie's efforts to help Peg, the gray-haired woman moved to the corner and emotionally fell apart. She garnered just enough composure to answer Victor's question and then retreated once again within herself.

Victor couldn't think of anything but his wife's condition, so further consideration regarding the man on the floor was impossible for the time being. Two more EMTs arrived at the house, and all four moved with serious haste, doing their best to stabilize the unconscious woman, preparing her for transport. Fifteen minutes later, the bleeding temporarily halted; Peg was strapped securely on the transport gurney and moved into the ambulance. They left for the ten-minute drive to Hayes Hospital.

The ambulance had no extra room for Victor, but the second emergency vehicle did and made him the offer. Victor, anxious to stay as close to his wife as possible, accepted and wanted to go immediately.

As he began to move outside, a young policeman, Sergeant Stone, gently grabbed Victor by the arm. "Sir, I know you want to leave right away, but if you would, could you tell me if you know the dead man?" As Stone spoke, he motioned to the section of the living room floor where the body was sprawled out.

Victor hurriedly replied, "Yeah, sure. I'll look." It still wasn't computing with Victor what Maggie had actually said; that the dead man had shot his wife. "Let's go, let's look quickly."

"Sir, sir, sir, please follow me carefully. This is a crime scene and I don't want to disrupt anything." The Sergeant carefully guided Victor around the broken furniture and asked him to stand at a distance, close enough to identify, but not too close to touch anything of significance.

Stone carefully turned the body over, so Victor could see the bloody face. As the Sergeant was doing this, Victor glanced over at Maggie, standing stoically in the corner. It was at that moment, that what she had said earlier sunk in. *The man on the floor shot his wife.*

Fear turned immediately to raging anger. He wanted to attack the lifeless form, now coming into view, but common sense prevailed, and he remained stationary. He glared downward at the dead man, half expecting to see a skinny face, with thin lips. If this were the case, he didn't know if he could contain himself.

But it wasn't the case. The lifeless person facing him was not one he had ever seen. This challenged his inner anger and, for a moment, simply confused the big man.

"I have never seen him before, Officer. I don't know who that piece of garbage is. Can I go now, Sir?"

"Yeah, go ahead, Mr. Drueding. I hope your wife is alright, sir."

Victor ran out of the house and got into the back of the EMT's van. Ten minutes later, they were at the entrance of the Emergency Wing of Hayes Hospital.

Chapter 48

One week after visiting the closed offices of Community Betterment, Steed was convinced that Mr. Freeport had abandoned him. There had been no communication, and it was time to face reality. It was at this point that Steed realized, without a doubt, he was on his own.

His frustration revisited him with regularity, and he suffered in a constant state of anger. His existence was consumed with the emotional impact of betrayal. His internal heat would begin to cool, only to reemerge and heighten to new levels.

He sat on his couch for days and hours on end, until finally, he concluded he must get on the move. Any action was better than none. But what actions should he take? He was not the professional plotter and planner; that was Raymond Freeport. Eriq was the streetwise operator. The con man. His proficiency was in the carrying out of orders, not giving them. He was the instrument in executing plans, not the planner. But he knew this must change.

He must become Raymond Freeport. But without the money of Raymond Freeport. Fortunately for Steed, he had a loyal assistant in Max. Max knew practically everything Steed knew about the goings-on of the past few years. Although Max was technically paid by Raymond Freeport, he had never met the man. So, his loyalties lay with Steed.

Steed had never respected Max very much, but Steed knew he was dependable and now saw the man as essential to his future. He could not do everything by himself, and Max would comply with any demands Steed put forward. That would include accepting very little compensation until the chopper was found. The chopper stash would be used, in part, to pay Max.

Steed settled on a simple plan—find the pilot, and before killing him, extract from him the location of the helicopter. Torturing the man for this information would be incredibly satisfying for the twisted thin man. Once the pilot was dead, he would find his wife and kill her. All in all, that would make for one incredibly enjoyable day.

He would possess the helicopter and the wealth contained within the secret compartment. He would then search out, locate, and kill the son of a bitch, that for so many years he had put his faith in. He would end the life of Raymond Freeport.

First things first. Steed needed to find Drueding. Odds were he was back in Missouri with his family, so he began his investigation with that assumption.

He didn't know much about technology, or the internet, but he knew these tools would help his efforts. Although he owned a computer, he wasn't particularly skilled in the use of it. Steed would retrieve the occasional email, and that was about it. However, he knew where the library was. And there, he would have access to a laptop, and the help he needed to use one.

He had been told hundreds of times, that to find anything at all, all you had to do was "surf the web". He didn't know what that bullshit meant, but if it gave him the information he needed, he sure as hell would learn to "surf".

He planned to sweet talk a librarian into helping him. She would be swept up by his charm and wit and guide him through the complexities of technology. In so doing, she would, unwittingly, assist the psychopath in his plot to murder.

The imagery of it all pleased Steed to no end. Facing a mirror on the wall, he stared at his reflection. He certainly knew how to make himself smile.

Chapter 49

Peg was rushed into the Emergency Room at Hayes. She had lost consciousness at the house, but her heart never stopped. Maggie had applied pressure on the wound in her lower right abdomen, but the houseguest had no further idea what to do to help her friend. Even given Maggie's efforts, Peg had lost much blood, coupled with oxygen depletion from being choked.

The paramedics followed normal protocol and did what they could to stabilize Peg for transportation to the hospital. They gave the injured woman oxygen and temporarily stopped the bleeding. Fortunately for Peg, although living in the outskirts of Centerville, the hospital was only a ten-minute drive. The town was that small. And in her case, every second was critical.

Victor was not far behind the ambulance. The van he traveled in pulled up to the Emergency Room entrance moments after his wife's arrival. Victor jumped from the vehicle and was met on the walkway by yet another policeman.

The cop was in plain clothes, but an ID badge, hung from a lanyard around his neck, indicated he was a policeman. "Mr. Drueding, my name is Detective Richards. I know you want to go to your wife, but may I have a quick word with you? It'll be a few minutes before they'll let you see her anyway."

Victor was irritated by the interception, as he was being asked once again to delay being with his badly injured wife. However, he knew his standing with the town's police department was on shaky grounds to begin with, and figured a little cooperation, as aggravating as it was, it wasn't a bad idea. Deep inside, he also knew, he and his family may be needing them.

"Sure, how can I help you?"

"Mr. Drueding, I just spoke to Sergeant Stone, and he said you could not identify the assailant, is that correct?"

"Right, never saw his dead ass before."

"Do you have any possible idea why anyone would want to hurt your wife, or even be at your mother-in-law's house for any reason at all?"

Victor's first instinct was to tell the truth, but he couldn't bring himself to do so. "No clue," he responded, "We just moved back here, and I, for one, don't even know that many people in town. The only folks that probably really aren't glad to see me are the cops here. I've had a little history on occasion. Maybe you've heard."

"I have, sir, but we're still the good guys. Listen, go ahead and see your wife, but please give me a call when you're done." The officer gave Victor a card with his name and information on it. "We'll have a statement by then from the lady who was in the house. And I really must talk to you further. This is a very dangerous situation, Mr. Drueding, and we must find out what it's all about. That okay?"

"Yeah, for sure. I'll call you when I leave here."

The detective put out his hand and Victor shook it. Victor wasn't one to make eye contact on a regular basis, but he briefly did so. The veteran detective had a look of genuine sympathy and concern. It was the first moment since he and his wife's return to Missouri, that Victor had any inclination at all, to maybe reach out, for help. Maybe.

Chapter 50

Dot was working at the department store when the call came. The Centerville police captain made the phone call, identifying himself to the store's operator, and given instant access to Peg's mother. Under normal circumstances, salespeople were denied personal calls, but when the caller is the captain of the town's police force, exceptions are made.

The captain attempted to convey his message, to the mother of the seriously injured woman, in a way that was not devastating. He tried his best but failed miserably. A fellow saleswoman witnessed Dot's physical reaction and described it as frightening. Dot began to quiver uncontrollably and lost all color in her face. She dropped the phone and slumped to the ground. Her coworkers rushed to her and were at the brink of calling an ambulance, when she began to come around.

Once settled somewhat, Dot asked for the rest of the day off. Her manager, who had been assisting in the effort to comfort her, told Dot to take as much time as needed. Another store employee was enlisted to drive Dot back to her home, as she was in no condition to drive herself. Her car could be retrieved at a later time.

Dot had been told by the police captain that her daughter was in the Emergency Room at Hayes Hospital, and that for the next few hours, at least, she would not be able to see her. He suggested she return to her house, before going to the hospital. The police there would give her more information and would transport her to the hospital. What he did not spell out to the older woman was that he wanted her in the protection of the police department as soon as possible.

Within a short time from receiving the captain's phone call, Dot arrived at her beloved home. Already, the house had a surreal appearance to it. Besides the yellow police tape that surrounded it, three squad cars were parked at odd angles to the house. Even in her unstable condition, Dot could not help but think these vehicles were unnecessarily driven into these contrived positions. It seemed to her that the police department was expecting the media, and the cars presented themselves as parked in the heat of action. This wasn't the case however. The police wanted as little attention paid to this scene as possible. There were too many unanswered questions.

A policeman was at the front porch to receive the owner of the house. He introduced himself as Sergeant Stone, and he escorted Dot through the front door. The body of the deceased man had been taken away, but with that exception, the living room had remained untouched. Dot's head swiveled from one direction to the other, shocked at the scene in front of her. Her nerves, that had never totally relaxed from the time she took the phone call, now became extremely tense once again. She kept repeating, "Oh, my God. Oh, my God," as she scanned the central room of her sanctuary.

Finally, she looked downward, to the rug. The broken remains of the coffee table were apparent the moment she walked into the house, but she had not noticed the rug. Blood stains covered two separate areas. She put her right hand over her mouth, in an effort to contain an outburst. She gasped, as she turned to the young policeman who had led her in. "That's enough," she blurted, and ran out through the front door.

Sergeant Stone followed her with an urgency in his step. He was afraid of many possibilities and hoped he could contain the woman, and possibly calm her down. Although he hadn't experienced such outcomes firsthand, he had heard from other officers about older family members having suffered heart attacks at the scene of a tragic family occurrence. He was also concerned that in her discombobulated state, the woman might simply take a fall, if nothing else. A broken hip, in certain instances, were as life changing as a heart attack.

A female officer, who had been in the kitchen taking a deposition from Maggie Crotty, appeared at the front door and asked Stone if he needed assistance. He yelled over his shoulder, "Please, Shirley, please come out here if you would." Officer Shirley Duffy hustled down the front steps and immediately put her arms around Dot. Stone moved a step back, quickly realizing he was a second stringer when it came to emotional comfort. Although Duffy had only been a policewoman for the past year, her natural instincts in this situation made Stone feel an inadequacy he had yet to experience in police work. He held back and watched, as Duffy slowly diffused Dot's heightened anxiety.

After a period of time, the three individuals moved to the porch steps and sat down. Dot had calmed considerably and apologized to the two police officers. Stone quickly responded, "No need to apologize, Mrs. Collins. Your reaction to everything is perfectly normal. If you are up to it, we have a few things to go over, but we won't rush you. And if you need anything at all, just ask us."

Dot took a deep breath and looked at the two young officers of the law. "I'm okay now. Please what is it you need to know?"

Officer Stone stood up and softly replied to the distressed, but now more composed woman. "Mrs. Collins, it is critical we find out who did this to your daughter. In order to do so, we have to secure your house for a few days and analyze every detail we can. We can learn much from the crime scene, but we need some time and the right experts to come in and do their job. So, one thing I ask of you, is if we can keep your home empty for the time we need to do the job?"

"You want all of us to stay away, is that it?"

"Yes, just for the time being. Is that okay with you?"

"It's fine, but where do we go?"

"We were hoping you could find housing for the kids, you, and your son-in-law. Is that possible? Maybe with friends of the family? If not, ma'am, we'll find something for you."

"I can try. I think I can. But please, do everything in your power to find out who this devil is, and why he would do such a thing to my daughter." She began to weep once again, but now quietly.

"I promise we will, Mrs. Collins. I promise we will."

After interviewing the older woman for a short while longer, Officer Duffy escorted Dot to the back of the house to her bedroom, where Dot collected some clothes and other personal items. The police officers sensitively suggested that until her home was cleaned up and back to a semblance of normalcy, it was not healthy that she return to what effectively was a crime scene.

Dot's luggage packed, they once again found the female officer. Shirley Duffy comforted the woman, hoping to keep her mind from focusing on her home and the assault on her daughter. They left the house, again by the back door, and Officer Duffy drove Dot to the Emergency Room of Hayes Hospital, where predictably, she fell apart once again.

Chapter 51

Victor, Dot, and Maggie finally all caught up with one another at Hayes Hospital. They were ushered into a private waiting room reserved for immediate family members. The rules were not very rigid however, and they certainly made an exception for Maggie, a close friend of the family. Maggie had been interviewed at the scene of the crime and for a short time down at the police station. From there, she drove directly to the Emergency Room.

The three boys were deliberately kept away from the very volatile situation. There was barely an opportunity for Peg's husband or mother to lay eyes on her, and when they did, it was extremely upsetting. So, it was decided that the boys would remain at friends' homes, until hopefully, at a better time, and under more hopeful expectations, it was safe to visit.

After a couple of hours, Victor left the Emergency Room with the promise he would be called immediately upon any change in Peg's condition. He stopped in the cafeteria on the first floor, for a cup of coffee and to sit quietly for a few moments. The tables around him were mostly empty of hospital staff and visitors, yet the last sensation Victor felt was that of a quiet moment. His mind raced in so many directions, he couldn't grab hold of a single thought.

He had always considered that bad guys could be hunting them, but he wasn't certain that this is what could happen. The dead man was a stranger to him, and the possibility was that this terrible event was unrelated to San Diego. But how would he know? And who could he turn to for help?

After finishing his coffee, he leaned back and retrieved Detective Richards' card from his wallet. It wasn't that Victor was anxious to be grilled by the detective, but he felt he needed to speak to someone, about anything. His head was spinning so out of control, he felt that talking to someone, anyone, would be better than living within himself right now. And possibly this was the time to follow Maggie's advice. Maybe now was the time to tell someone in authority the truth.

He pulled out his cell phone and dialed the detective's number. After two rings, a deep voice came over the receiver, "Richards here."

"Detective Richards, this is Victor Drueding. I told you I'd call."

"How's your wife, Mr. Drueding?"

"Unconscious. Possibly in a coma. I don't know. Not good right now. I do know that. The hospital told me to go home and get some rest. They will call me if anything changes, and if I don't hear from them, I'll just come back in the morning."

"Mr. Drueding, I want to speak to you about that. We need to secure the house for possibly a few days. We're helping Mrs. Collins find a place for her and your boys to stay for that period of time. I didn't want to get into this when I saw you outside the ER, but I have no choice in the matter. The house is a crime scene, and we have a lot to accomplish before you can return."

Victor rubbed his face with his left hand, once again hearing something that was totally unexpected. He fought the urge to react angrily, but rather resigned himself to handle calmly, whatever was to come.

"Let's talk," said Victor.

Detective Richards drove to the hospital and picked up Victor, who was waiting for him just outside the main entranceway. Rather than return to the police station where Victor would understandably feel uncomfortable, he drove to the only Italian restaurant in town, where they could sit and talk in private. Richards figured, that if the byproduct of having a discussion at an excellent Italian restaurant was enjoying a dish of chicken marsala at the same time, well then, so be it. The job had to have certain perks, didn't it? And he loved to eat.

Richards requested a table well removed from the mainstream foot traffic. They were seated in a corner of the restaurant where there was no passerby activity at all. The fact of the matter was that this was not the first time the Detective had used this table for a similar purpose.

A waitress stopped by their table and took their dinner order. The Detective settled on his favorite fare, chicken marsala. Victor wasn't hungry, but ordered a tuna sandwich, just to have something in front of him. They both asked for coffee. When the waitress left them, Richards took out a pen, a small flip-up note pad, and sat back in his chair.

"Victor, I know this is hard for you. You can tell me what you want, but the more you tell me, the better. I know you have a heavy heart now, and I won't burden it anymore. Please believe me, I have one objective right now—to find out who the son of a bitch was that hurt your wife. And if there are more guilty people involved, I want to find those sons of bitches too. I am not interested in hurting you or your family in the least."

"I have a lot to tell you," said the big man in a quiet and somber tone. "And maybe I'll be in trouble after I do. But, know this, everything I'm about to say was of my own doing. My wife knew a little, but not much about it. My mother-in-law knew nothing. My kids knew nothing. The woman, Maggie, at the house, had nothing to do with anything, except hopefully saving my wife's life."

Victor's large hands rubbed at his temples, as if he was contemplating how to even begin the story he was about to tell. Victor looked the Detective in the eyes, and said, "I think you're going to need a bigger note pad."

Dinner was delivered, and the chicken marsala looked and smelled delicious. Detective Richards stopped scribbling notes after a few minutes, as the mini pad was highly inadequate for transcribing what he was listening to. After only a short time into Victor's story, Richards began to regret the setting for their meeting. He realized he had left his recorder back at the station. But more importantly, Detective Richards had become shockingly aware of the possible magnitude of the situation surrounding the shooting of this big man's wife.

Victor had never spoken so many consecutive words and sentences in his life. He described, in great detail, the events of the previous year—from when he first met Eriq Steed at his and Peg's apartment, until he last saw the skinny monster staring up at him, as he escaped the murder scene at the helipad.

He didn't attempt to skew the facts with claims of innocence. He knew from the beginning what he was doing was wrong. He did, however, feel that there were worse things in the world than delivering medicines to third world markets, no matter what the law said, or who profited.

When he finished the full account of events, including their journey by helicopter to Centerville, Missouri, Victor's one-man audience was awestruck. Detective Richards thought he had heard it all, up until this very moment. He now knew the possibilities of plot lines were well beyond his comprehension. In a million years, he would never have concocted what he had just been told. He sat across from a sad and solemn man, who had just emptied himself of heavy secrets. It was now the law enforcer's turn to react. He knew he must transition from the role of attentive listener to his role as policeman. He sat in silent contemplation, staring at the plate of chicken marsala. Then he snapped suddenly into the moment.

The detective pulled his cell phone from his inside sport coat pocket and hurriedly placed a call. The female voice at the other end of the line was loud enough for Victor to hear her as well. "Hayes Hospital, Emergency Room."

"This is Detective Richards from the police department. I need to speak to the doctor in charge of the Emergency Room right now."

A minute later, a man's voice was heard. "This is Doctor Murray. Can I help you?"

"Ted, this is Ben Richards, thanks for picking up. We've got a situation concerning a patient of yours."

Dr. Ted Murray had known Ben Richards for three years. The Emergency Room at Hayes Hospital had naturally been common ground for the police department and hospital staff, with victims of auto accidents, drug overdoses, domestic violence, and other unfortunate occurrences, bringing the two worlds together. This was one of those times.

"Let me guess. The Drueding woman?"

"The very one. Listen, Ted, some background to the event has surfaced, and I need you to put a tight lid on all information getting out on anything relating to the woman. Tell me it's not too late to do this?"

"Not at all, Ben. Our protocol kicked in as soon as she arrived. We just assumed the department would be calling, but I'm glad you confirmed it. Any more I should know?"

"Not yet, but I know it's serious shit. Double up on the blackout instructions, if you would. I'll be back to you soon enough. Okay?"

"Will do, guy. Hope all works out."

"Me too. Talk to you later." Detective Ben Richards put his phone down and looked across the table at Victor. "Mr. Drueding, why don't you call your mother-in-law, find out where she and your boys will be staying tonight, and then see if you can find a place as well. I'll stay with you while you get those addresses for me and then drive you to wherever you have to go."

"I think I can crash at the airfield. There's a cot and shower there. I know the manager won't mind, but I'll give Teddy a shout to confirm anyway. Why the orders to the doctor? What are you thinking?"

"I'm thinking I phone the Bureau in San Diego, my friend. We're going to need all the help we can get. If I interpreted your story correctly, we need the feds to get involved pronto. You might be in some trouble yourself, for the taxi service you gave those shitheads to Mexico, but your role is nothing compared to what we know they've done. And we've got to find out fast if your wife's shooter was one of them, or just an unlucky coincidence. You did the right thing to tell me, Mr. Drueding, but now you're going to have to trust me. Okay?"

Victor's pulse picked up as he listened to the detective, but in some ways, his telling the story and the policeman's reaction to it gave him a bit of relief. For months, he had carried the weight of untold dark secrets. Now, he had finally shared them. And sharing them seemed like the right thing to do.

They stood up and headed for the front door of the restaurant.

The plate of chicken marsala sat on the table, uneaten and cold.

Chapter 52

Detective Richards returned to the station and immediately called the Federal Bureau office in San Diego. He hadn't had much experience with federal agencies, as his territory was a relatively tame environment. Murders and felonies of varied descriptions did occur, but to a far lesser degree, than in the larger populated cities and towns throughout Missouri. And certainly, compared to the large metropolitan areas in the country. Most crimes in Richards' territory did not involve interstate activities or issues that would necessarily bring in the feds.

The bureau in San Diego was a large operation, coping with a laundry list of crimes. California was big to begin with, with the myriad of problems that come with a burgeoning population. Add to that the fact that San Diego neighbored another country, and you have complexities in crimes that were totally foreign to the little rural region familiar to Detective Richards.

Richards was put on hold for what seemed to be forever; then a young man's voice came on the line. "Agent Robert McKenna here. How can I help you?"

"Agent McKenna, this is Detective Richards, from the Centerville, Missouri Police Department. I have a little situation out here that may have a connection to your backyard. I thought I would make contact with your office and see what you think."

"Hit me with it, sir. I'll be glad to give you my thoughts."

Richards recounted the story that Victor Drueding had told him, adding to his first-hand details relating to the shooting of Peg Drueding. There were obviously many huge gaps in the events he described, beginning in San Diego and continuing in Missouri. Richards read from his notes, as McKenna took his own, but each aware that their conversation was taped, for both of their benefits.

When the detective was done speaking, Agent McKenna sighed. "There's a lot to digest here, sir. Let me do some homework and see if what you gave me could be pieces to one of the many puzzles out here that we're trying to solve. Give me a couple of numbers by which to reach you, and I'll look into this. I have to say, however, that as a relatively new agent, I'm given a lot of leads that go absolutely nowhere. Many times, the stories you're told, are just that, stories."

"Well, the shooting wasn't a story. The woman is in a coma in the local hospital, from a gunshot wound. Why would her husband bullshit me?"

"Sir, he might be as truthful as the Pope, but a lot of times, stories are made up, in great detail, so the real trail, the real truth, is never considered. But listen, I'm taking what you said absolutely seriously, and I'll start to look into it."

"Thank you, Agent. Why don't I shoot you an email with my pertinent info, and we can always connect with one another, at any time. Sound alright?"

"Sounds great, sir."

Email addresses were exchanged, and the men thanked one another. When the conversation was over, Richards sat back in his chair, and thought, "Shit, I thought whoever I spoke to would get as excited about this thing as I am. I forget there's a whole lot of other bad crap happening in the world." He left the station frustrated, but committed to prioritizing this case, as he was certain Victor Drueding was telling him the truth.

Chapter 53

April 7

Dean woke up at Kane's home early Saturday morning. He hadn't slept well and finally gave up pretending he might go back to sleep. The bed was partially to blame. It was as soft as a sponge, and he tossed and turned all night. His mind had trouble settling to begin with, so the added problem of the bed rendered his efforts to sleep useless.

His life, which was precariously being lived, on a normal day, had now taken a turn that infused him with anxieties he had never experienced before.

His mom lay in a hospital bed, clinging to life. His father told Dean and his younger brothers they were not to go to the hospital until their mother improved. If their mother improved. "My mother could die," was the awful thought that kept running through his mind. Up until a few months ago, Dean had been living without her in his everyday life, but always knew, subconsciously, she would be there if needed. She had lived many states away, but available nonetheless. Dean loved his grandmother, and appreciated her, but she wasn't his mother.

Neither Dean nor his brothers were close to their dad. All they ever felt was a remote connection to him. The normal father–son relationship did not exist. Their father had never played catch with them, never took them to ballgames, or amusement parks. Dean couldn't remember the last time he had eaten a meal with his father, even though it may have taken place in the recent past. If it had taken place, his father was quiet.

When they did sit down together as a family, the only voices he could remember were that of his mother and grandmother. Even when his father was physically present, he was not engaged. Or simply not interested.

And now his mother might never open her eyes again. A wave of panic set in, and he experienced a nervousness he had never felt before. Being careful not to awaken Kane's parents, Dean tiptoed quietly to his friend's bedroom and woke him up. He whispered to the groggy boy, to get up and dressed, saying, "We're out of here."

Once outside, on this brisk, rainy morning, the boys hustled their way to Worm's house. Hunched over, to protect themselves from the cold rain, they moved as quickly as they could. In the distance, clouds were breaking, blue sky popping through in patches.

Worm's bedroom was on the ground floor, and it would not be the first time they tapped on his window. Worm grabbed at any excuse to leave his house, and today was no different, even though he was barely awake. Within minutes, Worm slid out of his bedroom window, looking even more disheveled than his usual self.

The three took their usual route downtown. As was almost always the case, they had absolutely no plans in mind, along with no money. Their options were few. This was a position they found themselves in on multiple occasions. It generally did not lead to a good outcome.

The rain lightened along with the sky, but the chill remained. They arrived at the closed bike shop and leaned against its walls, as was their habit. They talked about the school they hated, and the losers they knew. They complained about other things as well, before coming around to what was really on all their minds.

Kane brought up the subject. "You gonna see your mom today, Dean?"

"Maybe, but maybe not. My dad and their friend from New Mexico are there. Stayed at the hospital all night, I'm sure. Plus, I'm afraid when I go, there will be no change. The whole thing scares the crap out of me."

"What exactly happened to her?" Worm spoke up.

"They're not telling me much. She's bleeding internally or something. Unconscious. Doctors are saying she is in a coma."

Worm followed up. "So why aren't you staying at your house? Your grandma's there, right?"

"Something about my mother falling, and blood all over the place. Don't want to freak us out until it's all cleaned up. I don't really know. But no one's there. Everyone is spread out."

"Shit, man. Sorry about that."

"Yeah, I know. It wouldn't bother me to stay there, but they said something about insurance and investigations, so they don't want anyone touching anything. My brothers are at their friends' homes too. Really sucks because I want to be home."

Kane, leaning against the wall, and shaking from the cold, said, "Crap, I wish I had thrown a coat on. Freezing my ass off."

Dean glanced up and down the street, as if looking for something that wasn't there. His nervousness was very apparent to his companions. Then, in an abrupt outburst, he exclaimed, "Screw it. Let's go to my house. We just won't mess anything up. At least it's something to do and gets us out of this damn cold."

The other two boys simultaneously reacted. "Good idea," they both said. The three turned in the direction of Dean's grandmother's house and began the trek to the outskirts of town. Even the simple act of moving gave the boys a sense of mission. A mission that would have been best aborted.

Chapter 54

Dean's grandmother's house appeared abandoned, which wasn't surprising to the boy. He was told it would be at least one week before they could move back in. The three boys walked to the back of the house, and Dean retrieved the backdoor key from a hook tucked under the lower portion of the gutter downspout. The backdoor opened into the kitchen, which was where the three of them planned to stay.

Dean was not at all interested in pushing his luck when it came to this situation. He was certainly not at all clear about the details surrounding his mother's injury or what caused it, but he knew the intensity his father felt about everything now, and he was not about to test him. They would spend some time exclusively within the kitchen, and then move on.

What Dean could not have anticipated was the impact being in the house would have on him. When he had the idea of going home with his friends, he figured it would be a relaxing thing to do. However, once in the house, he felt a strange sensation, as if it was a foreign place. And although nothing prohibited him from walking from the kitchen into the living room, an uncomfortable feeling kept him from doing so. He felt as if something he may find one room away would frighten him more than he already was. His nerves began to get the better of him once again.

The three sat around the kitchen table and, for a prolonged period of time, didn't say a word. Dean got up and walked to the refrigerator. He was hoping there might be sodas of some kind that he and his friends could have, but there were none. There was, however, something else. Beer. He stared at three six-packs of a brand he had never heard of, something his father obviously enjoyed. He stared at the beer for a couple of minutes, then thought, "If we each just have one, my dad will never know. He's got other things on his mind now. Plus, the woman from New Mexico drinks beer. He won't have a clue."

He looked back at his friends, and asked, "You guys want a beer?" Two heads shook up and down.

Three skinny fourteen-year-old boys, who had not even eaten breakfast, drank beer instead. The result was inevitable. They became, very quickly, three drunken fourteen-year-olds. Dean's smaller associates each consumed one can, but he enjoyed the pleasurable feeling far too much for a single beer. It gave him a sense of relief he hadn't felt for two days. He barely noticed downing another.

The boys fell all over each other, laughing at anything and everything. Dean's nervousness was erased after the first sip of the first beer and erupted into giddiness after two. If there was one redeeming factor, it was that the boys were walking. Even riding their bicycles would have been challenging and possibly dangerous in their intoxicated condition.

Had they stayed in the kitchen, things may have been okay. But they didn't. Their energy levels elevated, the small kitchen became too limiting, and they banged their way out the back door. They ran erratically, but in the general direction of the rail yard. Pushing one another as they went, the smaller Worm spent almost as much time on the ground as he did on his scampering feet. He laughed even harder when knocked off balance by either of the other two. The more he landed on the wet grass or gravel, the more out of control was all of their laughter.

After fifteen minutes of running and roughhouse, they slowed, and took a few moments to catch their breaths. While doing so, they noticed two silhouettes of what seemed to be younger boys, walking in their general direction. It was Dean who first realized that the larger of the two boys was a schoolmate of his. He was also the son of the man who humiliated his father at a school event, a couple of years earlier. The boy's name was Stan Johnson. And as was usually the case in the schoolyard, the other boy accompanying Johnson, was his best friend, Fred Munroe.

Dean, as well as every other person in town, knew these boys to be highly regarded Youth League baseball players. They were popular among their schoolmates as well as the community at large. These were boys from established and well-regarded families, whose lives seemed charmed.

Upon the realization of who they had come across, a sense of jealousy overcame Dean, fueled as much by his inebriation than anything else. His jealousy morphed into anger almost immediately.

Chapter 55

Dean and his friends veered purposely into the direction of the two younger boys. When they were close to them, Dean called out. "Does mommy know you babies are out of the house?" Worm and Kane dutifully laughed in an over exaggerated fashion.

Johnson, the taller of the two boys, immediately replied, "Leave us alone, Dean." It was at that point that Dean noticed Stan Johnson was, oddly enough, walking on a rail of the tracks. He continued to balance on the rail as he scanned Dean and his friends. This calmness on the part of the younger boy irritated Dean, as most younger kids would have felt intimidated by him. Not these boys however.

Dean yelled more threatening comments that were met with a total lack of concern by the younger twosome. Dean became genuinely angry. He looked at Worm and Kane and nodded toward the youngsters. Dean's friends, interpreting the nonverbal command, grabbed both Stan and his friend Freddie Munroe. Munroe, the only African American student in school, was known throughout town to be an incredibly gifted athlete. His small frame belied his toughness and athleticism. Nonetheless, even the less physical Worm had a considerable size advantage, and held Munroe easily.

Dean moved closer to Munroe and began to taunt him, hoping to frighten the boy. But in return, Dean was on the receiving end of Freddie's own verbal assault. "Go to hell, you piece of crap. Hit me all you want, you loser," Munroe yelled at Dean, as he struggled to free himself from Worm's grasp.

This unexpected barrage of bravado by the small captive pissed Dean off. His nerves, already wracked by his mother's uncertain condition, were now frayed even more by the insolence of this fearless little boy. In his intoxicated state, Dean lost control and was intent on teaching Munroe a lesson. As Dean moved toward him, he heard a voice scream at the top of his lungs, "Hold it, listen!"

Dean stopped and turned in Johnson's direction. "Dean, listen!" Johnson cried out once again. The older boys fell silent for a short moment, wondering what Johnson meant. It then became apparent. They all heard it. A rumbling that all youngsters from Centerville were familiar with. The sound of a train approaching. A freight train.

Dean paused, puzzled by Johnson's outcry. Then, figuring his victim was searching for anything to keep Dean from punching his friend, he smiled and mockingly echoed, "Hold it, listen. You're a joke, Stanny, what could you possibly be thinking?"

"I'm thinking we jump, you fat ass tub of lard," Stan yelled back. "I'm thinking we jump."

Now, Dean knew exactly what the younger boy meant. In Centerville, bored adolescents had invented "train jumping," a highly dangerous, extreme activity, in order to obtain bragging rights and assert one's courage.

The act was as labeled. When a freight train slowed while passing through the city limits, a crazy young person would run alongside of it and attempt to jump aboard. Injuries were predictable, but the allure grew with each and every broken bone, open gash, and bleeding body. All badges of courage. All stories to tell your friends, certainly not to your folks.

But as drunk as Dean was, he was not stupid. He would not be goaded into putting himself at risk. "Nice try, Stanny Boy, but the only one who's jumping is your little friend here. Hold Stanny down, boys."

Worm released Fred and joined Kane in restraining Stan. While still struggling, Stan was now further secured by the two boys. Fred found himself surprisingly freed altogether.

Dean yelled to Fred, "Hey little dip shit, run away, and we'll pummel Stanny for your trouble. And before your friend tells you 'it's okay, Freddie, run,' know that when he comes to, battered and beat to shit, he'll always blame his chicken shit friend who betrayed him. So, little turd, you are going to jump…or else."

The train rumbled toward them. In a minute, it would be upon them.

Stan pulled at his captors, then accepting they had a lock on him, screamed out to Dean. "No, you shit. I'm the one who knows the punk that you are and the pathetic family you come from. You hate my father, fine, then hate me. You know Fred's too small to do this, you thick-skulled pig."

Stan struck a raw nerve and Dean became incensed. "Get that Black kid now and hold him for all you're worth," he hollered, over what was becoming a thundering loud locomotive. He directed Kane and Worm to drag Stan over, closer to his friend. Then, they grabbed Fred and released Stan. The hostage switch was made. Now it was Fred who was held by Dean's companions, and Stan who was freed.

"Jump now, Johnson. Jump now or I swear we'll kill this little bastard."

Fred yelled to Stan not to do it, but his words were drowned out by the stampeding train. Stan, believing that Dean was out of control, and would definitely hurt Fred, committed himself to do the unthinkable. He would attempt to "jump" the train.

He began running parallel to the locomotive in an effort to match the speed of the giant machine. As he ran, he angled closer to the train, scanning the side, for both a handhold and foothold. Finally, he spotted a metal bar that was within reach. He ran faster, in order to make the grab. He extended his arms and lunged toward the steel monster. And within a flash, Stan Johnson's body disappeared.

Chapter 56

The scene was surreal. The train had passed. Four boys were standing exactly where they had been standing only seconds before, when the train approached. One boy, who had stood with them only moments before, was nowhere to be seen.

Dean's head swiveled from left to right and back again. "Hey, Johnson, where the hell are you guy?" he yelled as loudly as he could. Whatever beer buzz he had felt was gone, replaced with a sense of fright. His pulse raced as he scanned the landscape for the boy he knew he had placed in jeopardy.

Fred shook off his captors, who had lightened their hold on him anyway. The three of them stood dumbstruck. Johnson had been running alongside the train, seemed to make the jump, and then instantly disappeared.

Worm and Kane looked at Dean and clearly noticed his nervous expression, something they had never seen before. They both knew and trusted their leader enough to know that if he was worried, they should probably be worried too. Dean turned to them and sharply yelled, "Look for Johnson. For God's sake, look for that kid!"

Dean and his friends scrambled around in all directions, perusing their immediate surroundings. For his part, Fred took off, running along the same path his friend had jogged, just moments before. His heart pounded, and he fought back the urge to faint. Then, to his left, he noticed a dark form at the bottom of the gravel filled ravine. He screamed, "I see him! I see him!"

Fred tripped and stumbled his way down the hill and reached Stan in thirty frightening seconds. His friend was face down, lying in a pool of blood. He knelt next to Stan and was shocked to see his friend terribly injured. He turned and cried out, "Go for help...go...go...go! Get help, get an ambulance...go...go...go!"

All three boys, to their credit, turned immediately, and with determination of purpose, ran as fast as their out-of-shape bodies could move, looking for help. A car came into view, driven by a middle-aged man. They waved him down. He pulled over, and using his CB radio, called 911.

An ambulance arrived twenty long minutes later, and EMTs rushed to Stan's body. After administering emergency care in assessing and stabilizing Stan, they carried him up the steep ravine that rose to the tracks and placed him in the ambulance. Fred climbed the hill, behind the medics carrying his friend, and stood, drained and weak, as he watched the ambulance drive away.

Thirty feet away, the other three boys also stood, all shaken by what they had just witnessed. The leader of the three felt a fear even greater than what he had felt only days before. He knew he was responsible for Stan's condition. A sense of dread and self-loathing overcame him.

Dean no longer felt strong and in control. He felt alone. He felt worthless. He wished it was him in the ambulance, and not the young boy he had put there. Dean knew that Stan's life may never be the same, if he lived at all. He also knew his life would never be the same. Dean stared into the distance with no particular focus. And although he was frightened, he no longer could feel any sympathy...for himself.

Chapter 57

Victor received the call while sitting with Maggie in Peg's ICU room. It seemed strange that anyone would phone him while visiting his comatose wife. He walked out the door to the nurse's station and was directed to a phone sitting on a desk against the wall. "When you pick up, push the blinking button, sir," directed a very young-looking RN.

"Drueding." Victor quietly said into the receiver.

"Mr. Drueding, It's Ben Richards, down at the police station. Sorry to call you at the hospital, but it's something important."

"Yeah, what is it?"

"Your son, Dean, Mr. Drueding. I don't know if he's in any trouble, but we brought him and two of his friends down here a short while ago. I've been hesitating to call you at all, knowing everything you're going through, but I figured I had no alternative." He paused, as if to consider how he would describe the situation concerning the train and the young boy's injuries. It struck Richards how ironic it was that the young Johnson boy was probably being tended to, only a short distance from where Drueding stood at this very moment. The Emergency Room was not far from the ICU.

Victor almost dropped the phone. He didn't know how much more his heart could take. For months, his nerves had been frayed from constant anxiety, followed by a short respite. Then, the tragic assault to his wife, with it's uncertain, and possible horrific outcome, yet to be known. Now, his son was sitting in the town's police department. "What more?" he thought. When would all of this catch up to his own health? He figured he must have had an ulcer already. "What next?"

Before the detective found the words to continue, Victor asked solemnly, "Should I just come down there, Detective?"

"I'm sorry to even have to ask you to, but it's probably best. Do you have a way to get here? I'll be glad to come over and pick you up."

"Nah, I'm with a good friend of ours. She'll bring me down there. Give me a half hour and I'll be there. That okay?"

"Sure, that's fine, Mr. Drueding. Just ask for me when you get here. And thanks."

Victor walked back into Peg's room and sat for a few minutes, while he quietly asked Maggie if she would give him a ride to the police station. She nodded in the affirmative. They turned once again to the injured woman, lying unconsciously in bed, and continued to chat casually with her.

Immediately upon their initial visit with Peg, it had been recommended that they communicate with her in a normal fashion, with the hope of making a connection. They were told that people would oftentimes come out of a comatose state and confirm having heard conversations, however vague a memory it may have been.

Ten minutes later, after telling Peg they would be gone for a short while, they left the hospital. If there was any change at all in Peg's condition, a nurse knew how to reach them. The fact of the matter was, there was no location in Centerville more than a quick drive to any other location, so they were very accessible in any event.

As Victor and Maggie entered the police station, they immediately saw Detective Richards, who was obviously waiting for them. He hurried over to his visitors and thanked them once again for coming. As Victor was about to introduce Maggie to Richards, she interrupted him, and said, "The detective and I have already met, Victor. You remember, I killed the bad guy the other day. I spent quality time in this fine establishment on Thursday afternoon."

Both Victor and Richards looked at Maggie, who although sounded altogether serious, was obviously making a little light of the situation. She always knew her audience well, as both men caught themselves beginning to grin and then thought better of it.

The detective refocused on Victor. "Here's the short of it, Mr. Drueding. Your son and two of his friends were with two other younger boys, out near the railroad track earlier today. A train came through and one of the two younger boys tried to jump it. The new and ultra-stupid game some genius kid made up a while back. Anyway, the boy today got badly hurt and is in the Emergency Room at Hayes. There is a possibility that your son and his friends somewhat forced this boy into doing it. So, we're checking things out."

Victor took a few moments to process what he just heard. "How the hell do you force someone to jump a friggin' train?" he asked, puzzled at the whole story. "Did he pick the kid up and throw him at the train? Did he push him into the train? I don't even get what you're saying." There was obvious irritation in his voice, as his emotional condition had no margin for patience.

"I know, I know, Victor." Detective Richards was himself somewhat stressed out by the events of the past few days, coupled with the story Victor had stunned him with at the restaurant. He even failed to notice that he called Victor by his first name, an infraction of a discipline he had always adhered to, when working with witnesses or other people of interest. "That's why I told you over the phone that I don't even know if Dean or his friends are in trouble. Could have simply been a 'dare' or accusing another of being a chicken shit if they didn't jump. We just don't know right now." He glanced over at Maggie and said, "Sorry for the language, ma'am."

"I don't give a shit," she replied in a deadpanned manner.

There was another pause. Neither of the two men even attempted to fight their response mechanisms now, and both laughed simultaneously. A short burst for sure, but one so necessary, as they turned toward the woman with a hint of appreciation in their eyes.

Detective Richards, again composed, pointed down the hall. "They're down there. We haven't made things uncomfortable for them at all. In fact, they're in a room with a little television set turned on. We told them, because someone got hurt, we just had to get their versions of what happened. But frankly, Mr. Drueding, I instructed our guys not to question anyone until you had a chance to speak with your son. I really believe this is just stupid kid stuff, that ended badly. But why don't I set another room up for you and your boy and give you some privacy."

"I appreciate that, Detective."

Dean left his friends in the room with the television and walked down the hall to a small office. In the office sat his father. The boy's pulse quickened as he now knew that his father knew. A father that in the past was not overly forgiving to his sons.

Victor was seated and didn't stand to receive the boy. His demeanor was that of a man laying eyes on another, younger human being, for the first time. No familiarity was shown at all. He pointed to a chair on the opposite wall, and Dean reluctantly sat down.

"Dean," he said, "I don't have the patience, time, or interest, in hearing one word of bullshit. Tell me exactly what happened, no matter how bad it was, no matter how bad it makes you look. I'll know if you are kidding me. The cops here may not know, but believe me, I'll know. So, think about what you are going to say, and damn, well, tell me the absolute truth."

The words struck Dean like a sledge hammer. He was looking into the eyes of the only person in the world he feared. He knew his father meant every word he had just said. He knew his father was hurting because of Dean's mother's condition, and he would not be able to feel one ounce of pity for his son. The truth was not going to be met with sympathy. His father may react to what he was about to hear, by simply giving up on his son. The boy's body began to feel weak, and he felt faint.

Victor did not move. He showed no emotion. He just stared at the fourteen-year-old boy across from him. Finally, he said quietly, "I don't have all day. Tell me now."

Dean felt defeated on all fronts. He had lost all sense of self-worth when he saw Stan Johnson lying in the gravel at the bottom of the ravine. It struck him at that moment that he was living in his own little "make believe" world. He knew that his bloated, artificial sense of self-importance was able to exist at all, because two other young and dumb boys gave it credence. Now all that was washed away. He didn't even know who Dean Drueding even was.

He started his story by admitting to taking the beer from his grandmother's home, and after drinking them, going with his friends to prowl around the rail yard, eventually stumbling across Stan and his friend, Fred. He found himself turning angry when he spotted Stan. He told himself at that moment that it was because Stan's father fought his own father, at a parents' sports assembly at school. For a time thereafter, he was teased that Stan's father won the fight.

Dean admitted that the fight at school was only a small part of his angst. The larger reason was the knowledge that Stan Johnson was everything he was not. Stan was popular at school and a terrific athlete. Everyone looked up to Stan Johnson. The only people who looked up to Dean were two very broken boys themselves.

As he listened to Dean's story, Victor's emotions turned from anger and disgust, to something he had never felt regarding the boy in front of him—sadness. Dean continued describing the scene at the tracks, as it played out only hours before, clearly and exclusively taking the blame for the injury inflicted on the popular younger boy. No, the injured boy wasn't pushed or thrown, but he may as well have been. And whatever was Stan Johnson's fate, it was Dean Drueding's fault.

When he finished telling the story, he hung his head and remained motionless. He didn't cry. He didn't make any sound. He just felt empty.

Victor stood up, stepped over to his son, and put his right hand on Dean's left shoulder. He didn't say a word, because truthfully, he didn't know what to say. The Drueding men were cut from similar DNA. Warmth was not a feature they naturally exhibited.

"Dean, stay here for a few moments. I'm going out to speak to one of the policemen. I have a feeling he's going to tell us to go home."

"No," Dean blurted out. "Not yet. Please, please, Dad, please sit down."

Victor was stunned by his son's reaction but found himself doing exactly what Dean instructed. "What's wrong, Dean?" he asked, this time with a sincerity not commonly shown by the big man.

"I have something else to tell you. Something as bad as what I did to Stan."

"Is someone else hurt?" Victor asked, now with an urgency in his voice.

"Not physically. But maybe. I don't know."

"Tell me, Dean. Tell me now."

"I stole some stuff."

Dean continued with his confession of the robbery of Charlie Mann. Victor's facial expression conveyed his upset with this unsettling story. Although he never served in the service of his country, he was empathetic to the plight of any and all disenfranchised veterans, especially those who returned from Vietnam. Hearing that his son stole the memories of this old man bothered Victor to his core. How could a son of his do this? What did he do wrong as a father? He knew the answers to those questions instantly. He had been a terrible father.

At that precise moment, Victor pledged to himself to change, to be there for his sons from this moment forward, and hopefully become a better person himself in the process.

As he was about to respond to his boy, they were interrupted by a knock at the door.

Victor yelled, "Come on in."

It was Detective Richards. "Victor," the detective said, with a serious expression on his face, "You have a phone call. It's the hospital."

Victor's face flushed, as if his blood pressure spiked with the news. Thoughts of Dean's transgressions instantly dissolved, as he nervously followed the detective out the door and toward the front desk.

Dean, seeing and sensing his father's concern, instantly became fearful. He followed his father and the detective down the hall and found himself praying that his father would not receive terrible news.

Victor was handed the phone. "Victor Drueding," he said, and listened intently, while staring straight ahead at a blank wall.

Dean anxiously watched his father and began to shudder, as Victor slowly placed the phone back onto the receiver. He turned to Detective Richards, and then to the young boy. "Your mother just woke up, son. Mom just woke up."

Detective Richards, disregarding protocol, placed an arm around one of the big man's shoulders. "Thank God, Victor. Thank God." He noticed Victor's body quivering and stepped back, giving Victor room to recover and compose himself.

"You get out of here, Victor, and take your son with you. Your friend is out in the waiting room. You all get to the hospital." Victor shook his head in agreement, unable as yet to speak. He put out his hand, and his young son took it. They walked down the short corridor to the waiting room and disappeared from Detective Richard's view.

Seconds later, a female's voice was heard screaming in excitement. Every cop in the police station heard the ear-piercing sound, and all became immediately alert. Richards found himself instinctively calling out, "It's okay, boys, it's no problem." All heads turned back to what they were doing.

Richards walked toward his office, shaking his head and smiling to himself. He thought, "How little does this sleepy town of ours know about the drama playing out in the life of one single family."

At the same time he felt relieved about the phone call of only moments prior, he also harbored a less optimistic concern for the future. "It's not over," he thought. He couldn't put his finger on why, but he kept thinking. "It's not over."

Chapter 58

Victor, Maggie, and Dean arrived at the hospital ten minutes after leaving the police station. The three hustled to the ICU, where a familiar face behind the desk nodded approval for all three to proceed to the room. Down the hall, they entered Peg's room, to find two nurses and a doctor surrounding the bed, obstructing their view. Upon hearing the sound of shuffling shoes behind them, the three health-care providers turned toward the door and smiled in unison. A nurse stepped aside, and the three visitors caught a clear view of the patient lying in the bed, with opened eyes, looking in their direction.

Dean immediately rushed toward his mother while releasing all the tension he had harbored from the day's terrible events. The sheer sight of her gave him a degree of comfort he desperately needed. Though his mother was barely conscious, it didn't matter. Her eyes upon his was enough. He bent over the bed and kissed her on the forehead.

Maggie put her arm around the big man's waist and pulled him toward her. The doctor approached them and quietly uttered, "We have a way to go, but this is a very good sign. Visit for a while, but please not too long. She'll tire easily."

Victor tried to thank the doctor, but was too shaken to speak, so he offered his right hand, and the doctor shook it happily. After nodding to Maggie, the physician left the room. The two nurses finished checking Peg's vital signs and the lines connected to her. When finished, the older of the two placed her hand on Dean's head and gently mussed his hair. Maggie and Victor whispered "thank you" to both of them as they departed.

A breathing tube prohibited Peg from speaking, if she had been able to do so at all, in her weakened condition. Nevertheless, the three pulled chairs up to the bed and made small talk to a receptive, appreciative, and most importantly, awake patient.

Although in a lethargic fog, Peg noticed Dean's apparent anxiousness and looked toward Maggie, making a gesture for something to write on. Catching her meaning immediately, Maggie grabbed a chart from the end of the bed and flipped over the top page, yielding a clean sheet. She held the clipboard close to Peg's right hand and placed a pen between Peg's forefinger and thumb.

Peg's grip was weak, but had only a few words to convey, and summoned the strength to do so. Staring intently at the page, she worked hard to write in a legible manner. Once finished, she looked toward her son and back to her message. Dean reached out his hand and turned the chart, so he could see what she wrote.

He read it once, looked at his mother, and solemnly acknowledged her meaning. Although Peg could not have known recent events, she clearly saw the turmoil reflected in her young boy's eyes. She knew something was terribly wrong and that he needed something from her. So, she gave him what she could.

Dean stood up straight and mouthed the words, "I will." His mother's lips turned up ever so slightly at the corners, as she felt a slight tinge of satisfaction, from her minor effort to help her boy. She knew it wasn't much, but it was all she could provide at this moment in time.

The younger nurse reentered the room and asked politely and sensitively if they would let Peg rest for a while. All three were quick to respond, touching and kissing their mother, wife, and friend. As they exited the room, they once again thanked the RN for everything.

Once again, the nurse checked readings and lines, and while straightening out the bed covers, spoke to Peg encouragingly. As she rounded the bed, she noticed the chart sitting on Peg's legs. "What's this doing here, ma'am?" she exclaimed, as she smiled, knowing family members often fumbled with the patient's chart. "Let's put this back where it belongs."

As she was about to place it on the hook embedded on the footboard of the hospital bed, she noticed the top sheet was turned over. She began to correct the sheet's position, when she saw a few words scribbled on the page's backside. Although the handwriting was feeble, it was easily legible. *Be good. Just be good.*

The nurse looked up at Peg and found her asleep, tired out from her experience of reentering the conscious world. The young woman touched the bedspread covering Peg's left foot, grinned at the older woman in front of her, and softly said, "I'm sure he will, mom. I'm sure he will."

As Victor, Maggie, and Dean made their way out of the ICU, Dean noticed a sign indicating the direction to the Emergency Room area. He stopped and stared at the sign. He froze in place.

Noticing they were no longer all together, Victor stopped and turned around. Seeing his son standing still, thirty feet behind them, he said in a soft, but audible tone, "Hey, what's up?"

His father's voice snapped Dean out of a mini trance, his eyes and attention having been fixed on the sign. "Oh," he responded and then remained silent for a few moments longer. He finally turned toward his father and said, in a hesitating fashion, "I've got something I have to do. Can I catch up to you guys in a little while?"

Victor noticed the sign his son was looking at and knew then what was on his mind. "Do you want me to come with you, Dean?"

"No, Dad. I've got to do this alone. That okay?"

"It's okay, boy. You know where Maggie and I will be. Catch up to us when you're done.

Okay?"

"Okay."

Victor and Maggie continued on their way, while the fourteen-year-old boy opened the door leading into the Emergency Room wing of the hospital. As he walked down the corridor to the waiting area of the ER, he came upon a series of Patient Family Rooms designed to give the immediate families a place to collect in private. After going by two empty units, Dean stopped. He looked into the third private room and, through a small window, saw a couple sitting, obviously distressed.

He had seen this couple at various school events. He recognized them. They were Stan Johnson's parents. Dean walked to the door leading into the room. It was open by about six inches. He quietly pushed it open wide. The young couple looked up at him.

Dean entered the private room. And began to speak to Brian and Sandy Johnson.

Chapter 59

Victor and Dean knocked on Charlie Mann's door, one week after Dean had confessed to his father what he and his friends had done. They would have been at the old soldier's door sooner, but it took a week of requesting, demanding, and finally, threatening his two friends to return to Dean all of the possessions they held of Mr. Mann's.

When Dean first approached them about returning the stolen goods, he made it very clear to his friends, that he would not mention their names to Mr. Mann. He told both Kane and Worm that he simply had a change of heart and realized the awful consequences of what they had done. The older man had risked his young life many years ago, and they had stolen the possessions that connected him to the memories of that fateful time.

Kane and Worm were not impressed with Dean's initial pleas to return the bounty. In fact, they had come to consider the items of

Charlie Mann's their very own property. Kane reminded Dean of the old adage, "possession is 90 percent of the law." This forced Dean to play his trump card, telling them if they did not give back the goods, his father would be visiting their homes to discuss the situation with their parents.

Dean wasn't sure who frightened his friends more—their parents or his father. But if he had to bet, his money would have been on his dad. He was scary looking and had a less than stellar reputation in the town of Centerville. Whatever the motivating factor was, promises were made to retrieve and return the stolen property within days. Although Dean didn't know why it would take days to act upon his request, he figured the main objective was achieved, and he and his father would visit Mr. Mann's soon enough.

April 14, Saturday

They waited until late afternoon, with the presumption Mr. Mann would be back home from whatever outside activities he may have had. They were correct in this assumption. Charlie Mann answered their knock at the door at 4:30 Saturday afternoon.

Mann wasn't accustomed to visitors, whether in the morning or in the afternoon. Before answering the door, he peeked through the side of his living room shade and noticed two men. If it wasn't for the fact that one of the figures was obviously a young boy, there would have been no way in hell he would have opened the door. Still, he opened it with some trepidation, as he clearly noticed the sheer size of the other figure.

"Can I help you, gentlemen?" Charlie asked, with a forced posture of confidence and bravado, although he didn't feel either.

Victor spoke quickly, knowing his son was feeling a mixture of nerves and fear. "Hello, Mr. Mann, my name is Victor Drueding and this is my son, Dean. My son has something to tell you, and I came along for support, because this is very difficult for him to do."

Charlie shifted his gaze from the older and larger man to the younger and smaller boy. His anxiety level dropped precipitously as he listened to Victor speak, and he shook off all concerns regarding ill intent on the part of his visitors.

The veteran read the uneasiness in the boy and figured he was the prankster who took a baseball bat to his mailbox post last year, or who egged his house the previous Halloween. Whatever it was, it did seem like a good idea to admit your transgression with your large daddy at your side. That thought somewhat amused Charlie; that anyone might be the least bit intimidated by this old, broken-down version of himself. At the same time, he actually felt somewhat special that he was part of a life lesson the father was imparting on the son.

Still, the boy appeared to be a nervous wreck, and the veteran spoke in a tone meant to settle the young lad. "Son, I'm all ears, and know that whatever it is, things usually seem far worse than they actually are."

Dean looked up at his father, who was staring forward. Victor was not in the least interested in easing the way for his boy; not for this situation. He was there for Dean, singularly to induce the young man to do the right thing. He would not allow his son to give in to his instincts and run for the hills. He had to follow through. He had to take his medicine.

Dean hung his head and mumbled a few inaudible words. Charlie strained to hear what was said, and figured once again, that his hearing was slipping. But that was not the case, at least in this instance. Victor did not hear the words either. He nudged his son and quietly instructed him to repeat what he had said, but louder and more clearly.

Dean lifted his head, glanced at Mr. Charlie Mann, and though every nerve in his body screamed in agony, announced clearly, "I stole your war souvenirs, sir. I stole a bunch of your stuff and I've brought it back to you today. I'm sorry. That's why I'm here." He turned and picked up two large plastic garbage bags. "Here," he said, "It's all in good shape and it's all here."

Charlie Mann was not a healthy man and was emotionally and psychologically unstable. Since his return from Vietnam, he lived in a fragile condition, never fully recovering, yet never a threat to anyone other than himself. The robbery had caused Charlie great despair, although he never reported it. The truth was that the old soldier always found a reason to blame himself for whatever went wrong in his life; his fragile psyche always ready to accept guilt, no matter how unfair to the old man.

So, when the boy and his father announced the reason for visiting Charlie, the veteran met the news with a stunned expression. He looked puzzled for a moment and then appeared weakened. He felt his strength drain from his body and leaned against the door's threshold, so he would not collapse. Victor noticed the strain on the older man's face and grabbed his right arm, hoping to steady him. "I've got you, sir. Why don't you sit down somewhere?" He looked around and realized that probably meant moving inside, but was not about to suggest that option.

"Help me go in," Charlie feebly instructed. "I just feel weak. The couch is right there." Victor supported the slight man as they slowly shuffled their way inside, to a beat-up brown sofa positioned against the right-hand wall of the living room.

Dean continued to stand his ground on the top of the steps outside. When the screen door shut, his father and Mr. Mann disappeared from sight. He didn't feel entitled to follow them in, so he just stood there and guarded the garbage bags containing the precious cargo.

Victor sat next to Charlie on the sofa and spoke to him about mundane things, in a casual, conversational tone. He didn't outwardly show concern for the physical or mental state of the man, rather he acted as though Charlie and he were just old friends, shooting the breeze about nothing.

At one point, Victor deliberately turned his head toward the front door, with the intention that Charlie noticed. Then Victor uttered, "Oh" as if he was surprised to see his son still standing outside and asked Charlie if it was okay to ask Dean to come into the house. Charlie followed Victor's glance toward the door, and upon seeing the small silhouette standing just outside, said, "Of course, tell him to come in."

Dean had been listening intently to the conversation within the room as his father helped Mr. Mann to the couch. Immediately, he picked up the two garbage bags and entered the home. He sat in an overstuffed chair across from the two men, placing the bags on the floor in front of him. Charlie noticed the bags, and it reminded him what Dean had admitted to, only a short time before. Charlie's mind and body slowly settled, as the sense of dread he had felt, dissipated.

"So, that's my stuff, son?"

"Yes, sir, all of it."

"Would you mind taking the things out? Right now, I can't remember exactly what was missing."

To Victor, Charlie's mood seemed passive and somewhat disconnected. It was a state he had found himself in on many occasions over the years and felt an unexpected empathy toward the older man. He put his large right arm around the shoulders of the frail body next to him and said softly, "Charlie, we'll look at everything closely and make sure all the items are in the condition they were. Also, Charlie, if you want, either Dean or I will come over to your house on a regular basis, only if you want, and help you do whatever chores you need to have done. Does that sound okay, Charlie?"

Charlie looked up at Victor's face and with a slight uptick in his energy level, replied, "That would be very nice of you." Looking over at Dean now, he repeated, "That would be very nice of you too, son." Dean, for the first time since arriving at Mr. Mann's house, stared directly into the eyes of the veteran and shook his head to the affirmative. "I'd be happy to do so, sir. I would really like to do that." He turned toward his father realizing this was a side of his father he had never seen or experienced. His father nodded to him and gave him a barely perceivable hint of a grin.

Victor pulled his arm back, leaned over, and grabbed one of the bags. "Now, let's see what we've got here, Mr. Mann." One by one, Victor pulled out the war memorabilia. As he did so, Charlie described what the object was, where he came in possession of it, and what it meant to him.

One of the items was the hunting knife that Dean remembered when they were dividing up the loot at Kane's house. He lost this item to Worm however and was, at this moment, happy that Worm had included it in the return, as Dean would not have remembered it otherwise. Charlie told the story of the Battle of Hamburger Hill in May of 1969 and how a young private gave him this knife, as a *thank you* for helping him stay alive.

One by one, the stories came and went. Both Dean and his father were riveted by each and every one of them. Charlie became more engaged and alert as the afternoon wore on. He never even had this level of attention and connection at the VFW, as important as that community was to him.

When the bags were empty, Dean reached into his pocket and pulled out the box. He stood up, took two steps toward the couch, and reaching out, placed the box holding the medal into the old man's hand. Without knowing exactly why, Dean already knew that this would be the most cherished of the items he stole. The young boy's mood darkened again, as a wave of unbearable guilt rushed over him. He backed up, his head down, and stood quietly.

Charlie opened the box and peered at the Purple Heart. It was in as pristine condition as it had been when it sat in his bureau drawer. He stared at it for a few minutes, as Dean and his father looked on quietly, allowing the man his memories. Charlie then stood up, on his own, making a gesture to Victor that he was okay. He walked into his kitchen with the box, and a drawer was heard opening and closing.

He returned, the box still in one hand; in his other, something else. He sat back down on the couch, placing the Purple Heart on the end table next to him. He looked over at Dean. "Dean, you're probably a little young for this, but I want to give you something in front of your dad." Turning directly to the big man, he continued, "Victor, you can take this from your son and give it to him at a later date, if you think it wise. I want Dean to have this, for showing bravery coming here today and admitting what he admitted to me. It takes guts to do that."

The frail veteran reached out and grabbed the hunting knife, that had been given him so many years ago. He took the knife and inserted it into the item he had just brought out from the other room—a sheath. Not a normal sheath, but as he illustrated to Dean, a leather sheath with a strap, allowing it to be belted around a person's calf. Dean had thought the knife was incredibly cool by itself, but this added feature made it Rambo cool.

Charlie extended the sheathed knife in Dean's direction, and said, "Here, I want you to have it. Again, your father can take it from you the moment you leave this house, but it's yours. The private from Hamburger Hill would have liked this. If I die, and the knife was found in a closet by some family vulture, the story of the knife would have died with me. But it will stay alive with you. Someday, pass it on to someone else that exhibits courage. Deal?"

Dean held the knife in his hands and felt a mixture of emotions he never knew existed. He looked up at Mr. Mann, then to his father, and back to the veteran. "Deal, sir. Thank you."

A short time later, they said goodbye to Mr. Mann, promising once again to be around on a regular basis. Victor gave Charlie his phone number and thanked him for everything. The old veteran stood at the doorway and watched them until they were out of sight. He moved back inside the house, sitting once again on the couch. He picked up the box containing his Purple Heart and opened it. He stared at the medal and thought back to a day when he was a young soldier.

And for a few moments, a wave of pride washed over him.

Chapter 60

San Diego
April 11, Wednesday

Steed discovered a newfound respect for the internet. With the introductory lesson given to him by a friendly librarian, he was able to run searches for the location of the person he sought. Additionally, having met the pilot's wife at their apartment the year before, he was able to cross reference her information to the pilot's. Steed primarily targeted the state of Missouri as it was the likely place to find them. Ultimately, he found the pilot and his wife in Centerville, Missouri.

Steed revisited the library, asking the librarian for further assistance. She was able to do a deeper forensic dive into all information relating to Victor Drueding. Steed told her that Drueding was a long-lost family member, who he wanted to surprise, after almost twenty years.

In truth, Steed figured the more information he had on the pilot, the more believable his backstory would be, when speaking to anyone in Centerville. He would be winging it enough. The more he knew, the better.

He summoned Max and told him to prepare for a road trip. The following Tuesday, they would drive to Missouri. Steed would use the next few days to plan the trip, traveling as much "off the grid" as possible, leaving little evidence of their movement. Once in Centerville, they would settle on a final plan of action.

The thought of capturing the man who stole the helicopter gave Eriq Steed chills. He would extract from the pilot the whereabouts of the chopper and then enjoy settling all debts with the thief, in a creative and satisfying manner. Steed would deal with the pilot's wife as well. These situations almost always involved collateral damage.

His mood sky high, Steed rummaged around his apartment for an item he hoped he'd have the opportunity to use. In a drawer in the bathroom, he found it. The metal scalpel could be hidden easily, along with his hand gun. If things did not go smoothly, the gun would have to do. If all went well, the scalpel.

Using the surgical instrument meant inflicting the pain and suffering well earned by the large, stupid man. Steed didn't just want to kill the man. He wanted to punish him.

As his twisted mind imagined the scene he hoped to be played out in the little rural town he was heading to, Steed began to smile. He waved the scalpel in front of him, and thought, "Maybe I should have been a surgeon." He smiled widely and made himself laugh. His oversized teeth impressing no one, as he danced around his small apartment, all by himself.

Chapter 61

April 16, Monday

Detective Richards received the phone call at the station.

"Richards here. How can I help you?"

"Detective, it's Agent McKenna out in San Diego. Got a moment?"

"Absolutely, what gives?"

"I checked around, and there very well may be something to what you told me. We have our share of missing people, of course, but most have family members who have filed reports. Then, there are peripheral cases, where the odd call comes in, reporting an apartment tenant who didn't return, or someone simply disappeared from a job. The common denominator with these reports is that no family members seem to even exist. No formal reporting of any kind."

"Agent McKenna, how does that help us?"

"Well, first, let me say, call me Bob. The Agent McKenna thing still throws me for a loop. Sounds like someone I don't even know. That okay with you?"

"Good by me. And I'm Ben."

"Great. Here's the thing, Ben. A couple was reported not returning to their apartment building around the same time you say a murder took place at that helipad you mentioned. I visited the residence and spoke to the super. Says a very nice couple, and not at all the type to skip out on paying rent. Also, who skips out paying rent and leaves all their furniture in the apartment?"

"Unless it's shit furniture."

"True enough, but still not a normal thing. I also checked out the helipad you mentioned. Otay County sold an old army helipad installation to a non-profit, or something like that, about five years ago. County officials said some eccentric old bird wanted to have it in order to preserve it, or some story along those lines. The official doesn't think it was ever used as an operational helipad, but he said they frankly never paid much attention to it. We're trying to locate the owner and tell him we'd like to take a look at it."

"So, Bob, is this enough to continue looking into my guy's story."

"Bet your ass it is. And I'd like to come out there and speak to him, if you don't mind."

Richards' reaction even surprised himself. "Mind, God no. When can you be here?"

"How about this Thursday, the nineteenth. I want to visit your man. And tell him I'll want to see the helicopter. How's that sound?"

"That's great, Bob. See you Thursday."

"Look forward to it."

Chapter 62

April 16, Wednesday, late morning, Hayes Hospital

Victor, Maggie, and Dean spent the better part of two hours at the hospital visiting Peg, who had been recovering nicely. Assuming Victor and Maggie would be there, Detective Richards had phoned Victor early in the morning and asked if he and Maggie would meet with him after their visit. They scheduled to meet in the hospital cafeteria at twelve thirty in the afternoon.

Just before noon, Victor and his companions sat down at a cafeteria table with a variety of sandwiches, two cups of coffee, and a soda. Whenever Victor and Maggie discussed things around Dean, they were careful not to say too much. The boy knew something had happened in Dot's house, but did not know anywhere near the true story.

The town, surprisingly enough, had been kept in the dark as well. At least it seemed that way.

They chatted about Peg's condition for a while, each so happy that she was trending in the right direction. Dean, with his quiet and outwardly cool demeanor, was beyond elated with every tidbit of good news regarding his mother.

When conversation regarding Peg was over, Victor said, quite abruptly, "Maggie, before I forget, there's something I want to tell you that can't go any further than this table. Okay?"

"Not if you murdered someone," she lightly answered and then caught herself in the reflection of Victor's eyes. Joking related to murder and violence in general, probably inappropriate always, were definitely not timely these days, and especially in front of the boy. Maggie's peripheral vision spotted Dean totally consumed in wolfing down his tuna sandwich. She mouthed "sorry" to Victor, and he continued.

The big man rolled his eyes, conveying the fact that he knew Maggie was just being Maggie, and then proceeded to inform her that Dean and he were moving back to Dot's house that evening, having received permission from the Police Department. He went on to say that all investigations pertaining to the house were completed, and the green light was given for the family to return.

Victor asked Maggie not to tell Dot this fact for a few days, as he wanted a little time for Dean and him to spruce the place up. He figured it would be emotionally difficult enough for the elderly woman to return home; at least he wanted the house to look inviting and as clean and normal as possible.

"Once everyone is back in the house," he explained "the cops will drive by more frequently and keep a watch on the place. At least for a while."

Victor looked over at Dean and seeing that the boy was preoccupied with a magazine, he lowered his voice. "Also, Maggie, Dean's not going to return to school this year. A decision reached by everyone concerned, including Dean. I was able to get him a job at the airfield, so the move back to Dot's house couldn't have come at a better time. You know, the field is just down the road. He can roll out of bed and be there in minutes."

"Wow, I guess that's great," Maggie replied, with absolutely no conviction in her voice. "So, when does the rest of the fam return. Next week?"

"Yeah, the rest of the fam, including you. Please hang with us for a little while longer. We need you badly."

Maggie reached over and took the big man's hand. "Every now and then you say something that reminds me why I love you so much, you big lug. I'm not going anywhere. At least for now."

Before Victor and Maggie finished their sandwiches, Dean stood up and announced that he had to go to work. There was an upbeat tone to his voice that Maggie was unfamiliar with.

"What kind of work will you be doing, Dean?" she asked.

"I think I'm the gofer and the general clean-up guy. The job was described as doing anything and everything nobody else wants to do." Dean smiled after he said this, which was again, an oddity to Maggie. She couldn't remember ever seeing the boy smile.

"Well, do a good job doing what everyone else won't do," she said, kiddingly.

"I will, Maggie. I intend to work my butt off." He looked at his father, said goodbye to both adults, and left the cafeteria. Both Victor and Maggie watched the boy hustle away, looked at one another, and had the same thought. "This job might give the boy a sense of purpose and responsibility he simply needed, to thrive." Without saying a word, they looked at each other, both with hints of a grin.

No sooner than Dean was out of sight, Detective Richards appeared and sat down in the chair only minutes ago occupied by the young boy.

"How're the sandwiches here, lady and gent?"

"Not as good as served at the fine Italian restaurants you frequent," was Victor's retort.

"Well, the last time I met you at one of those, I left a perfectly good chicken marsala uneaten. And I blame you for that, sir."

"What's new? Everyone blames everything on me."

Richards chuckled and then immediately turned serious. "Listen, guys, the federal agent from San Diego is coming tomorrow. He'll want to speak to both of you at length. Especially you, Victor. So, I want both of you to be prepared. Go over everything in your minds tonight about what you know and experienced concerning all of this."

Richards looked around for a waitress and then realized he was in a cafeteria.

"Shit," he blurted out. "I need a coffee, but it'll wait. Victor, even if this means a little trouble for you, my friend, please be as forthcoming and truthful as you can be. This guy can be a powerhouse of a friend, and we need him and the resources of the federal government. Capeesh?"

Victor, with a deadpanned expression, pointed his very large right index finger in the policeman's face. "First, you look for a waitress in a hospital cafeteria and then you throw around Italian words, like you work for Interpol. Are you just trying to impress the hell out of us, or what?"

The detective glared at the large finger extended in his direction, his expression indicating acute displeasure. Maggie wasn't sure what she was witnessing but became uncomfortable with the change of atmosphere at the table.

Richards leaned forward, his face almost touching Victor's accusatory digit. In a low, deep voice, he proclaimed, "I took a chance even coming here, you behemoth. As I said, the last time I met you at an eatery, I never touched my chicken marsala. So, big boy, the way I see it, you owe me a dinner. Capeesh?"

Victor grinned every so slightly, and withdrew his finger. "Know this," he stated firmly, "When this shit is behind us, I'll be glad to buy you any dinner you want. Deal?"

The detective sat back in his chair and smiled.

"Deal, my friend."

Nothing more was said, but all three had the same concerning thought simultaneously

Chapter 63

April 19, Thursday

Federal Agent Robert McKenna flew to Missouri Thursday morning, arriving at Centerville Police Station at noon. He and Detective Richards sat together for two hours, discussing every aspect of what each other knew, in an effort to link Victor Drueding's story and his wife's shooting, to unsolved, incomplete mysteries, connected to the San Diego area.

None of the various incidents they discussed provided any hints of closure. Stories simply left off, dangling, with no ending. And this was exactly the reason for McKenna's visit. After meeting with his law enforcement counterpart, the Federal Agent planned to sit with Victor and Maggie, to draw every tidbit of information from their memory banks.

McKenna was trained to consume dates, names, descriptions of people, and any other information he could collect, in an effort to couple storylines and create hypothetical pictures, by merging that which previously seemed unrelated.

McKenna's instincts told him there was something very real and serious here. He was beginning to believe they were on the verge of uncovering a crime saga, much larger than delivering drugs to Mexico. He didn't know where his investigation would lead him but had an ominous feeling about what he would find.

The agent met with Maggie Crotty next. She arrived at three o'clock. Although Maggie was a primary figure in the shooting scene at Dot Collin's house, she really didn't have much to offer. She recounted who and what she saw, prior to killing the perpetrator. McKenna did press her, however, on everything Victor and Peg may have said while staying with her in Truth or Consequences, and anything else she could remember pertinent to his investigation. Maggie was totally forthright, as Victor had asked her to do so. She left having told the young agent everything she knew.

At five o'clock, Federal Agent Robert McKenna found himself sitting face to face with one of the largest men he had ever been in the company of. Victor Drueding began his account of the entire ordeal by going back to his origins at the airfield outside of San Diego. Working hand in hand, at a very young age, with his father, Victor described how he developed a love of all aircraft, especially helicopters.

He spoke of his youth, which was one he did not remember fondly. But when he met his future wife, Peg, he thought for a time he might find happiness after all. They probably should not have had children right away, but they did. The very abbreviated period of time when Victor felt the comfort of contentment faded when the children entered the picture, and his financial struggles grew.

The difficulty of life in his younger days, now continued into his adulthood. The result of having a wife and three children he was barely able to provide for cemented his sense of failure. His depression was feeding on itself, and they decided to let their children live with Peg's mother in Centerville.

Then, one day, a knock came at the door, and Eriq Steed walked into their lives, bringing with him an offer of hope.

Victor continued his story, with as much detail as he could recall, concerning the Mexican activity, his involvement, and all the other participants. He spoke with clarity, was concise, yet comprehensive. His voice only stammered once, while describing the scene at the helipad, seeing his associates murdered and their bodies lying on the ground, next to the smiling thin man. He would live with that memory, of witnessing the carnage below, forever.

McKenna listened intently. Fortunately, the tape recorder captured everything the big man said, as the agent found himself lost in Victor's incredible story. There was an innocence about it all, that McKenna was not accustomed to. He was used to the criminal mind, typically an inept one, spewing a contrived yarn, in order to shed a positive light on themselves. This was not the case. The man in front of him was emptying himself as if he were facing St. Peter at the gates. He held nothing back. It was truly a confession. No doubt the absolute truth. No matter what the consequences.

And maybe that was what the big man was thinking after all. What Maggie had said to him, only a few short months ago.

Chapter 64

April 20, Friday

Steed and Max arrived in Centerville late Friday afternoon. Steed had paid cash for a rental car in San Diego, using a driver's license and credit card obtained under one of his many aliases, for identification. Likewise, they paid cash when checking into a very small roadside motel, three towns removed from Centerville. They carried burner phones that they expected would have very short shelf lives. All efforts to minimize a paper trail.

Steed was conscious of the fact that two strangers walking around a small town like Centerville might draw attention, so leaving Max at the motel, he drove into Centerville by himself. He parked at what appeared to be a very active diner, where he assumed some people were sure to know everyone else's business. He was correct.

He struck it lucky with the first person he said "hello" to—his waitress. "Well, hello, ma'am," he said with the affable voice that tended to disarm people, especially women. The waitress responded in kind, and after Steed asked her for her recommendation from the menu, he placed his order accordingly.

He chatted her up during her occasional visit to his table, and when his meal was finished, he waited for her to come and collect his cash payment. He deliberately placed the bills in such a way, she would immediately notice the overly generous tip. "This is the best meal I have had in my two days of travel, ma'am. And the service you gave me was top shelf. Thank you very much."

"You're absolutely welcome, sir. Thank you very much," she noted, as she looked down at the bills spread out on the table. "You're quite kind. Where were you driving from, may I ask?"

"Elkhart, Indiana has been my home for the past few years, but as a sales road warrior, I am all over the place, Well, thanks again, ma'am. I'll be hitting the road as always."

"Well, nice meeting you. Good travels."

Steed stood up, and just as the waitress turned to walk away, called out to her. "Ma'am, I'm sorry, one last thing, if you don't mind."

The young woman turned around, and with a curious look on her face, responded, "Yes?"

"Ma'am, as I was reading the paper, waiting for my meal, I thought I heard two people say something about a man called Drueding. I know it's a long shot, but I have a good friend from my past called Victor Drueding, who I lost touch with years ago. For some reason, I think I heard that he moved to this neck of the woods. Again, total long shot, but would you possibly know a Victor Drueding?"

A knowing look appeared on her face, as she clearly had information for Steed. "Is he a large man?"

"Large? He's two of me. This is great. Does he really live around here?"

"Well, I don't know exactly where he lives, as I personally don't know him, but a Victor Drueding and his family live out near Pavilion Field, our small airport in town. Do you know where that is?"

"No clue, but that's okay, as unfortunately I have appointments tomorrow and the next day, so I have to hit the road anyway. But this is so cool. I'll be coming back this way in about a month, and I'll track him down by phone before I do. Thank you, thank you. I'm so happy I asked. And did you say, 'his family'? It has been so long, I didn't even know he was married."

"Yep. For sure. Wife and kids. In fact, his oldest son, Dean, works with him at the airfield. You can tell this is a small town, and you're lucky you're in a diner. Everybody knows everybody else's business." She smiled and then said, "Good luck finding your friend. I really have to get to my other tables. And again, thanks for the tip."

"Thank you, ma'am. You've made my day."

She turned around once again, as Steed mumbled to himself, "You've made my day, sister, more than you could ever know."

Back at the motel, Steed phoned Max's room, and confirmed to him that Drueding was indeed here in Centerville. Steed told his aide that he wanted to be alone for a while, in order to think. He laid on his bed and considered the possible scenarios that would play out.

The thin man had total confidence that he would react effectively to whatever circumstances presented themselves. His abilities to improvise, and create on the fly, had been proven many times over throughout his adult, criminal life. He would certainly have no problem manipulating the yokels of Centerville. In fact, it would be enjoyable.

After a while, a knock came at Steed's door, and Max's voice called out. "Quick question, boss." Steed opened the door, but did not invite Max in. "What do you need, Max?"

"Just would like to know the timetable. When and where?"

Steed grinned at his underling. "Get some sleep, Max. Tomorrow's the big day."

Chapter 65

April 21, Saturday, Noon

Dean worked all morning cleaning hangers and mowing various patches of lawn surrounding the group of buildings that made up the infrastructure of the airfield. Along with providing gofer service for the staff at Pavilion, he was slowly being acquainted and indoctrinated with the most basic of aircraft maintenance tasks. Soon, when he was trained sufficiently, he would add landing strip inspection to his repertoire of responsibilities.

It was impressed upon Dean by all at the airfield that conscientiousness and attention to detail were critical at all times in the service of equipment and people at the small airfield. To prove the seriousness of the field's demands on those in its employ, it was pointed out to Dean that something as seemingly innocuous as a pothole on a landing strip could cause a fatal crash.

Pavilion's manager, Teddy Thompson, took every newbie under his wing, with one objective. Teddy would not allow any new employee to continue forward in his or her tenure at Pavilion, until it was proven to him that every action taken by the rookie was in the very best interest of the lives of its clients and members, each and every day.

In Teddy's initial presentation to young Dean, he spoke of the type of person he sought to be part of his team. He pointed to a particular employee who exhibited the exact traits he was looking for. Teddy described how quickly he was impressed by the seriousness and professionalism of this individual. Within the first few days on the job, Teddy saw immediately, that this person not only had the knowledge of his craft but also had a fastidious attention to detail, to correctness, and to total accountability.

Dean asked if this person still worked at Pavilion, and Teddy replied, "He better still work at my airfield; I would be lost without him. And, by the way, he's your father."

Dean swelled with pride at that very moment. He was stunned by the realization that, until those words left Mr. Thompson's mouth, "by the way, he's your father," Dean had never really appreciated what his father did for a living. Over the past few weeks, Dean found himself beginning to see his father as he had never seen him before. And in doing so, he began to see his future self, hopefully as a better man. He had become convinced that his life's new direction was, without a doubt, worthwhile. He was finding appreciation where he never knew it existed. And in contrast, he faced the hard reality, that up until now, he had not been living a life, his parents, nor he, could be proud of.

It was lunchtime, and Dean was about to make the short walk home to his grandmother's house, for a quick sandwich and soda. As he was heading out of the hanger's main doors, he saw a figure walking toward him, waving in a friendly manner. Dean didn't know many of the people who owned planes, but figured the guy had a question regarding his aircraft. He decided immediately that he would not take the chance of possibly giving erroneous information. He would simply direct the man to the main office, although he knew no one of authority was there at the moment.

"Hello, young man," called out the stranger. "Where is everyone? I have questions regarding flight lessons." Dean was relieved to hear a question that he would not be expected to have any knowledge about. "Sir, you'll have to speak to Mr. Thompson. He's the manager here and would be the one to help you. If he's not around, I'm sure he'll be back soon."

The man put his hands into his windbreaker pockets, and shivered somewhat, although it certainly wasn't a cold day. "Any chance you can help me on something else, son?" He seemed to catch himself and then continued. "Sorry, I always hated it when people called me 'son'. What would your name be?"

"My name's Dean. I'll help you if I can, but there's not much I do here, except clean up. What do you need?"

"I'm also looking for a man named Victor. I hear he's an excellent aircraft mechanic. I intend to purchase a single engine plane and take lessons on that particular aircraft—the one I'll be flying. The idea being, when I get my license, I'll already be totally familiar with the airplane. Sounds pretty smart, huh?" The man smiled widely, indicating his last comment was a lighthearted one. "So, I'll be needing some basic aircraft mechanic instructions as well."

Dean was about to say that Victor was his father, when his concentration was broken by the sight of the man's unusual smile. In Dean's fourteen years, he had never seen such large teeth framed within such a skinny face. He just nodded to the man and replied, "He's not here either." Dean's stomach growled, reminding him he hadn't much time to get home and eat.

"Where would you suggest I wait for Mr. Thompson, Dean?" asked the thin man, now with an added familiar tone to his voice.

"Over at the office, sir. I'm going by there now, so I'll show you where to go."

"That would be great of you. You lead, I'll follow."

Dean and the stranger stepped into the small building that housed the airfield's office and spoke briefly to an elderly gentleman, there primarily to answer the phone and contact Mr. Thompson in the event of an emergency. Once again, Dean suggested to the visitor that he wait for the airfield manager at this location.

"Dean, where might you be going, son?" The skinny man asked, somewhat surprising Dean with the question.

"Just shooting over to my house for a quick sandwich and then coming back, sir. It's just a stone's throw from here," he replied, as he motioned with his right hand in the direction of his grandmother's house.

"Any chance your father might be there now, Dean? I'm really in a hurry and I would just like to shake his hand and possibly set up a meeting at another time. I'd be in and out in a flash. Okay if I come with you and see if dad is there? I won't stay but a sec."

Dean felt a little uncomfortable with the man's forwardness but didn't know how to say "no" without insulting him. "Sure, I guess," he found himself answering, although something didn't quite settle well with him.

"Super, then let's go. I'll have a short chat with dad, then back to my car, and out of your hair. How does that sound?" The smiley man laughed, as if amused by the mere sound of his own voice.

The young boy and the skinny man walked away from the office building and toward the path leading to Dot's home, while the boy's discomfort level continued to grow. Dean couldn't shake the thought that something the man had said seemed odd. But he just couldn't put his finger on what it was.

"So, this is where your grandmother lives, huh, Dean? Who else besides your father lives here?" The thin man acted the casual friend, while the young boy continued to feel the discomfort of a situation he didn't ask to be in. He didn't know this man and wondered how, all of a sudden, they were standing together in front of his grandmother's house.

"Did you hear me, Dean? Who else lives here?"

"Just me and my dad right now. My mother, grandmother, and my brothers are returning in a few days."

"Why? Where have they been?" The skinny man was now being openly pushy and had become very intimidating, staring directly at the boy with each question. He repeated himself, asking once again, "Why? Where have they been?"

"Visiting friends, sir." Dean, feeling very nervous now, still abided by the instructions given to him, not to divulge any information pertaining to his mother's injury or the whereabouts of his family. "I'll run in and see if my dad's home. But I kind of doubt he is." Dean hustled up the porch stairs, turned the knob of the unlocked door, and burst into the house.

Almost immediately, he turned back, with the intention of yelling out, that his dad was not around. As he did so, he bumped into the skinny man, who had evidently followed him up the steps. "Oh, sorry," Dean said with a surprised tone to his voice. "My dad isn't here and possibly he won't be around for some time."

"But I thought you said he would be right back?" The man smiled in such a way that now appeared menacing to the boy. Up until three weeks ago, Dean thought of his grandmother's house as his safe haven. If it were not for the realization that something bad happened to his mother, in this very room, he may have thought differently about his current situation. But now he clearly knew that the man standing next to him might be a bad person, and as the hair stood up on his arms, he felt the chill of fear overtaking him.

"I thought he would be sir, I'm sorry." He tried to hide the fact his body was beginning to quiver.

Chapter 66

April 21, Saturday, Noon

Detective Richards drove Agent McKenna and Maggie to Westford to visit the new photo laboratory connected to the Westford Police Department. This adjunct office was recently built, in an effort to enhance the abilities of surrounding police departments, in a broad range of investigations.

McKenna was hoping they might discover the identity of the man Maggie shot in Dot Collins' home. As Maggie was the only person, besides Peggy Drueding, who had seen the man alive, her input, along with photos of the deceased, could very well be critical in the investigation.

Victor was to have joined them, but asked if he could catch up with them, as he felt obliged to first visit his wife's mother. He had not had the chance to visit Dot in a few days and clearly knew she was still in a very fragile state. He planned to stop by Dot's friend's house, where she was still residing and check on her. McKenna understood completely but asked that Victor make his way to Westford as soon as he could.

The photo lab had updated technology, and the agent felt there was no better time than the present, to begin searching all avenues in their investigation, including possible facial recognition of the bad guys back in San Diego. Obviously, Victor was critical in this endeavor. One never knew who might be recognized as they scanned a criminal photo bank.

As Detective Richards was driving, McKenna, sitting in the back seat, laughed. "I've been in Missouri approximately forty-eight hours, and I've driven this route twice already."

Richards looked into the rear-view mirror. "What do you mean?"

"One of my guys and I had the helicopter transferred to a warehouse in Westford yesterday, where my buddy is doing forensics on it as we speak. We followed the flatbed that brought it there, and I'm now looking at the same scenery we passed yesterday. But I have to say, this is a nice part of the country."

"Sure is," chimed in Maggie, who was sitting in the front passenger seat. She turned around toward the young agent, and continued, "And by the way, I have never seen anyone fly a chopper like the big man. Victor is a talented pilot. I saw him hover, spin it, bank it like a hummingbird; up, down, and sideways. The guy can fly the shit out of that thing."

McKenna couldn't help but chuckle. "I'm not here looking for a pilot, Miss Crotty. My associate and I are here looking for murderers. But I'll keep Mr. Drueding's skill set in mind, in case the government is looking for a huge human to fly small aircraft for them."

Both Richards and Maggie laughed at the otherwise conservative young G-man actually cracking a joke. "Good one," Maggie blurted out. "You're starting to sound like a real live regular person. Better watch out or you'll lose your job."

"If you don't rat me out, I'll be fine. But that does bring up another thought, Miss Crotty." He changed his tone to indicate he was about to ask a serious question. "You don't have to answer this if you don't want to, but what do you make of Victor Drueding? I know you haven't known him for long, but you obviously made a connection with him and his wife, or you wouldn't have come out here to visit them. So, what do you think? What's with Mr. Drueding?"

Maggie turned again, this time away from the agent. She quietly stared out the front windshield for a full minute, considering how to answer the question. She knew what she wanted to convey but was contemplating how to say it.

"Mr. McKenna, Victor is a good man, but he is a conflicted man. He wants to do good, but life has not been easy for him. I think he went from being a lost young man, whose parents died far too young, to becoming a lost husband and father. He's talented in a limited field and is simply trying to find his way."

Maggie paused for a moment, as she struggled to remember something from the past. Then the memory came to her, and she continued her assessment of her friend.

"My dad used to say, 'that some people just needed to find the right seeds; plant them and watch them grow.' By that he meant, find the right path for yourself, dig in, work hard, and time would take care of the rest. The right seeds will produce a healthy and bountiful world for you, your family, and those around you."

Maggie again turned back toward the agent. "Blame my father for those sentiments. He was kind of a hippie, if you know what I mean." She smiled at the young man in the back seat, who was looking at her with all seriousness.

"Agent McKenna, I don't believe Victor ever really found or planted the right seeds for his life. I think he's still looking for them. But I know, in my heart, that Victor Drueding is a good man."

Richards looked over at Maggie and subtly nodded his head. "Son of a bitch," he uttered. "I think I actually understand what the hell you just said." He then smiled at the woman next to him, who grinned back at him, grabbed his right arm, and mouthed "thank you."

The young agent in the backseat remained silent.

They arrived at the Westford Police Department and within a short time were scanning through the photo database.

Chapter 67

"Dean, I really am in a hurry. I'll get out of your hair, but first phone around, if you must. We must find your father. Tell him someone is here to see him. It is business now, Dean, and your father would not want you to ignore a business opportunity for him, now would he?"

Dean hadn't a clue where his father was but felt calling someone might be a good idea in any event. He knew Maggie and his grandmother were staying with a friend of the family, not very far away, and figured it might help his situation. "I can try, sir."

"Excellent, my young man, excellent. Give it a whirl." The stranger looked around and spotted the house phone sitting on a wall table across the room. He pointed to the black phone and nodded for Dean to start making calls. Dean hustled over to the phone, and for a moment considered angling to the left, and running out of the house. However, this man gave the appearance of a person, who, although thin, was wiry and strong. If he chased Dean down and caught him, there was no telling what he would do.

He took the phone and called the number he had committed to memory; the phone number where his grandmother was now staying. The phone rang twice, and an older woman's voice answered. "Hi Grammy. It's Dean."

"Dean, I'm thrilled to hear your voice. How's the working man doing, kiddo?"

"Work's good, but that's not why I'm calling. Is Dad around by any chance? I've got an airport question for him."

"No, honey. He and Maggie drove over to the Westford Police Department to meet with a policeman from the west coast. I don't know exactly what they're doing, but it has to do with what we both know about. Know what I mean?"

"I know, but is there a way to get a hold of dad?"

"I suppose I could call the police station. Is it that important?"

"Kind of. I wish you would do that if you don't mind. I really need to talk to him. Someone is here to see him, and they don't have much time to wait around."

"Who's there, Dean?"

"I don't think you know him." Dean found himself lowering his voice, so as not to be heard across the room where the stranger was acting like he was flipping through and reading a magazine.

"I know everyone around here, kiddo. What does he look like?"

Dean lowered his voice even more now, and whispered, "Very thin, with a mouth full of huge teeth." He figured he whispered so softly that even his grandmother didn't hear what he had said.

She had heard and laughed, as she figured whoever was there was standing not far away from Dean. "You're a funny kid, Dean. I'll try to find your dad and have him call you. That okay? What's the phone number there?"

Dean was surprised by the question. His grandmother obviously knew the phone number of her own house. "Grammy, it's your phone number."

Dot was stunned, as she had figured her grandson was at the airfield. "Dean, someone is in the house that you don't know?" Her heart began to race. Then, unexpectedly, the front door opened, and in walked her son-in-law. "Dean, your father just walked in. Let me put him on the phone." She started to reach out and hand the phone to Victor, when she heard Dean's voice, louder now, and sounding very nervous.

"No, Grammy. Just tell him to come over here. Now." Then he hung up the phone.

Chapter 68

Victor looked bewildered the moment he entered the house and had a telephone thrust into his face. He heard Dot say, "your father just walked in," and presumed it was Dean on the other end of the line. Then, just as he reached out to take the phone from his mother in-law, she jerked it back and hung it up.

"Dot, what gives?" Victor asked, concerned by the expression on the older woman's face.

"That was Dean. He wanted you to know a man was with him, who wanted to speak to you. Dean doesn't know the guy and the boy seemed a little nervous."

"That's fine, Dot. Dean doesn't know most of the people who come through the airport. Remember, he just started working there." Victor now seemed to understand the situation and figured he'd make a quick stop at the airfield on his way to Westford, once he sat with his fragile mother-in-law for a few moments.

"No, that's not all, Victor. Dean whispered that the man was with him…in my house, not at the airfield. He's alone with a stranger in my house." Her face looked strained with worry.

Victor's eyes widened instantly, and his nerves awakened in a way that had become so familiar to him over the past many months.

"What else did he say, Dot? Tell me everything he said."

"Nothing really, Victor. I asked him what the man looked like, and again he whispered, 'A skinny man with big teeth.'"

Victor knocked over an end table as he lunged for the phone that was now sitting on the arm of Dot's chair. She looked shocked at his unexpected and almost violent motion.

Victor knew Dot's home phone number by heart and punched the buttons with urgency. The phone rang only once on the other end.

"Yes?" answered a familiar voice, that although expected, gave Victor's nervous system a jolt, as the hair on his arms stood up.

"I'll be there in minutes," was all the big man said.

"Be sure to knock," was the brief reply.

Victor placed the receiver down and glared at Dot for a few seconds. "I've got to go, Dot." He turned and walked briskly out of the house, consciously trying to control his breathing. He knew this was no time to lose his physical or mental control. This was not the time to panic.

Dot followed him to the door, and when his car pulled away, she rushed back to the phone.

Chapter 69

Dean looked at the man who just hung up the phone. "Was that my dad? Is he coming over?" Dean had succumbed to his fear. His knees were weak, and his heart pounded. Although he hadn't a clue what was going on, he knew he was in peril.

At that very moment, it struck Dean what the man had said earlier, that made him feel uneasy. Dean had never mentioned to the skinny man that Victor was his father. But the stranger knew this. Dean's senses swirled. Now, escaping from the house seemed to be the wise thing to do. Whatever the risk.

He ran toward the front door, but the stranger reacted with incredible quickness. He grabbed and held Dean in his arms, that were shockingly strong. The man turned Dean toward him and peered directly into his eyes. His lips turned up, and his large teeth now looked more ferocious than anything else.

"You're not going anywhere, my boy. You're staying here, and we'll wait for that son of a bitch of a father of yours. Then, the fun will begin."

Dean shook violently within the skinny man's grasp. "Who are you?" He cried out.

The stranger nestled the side of his face against the side of Dean's face and whispered. "My name is Steed, son. But you won't have to worry about that. For long."

Chapter 70

Victor knocked at the door, as he was instructed to do. The familiar voice answered, once again sending a chill through Victor's entire body. "Enter, pilot," the thin man instructed. Victor slowly turned the knob and pushed the door inward, very much expecting these could be the last seconds of his life. But he had no choice.

The door opened halfway when Victor saw his boy sitting, tied up on a kitchen chair that had been brought into the living room; a rope wrapped around his gaping mouth, enabling him to breath, but not much else. Directly behind Dean stood a lean man, smiling from ear to ear, almost suggesting an eager host awaiting his guests to arrive. And in many ways, that is exactly what Eriq Steed was.

In Steed's right hand was a semiautomatic pistol, the same weapon he used at the helipad; a nightmare Victor could never escape. But the extreme emotions Victor had experienced at the scene of the couple's deaths were now exceeded in pain and raw nerves, as he peered into the eyes of his oldest son.

Paralyzed in the moment, a surge of guilt compounded the fear, loathing, and self-debasement that weighed on Victor like heavy armor. His instinct was to plead to the murderer, who held his son captive, to shoot the father now, get it over with, and escape. Just allow his son to live.

Before Victor could react in any vocal or physical manner, Steed spoke up. "I've been waiting for this opportunity for months, pilot. You have damaged my life in a way you will never understand, but here, at this precise time, my psyche is healing by the moment. I wish we could visit for the entire afternoon, but unfortunately, I know time is short."

Steed pointed the gun toward another kitchen chair that was situated only a foot from where Dean was held. The gunman's left hand appeared from behind his back, holding what appeared to be a wad of rope. He flung it at Victor, the rope hitting the floor in front of where the big man stood.

"Let's get comfy, big guy. Sit down right here and do exactly what I tell you to do. If you don't do what I say, when I say it, or if you make any movement I find distasteful, I will unload a full clip into your bastard son's head. Got it, asshole?"

Chapter 71

Dot placed a call to the Westford Police Department, asking to speak to Detective Richards. The Detective had been scouring photos with Agent McKenna and Maggie in the annexed facility.

When the main desk advised him of the call, he picked up the extension just outside the viewing room in the Photo Lab.

"Richards here."

"Detective, this is Dot Collins," Dot's voice sounding frantic.

"Yes, ma'am. How can I help you?"

"It's Victor, Detective. He was here only a minute ago but ran out the door." Dot paused a moment to catch her breath. "Victor had just phoned my home and spoke to someone, but I'm not sure who."

Richards could hear the anxiety in her voice but was not at all clear to what she was getting at. "Is there a problem, Mrs. Collins?"

"Yes, sir, I think there is a problem. Victor's son, Dean, just called me saying he desperately needed to speak to his father. He was at my house, Detective." She stopped to breathe once again and collect her thoughts.

"And?" asked Richards, his brow now furrowed, as he strained to understand the urgency in her voice.

Dot continued. "Dean's not alone, sir. The boy sounded frightened. He told me he was in my house with a stranger."

"Who was the stranger?"

"I don't know, Detective. I told Dean I know everyone in town, and to describe him if he didn't know his name." Again, a pause.

Richards knew the older woman was laboring to relate her story, but he felt frustrated, none the less, with the stop-and-go conversation. "And?" he asked once again.

"Then my grandson whispered, 'He's a thin man with very large teeth.'" Before Dot could continue, the detective broke in, "Don't go anywhere, Mrs. Collins; stay right where you are." He slammed the phone down on the receiver.

McKenna could somewhat overhear half of the conversation from his vantage point in the lab and recognized the frustration on the part of the detective. Then, unexpectedly, he heard the crashing of the receiver on the phone bed. Richards' loud directive followed immediately. "McKenna, come with me. Hurry. Maggie, you stay here."

The two men ran down the hallway toward a side door, leaving Maggie standing alone and puzzled. She went to a nearby window and saw Richards' car race out of the parking lot and onto the road heading toward Centerville.

Chapter 72

Victor sat on the kitchen chair, situated next to Dean, with the wad of rope on his lap. Steed instructed the big man to tie each of his ankles to the two front metal legs of the inexpensive chair. As Victor tied himself, he noticed that Dean had his ankles tied to the legs of his chair as well; his forearms were strapped to the metal armrests.

When Victor was done securing his ankles in such a way that satisfied Steed, he was told to put his hands together behind his back. "I'm going around you and tie your hands. If you so much as twitch, I guarantee I'll have time to pull the gun out of my pocket and finish off your kid. Got it?" he screamed at the seated man. Victor immediately shook his head, still mentally swirling with fear and confusion.

Within minutes, Steed had secured Victor's wrists, walked around, and faced the father and son. "Well, I would say I have two peas in a pod," the skinny man happily chuckled, his casual attitude making him look and sound even more sinister than usual. "I have a quick text to send, and I'll be right back to you guys." He pulled out his cell phone and punched a message to his accomplice. When he was done, he stepped backwards, to the front door, and opened it a crack.

"I'm going to have a little company for a few moments, boys. But don't worry, I'll only be right outside. I'd say, 'don't do anything stupid,' but I don't think I have to. You can't." He laughed loudly, enjoying his own warped sense of humor. He slid one foot out the door, stuck his head through the opening, and looked around outside.

Max drove up to the front of the house, jumped out of the car, and ran up the porch steps. "Nobody in sight anywhere, boss. What do you want me to do?" Steed gave instructions to Max to pull the car around and park it on a narrow road behind the house. He was to leave the car and run back to the same vantage point he had just come from, watching for any cars coming in their direction. Steed was aware of the possibility that police would show, and Max was to alert Steed by phone if he spotted anything.

Steed didn't need much time. He would have the information he sought from the thief, within moments. The kid's presence assured Steed of that. When the pilot divulged the whereabouts of the chopper, Steed would escape out the back door, and to the car. Once he cut their throats.

If Max were to call, Steed would quickly finish his work, jump in the car, and wind his way through the back roads. He would meet Max at a predetermined location, and they would drive out of the area, never to return. The cops would find the bodies, but nothing more. Steed and Max would be gone.

The mystery of the father–son murders and Peg's shooting, ironically occurring at exactly the same spot, would become a folklore of tragedy. The town would become a focal point of law enforcement and crime analysis, no longer a sleepy midwestern community with barely a story to tell. While Centerville would be on the media map for terribly sad reasons, Steed and Max would be off the map, living in obscurity, in locations unknown.

As Steed and Max spoke quietly to one another just outside the front door, Victor made eye contact with his son. He whispered, "I'm so sorry, Dean." The ropes in Dean's mouth prohibited him from saying anything intelligible, but he wasn't interested in speaking at all. He opened his eyes wide, as he looked intently at his father and then deliberately turned his gaze downward. He quickly looked back up to his father and then down once again, in an effort to communicate that his father do likewise.

Victor understood and lowered his eyes toward the floor. He noticed Dean's right pant leg hitched up almost to his knee; the result of the boy's loosened right hand, having been grabbing and yanking at his jeans, all while the two killers were preoccupied. Victor's eyes were drawn to an unexpected sight. The top of a handle. The handle of a hunting knife sheathed along the boy's bare right calf. The knife given to him by the old soldier.

Victor's pulse began to race even faster than it had been. He looked upward again and saw the two figures still speaking. He knew time was very limited. He turned toward Dean, who had continued to pull at his ropes, as his father looked away. Dean had loosened his right leg ever so slightly, but enough to allow him to raise his calf upward. Simultaneously, he pushed his right arm toward the floor as far as he could, straining against the tension of the rope. His index finger reached the sheath's snap, and he was able to pop it. With one coordinated effort, between his right hand pushing downward, and his right calf pulling upward, he managed to make the desired contact.

He grabbed the mahogany handle of the carbon steel hunting knife, and thrusting his leg downward, unsheathed the knife. The gift that the soldier had given Charley Mann, as a *thank you* for getting him home alive, was securely held in the right hand of the fourteen-year-old boy.

Dean could not turn the knife and effectively cut the rope securing his right forearm, and he surmised there was no point in cutting the rope securing his leg. He looked at his father and then down at his dad's hands, tied behind the big man's back. Victor knew immediately what his boy was thinking. Victor shifted his tied hands toward his son, in a strained effort to give Dean an angle and opportunity to carve away at the rope.

Victor, his mouth still untied, as the monster needed him to talk, whispered to his son, "Just cut. Don't worry about me. Rope, skin, whatever. We have no time. Cut."

Dean shook his head in understanding. With as much torque and pressure as his small right hand and wrist could muster, he slid the cutting edge of the knife along the coils of rope wrapped around his father's wrist, slicing back and forth as fast as he could.

"Faster, cut." His father implored him once again, attempting to keep his voice as quiet as possible. The old veteran had bragged about the razor-sharp edge of the carbon steel blade but emphasized its danger if one was not too careful. The blade was doing its job but was also straying from the intended target in the process. Victor's skin was being torn by the erratic movement of the blade. Blood was flowing, but Victor barely felt the pain. There was no time for that.

As the strands of rope began to pop, a voice rang out, from the direction of the front door. "How're you boys doing over there? Did you miss me?" Steed had sent Max on his way, with their game plan well understood. His tone suggested he was enjoying every minute of his well thought-out strategy and was particularly happy with how everything was playing out.

"Well, guys, here's the plan." He pulled out what appeared to be a very thin knife from his back pants pocket. "As we unfortunately don't have much time, I am going to ask you, pilot, a couple of questions. You will answer my questions quickly, and truthfully, or you will watch as I use this handy scalpel on your son's face." Steed approached the two seated figures. Looking at the young boy, he asked, in a delighted tone, "That sounds like fun, you little shit?"

Steed, now standing between the father and son, placed the scalpel against Dean's right cheekbone. He turned and looked down at the father, about to make his first inquiry, when he noticed what appeared to be a pool of red on the floor.

Chapter 73

As the puddle of blood came into focus, Steed quizzically uttered, "What the hell?" He instinctively figured it was the result of the tightly tied rope having dug into the pilot's wrist. What else could it be? This amused the thin man. He must have been so amped up, and pulled the rope so hard, that it cut into his prisoner's skin. "Oh, well," he figured, "He'll be dead soon enough anyway."

As he turned his eyes from the pool of blood to Victor's face, he was about to tease the captive with a glib, torturous comment. As Steed began to speak, the big man violently yanked on the compromised ropes that tied his wrists, now sliced to thin fibers. His bloodied hands burst from their bonds, with a loud snap. The skinny man's expression was one of shock, as Victor swung his arms outward and caught his captor by the neck.

His feet bound to the legs of the kitchen chair, Victor's only hope was to maintain a grip around the murderer's throat. If the skinny man freed himself from Victor's grasp, both father and son would be at the mercy of an enraged devil.

Victor pulled the much lighter man toward him, and purposely leaned to his right, toppling both men over, and onto the floor. Steed held on to the scalpel, with the single intention of attacking the pilot's neck. If he could make contact, the razor-sharp blade would do the rest.

The men found themselves staring into the eyes of the other, with practically no space between them. The skinny man's face reflected a disgust for his adversary, as if he were insulted by this lesser man, now having the audacity to fight back. "I will carve him and his son up," was the fleeting thought of the depraved man, now struggling to free himself.

Propelled by a rush of adrenaline, the combatants fought to kill the other. Steed lunged the knife in the direction of Victor's head, but Victor purposely held his left elbow out, in a defensive posture. Nonetheless, the scalpel found the upper arm and shoulder of its target. As Steed's hand frantically jerked back and forth, shirt fabric began to shred, torn easily by the surgical instrument. Blood followed. Much blood.

Dean was witness to the lethal fight directly at his feet. He struggled wildly to somehow free himself and help his father. The boy's heart raced, powered by fear. A rush of sadness overcame him when he saw blood pour from his dad's upper arm. He couldn't bear seeing this bigger-than-life person, his father, being hurt. But he was helpless, a trapped spectator to a nightmare.

As Victor squeezed Steed's neck, he felt a searing pain in his upper arm and shoulder. He knew the scalpel was a short blade yet razor sharp. He also knew it was as lethal as any knife. And more strikes would be coming.

The muffled sound of a phone ringing could be heard in the chaos. The skinny man began jerking his legs violently, kicking Dean's lower body in the process. The maniac was trying to create enough torque, to wrench his neck out from the grasp of the pilot. Steed's body jerked wildly about, like a crazed animal.

Dean was frantic. He needed to do something. Anything. Although his hands, feet, and mouth were tied, he still could rock back and forth. Without hesitation, he swayed his upper body slightly backward and then, with all his might, drove it forward. His center of gravity caused the desired effect, as he toppled face first. His bound body and chair, landed upon the knees of the man trying to murder his father, containing his efforts to kick himself free.

Steed felt a weight land upon him and his hate grew all the more. "These two bastards will pay with their lives," raced across his mind. He tried to scream out but could not find the breath to do so. He swung the blade with increased intensity. Again, and again.

Victor cringed with each strike of the scalpel, his upper body cut repeatedly. He forced himself to focus singularly on one objective; he could not let go. He squeezed harder and forced his fingers deeper into the man's throat. His thumbs found the trachea, as he forcefully pressed inward. The big man's fingers, strengthened from a young age as he worked side by side with his father, dug into the sides of Steed's neck. Bone or cartilage, or both, made a crunching sound.

The thin man's efforts to kick himself free began to diminish, along with his energy. Sensing this, but without relaxing his hold, Victor allowed himself to stare into the devil's face. Steed's black eyes extruded outward, reflecting his loathing, even at this moment. His mouth was open wide, exhibiting his giant teeth; his tongue quivered, covered with a whitish foam.

Victor knew it was the end. But before he lightened his grip, solemn thoughts came to him. As he gazed into the face of the heinous creature, Victor recalled the image of the young, married couple, lying lifeless on the helipad floor, and his wife lying unconscious for days in the hospital. Kevin and Elaine didn't deserve their fate. Peg didn't deserve to be hurt. His son didn't deserve this horror. And how many others were destroyed by this wretched monster?

Steed's head lolled over to one side, limp, as life departed his body. Reactively, Victor pushed the dead man away. He didn't care to touch the evil thing another moment. The big man felt dazed and weak but refused to pass out. He heard the sound of his son's muted sobbing.

Then, the front door crashed open.

Chapter 74

McKenna was first through the door. There was no knocking this time. He unloaded one burst of gunfire into the doorknob, one second before he rammed his right shoulder into the upper panel and crashed through. Directly behind him, Richards, his gun held in his outstretched right hand, was ready to fire at any threatening adversary.

Through the cloud of wooden splinters and dust blasting inward from the exploded door, the two law enforcers were prepared to meet any resistance. But there was none. Instead, they confronted the least expected scenario. Three bodies laid in a human heap on the living room floor. Two seemed to be bound by ropes to the kitchen chairs. The third lay motionless, entangled between the others.

Richards was first to realize it was Victor and his son tied up and most likely injured. Blood was splattered on the clothes of Victor's upper body. Dean lay face down between the knees of the deceased body. The boy was gagged but could be heard making sounds of distress.

Within minutes, McKenna and Richards assured themselves that no one else was in the house, and they holstered their weapons.

Chapter 75

On the advice of young Federal Agent McKenna, Detective Richards made a call and instructed only two police cars, emergency lights off, come to the house. Of course, an ambulance was also summoned, as well as the coroner's vehicle, but again, instructions were clearly made to limit lights and any action that might attract attention.

Dot's house was positioned in such a way, that a number of vehicles could be on site, without garnering too much notice. There was really no reason to drive past the house, as there were no homes beyond hers. If cars were to arrive quietly, there was a chance very little would be seen by neighboring residents.

Agent McKenna was keen on keeping the public's awareness, surrounding this mysterious string of events, to a minimum. In his view, people were still at risk, as this ever-evolving crime puzzle was still clearly unsolved.

Within twenty minutes, the house was a beehive of activity. As Victor and his son were tended to, and the coroner and other law enforcers were carefully handling the gaunt-looking corpse of Mr. Eriq Steed, Agent McKenna's cell phone rang. He took a few steps toward the kitchen and answered the phone. "McKenna here." He listened for a short time and then turned back toward the detective who was kneeling over Steed, hoping to make eye contact. Unfortunately, Richards was looking downward and missed seeing the serious young agent smile.

The Federal agent had just learned that the second of the two arriving police cars spotted a suspicious-looking man ducking in and out of neighborhood yards. It was not a difficult task to apprehend the questionable character, and immediately, the very nervous forty-something began blabbering. He rambled on about participating in activities against his will. McKenna gave instructions that the man be held in the police vehicle and brought quietly to the house. As he placed his phone back into his pants pocket, McKenna finally did make the hoped-for eye contact with his counterpart. As he stared at Richards, he whispered the words, "We have a canary."

Within minutes, the squad car pulled up with Steed's associate, sitting handcuffed, in the back seat. His clothes, hands, and face were dirty from the spills he took trying to run away from the police. The disheveled-looking man had a very frightened look on his face. For good reason.

McKenna and Richards marched Max around the back of the house, and into the kitchen. From the time he was helped up, and out of the police car, Max was talking. It was as if the underling of the recently departed Eriq Steed was releasing bottled-up guilt he had been carrying around for a long, long, time. Once captured, he decided to sing.

Miranda Rights were read to Max immediately, although he didn't care. The suspect appeared almost irritated to have to take a break from his confession, in order to hear that "what he said could be used against him." Max was asked to take a breather, and Detective Richards again spelled out that he had the "right to remain silent."

"Okay, okay," was all Max uttered. Then he continued.

Agent McKenna and Detective Richards pulled out miniature recorders and let the man in front of them verbally spew forth. Max rattled off names that he knew of, mostly aliases, and as much as he knew of the operation. He said he was but a foot soldier; a soldier who knew the consequences of saying "no" to his superiors. He had been living in fear. At least that was his story.

His nervousness seemed to subside the more he divulged. He finally admitted he was glad the nightmare of the past few years was over. Whatever his fate, he stated, would be more peaceful than the life he had been living.

Once finished in the kitchen, a policeman took Max downtown.

The two lawmen reviewed what they had just heard. The dots were finally being connected.

Chapter 76

The next weeks brought further changes in the Drueding family. Victor and Dot were asked again, by law enforcement, to leave Dot's house for a while, as a new forensic investigation took place, this time concerning the death of Eriq Steed. Dot not only had no issue with this request, but she made it clear to her family and the police department, that she would never enter the house again.

The airfield nearby her home had always expressed interest in purchasing her property, and she asked if they still wanted it. They did. In the meantime, Dot made arrangements with her friend, who she was currently residing with, to remain living in her house on a permanent basis. Her friend was glad to have the company.

Peg continued on the mend, with a hospital departure date close at hand. Given Dot's position and the impending hospital discharge of his wife, Victor decided the best course of action was to rent an apartment, which he did in a very quick fashion. It was not a large space, but he felt it would meet the needs of his family, until future events played out. He wasn't even sure if he would be a free man this time the following year. He had admitted to every transgression he could remember committing and had no plans on even attempting to hide anything from anyone again.

He came to grips with the awful knowledge, that his life, and the lives of those closest to him, were shattered to the point of near-death for three of them. He faced the fact that he had failed as a husband and a father, but moreover, that he was responsible for placing his family, the few people in the world that valued him, in great peril.

Although Victor did not know what lay in store for him, he would at least do the right thing by his family, and by the law. Let the chips fall where they may. He only hoped his family would be okay.

One day, as Victor was moving a few possessions into the new apartment, he received an unexpected phone call. It was Pete Lynch, the manager of the airfield in Garden City, Kansas, the last stop he and Peg made, on their way to Centerville. Lynch got right to the point, and asked Victor if he thought his son, Dean, might be interested in staying in Garden City, with him and his son, for the following school year. Victor remembered Pete's son, Bucky, who he teased about "filling up the gas and checking the oil."

"Victor, the boys are basically the same age. It would be a great match, especially as I've heard Dean has taken to helicopters like his ol' man. They can both go to school and work part-time at my airfield. What do you think?"

Victor was caught off guard with this totally unexpected call, and before he responded to the man's question, asked, "How did you know about what's going on here, Pete?"

"I really don't. Let's just say someone who thinks fondly of you and your wife contacted me with the idea. I thought it over and think it's a super idea, not just for your boy, but for mine. And hell, if it doesn't work out, for whatever reason, I'll drive your son back to Centerville. What do we have to lose?"

"Let me speak to my son, Pete. I have to say, without having the time to think it over, it sounds like a pretty good idea to me. By the way, can I ask who contacted you?"

"You can ask," Pete said with a laugh, "But I promised not to say. Ask me again in a few months. I'm sure I will have forgotten my promise by then."

Victor was liking this guy more by the moment. "I'll know by then, anyway, Pete. Nobody around here can keep their mouths shut for that long. Thanks for the offer. Let me talk to my wife and Dean. I'll get back to you tomorrow."

"Sounds good, pal. Take care, big guy."

As Victor hung up the phone, a wave of relief swept over him. The person he worried the most about was Dean. His son had been through so much over the years, and especially of late. Sure, much of it was self-inflicted, but influenced so much by the cards he was dealt. If he could start again, in a new place, with a clean slate, what might be the outcome? It was a sliver of hope for his family that was desperately needed, not only for the son but also for the father.

Chapter 77

The apprehension of Steed's right-hand man did not provide a full and complete picture of the criminal activities of Raymond Freeport and Eriq Steed, but did provide critical pieces of the overall puzzle. This was all the federal agency needed. With the insight they now possessed, coupled with their forensic expertise and cutting-edge technology, it was only a matter of time for the balance of the pieces to fall into place.

Victor had already provided the location of the helipad, as much information as he could about the unfortunate couple who were murdered, and the Mexican beach's location. With this information, McKenna garnered support from his Mexican counterparts, and a joint effort was set in motion. In short order, low level players in Mexico were rounded up, as was remaining pharmaceutical inventory in their possession. This led directly to the identity of the drug's manufacturers, initiating further investigation into the underbelly of these massive corporations.

The Feds understood that Victor Drueding was compliant in his role connected to the newly unearthed crime network and activity. They also understood clearly that Victor was the key to their investigation. Additionally, they were sympathetic to the price the Drueding family had already paid.

After a number of behind closed-door meetings and quiet negotiations, it was decided by federal prosecutors, that no charges were to be pressed against Victor and Peg Drueding.

Chapter 78

July 21, Saturday, Late morning

Victor had just returned to the apartment from food shopping and dropping off the kids at the movie theater. He was putting groceries away, when a knock came at the door. Peg was still in bed, gaining strength by the day, but sleeping late most mornings. Victor hustled to the door, so the knocking wouldn't wake her.

The unexpected visitor was Agent Robert McKenna, dressed uncharacteristically, in very casual attire. Victor was about to say hello but found himself first scanning the man up and down. From his footwear, which were a black pair of high-top sneakers, to his tight blue jeans and a light gray sweatshirt, it just didn't seem to fit the same federal agent he had come to know. His dress was a total departure from the button-down, dark blue suits Victor was accustomed to seeing this young man wear. Victor's brief perusal of the person in front of him was to confirm, in fact, that this was McKenna.

"It's me, Victor. See, the Fed logo on my sweatshirt?" the federal agent offered lightheartedly, before Victor could say anything. "We're allowed to be human beings on alternate weekends. Sometimes."

Drueding looked McKenna in the eyes, which conveyed a very relaxed and cordial expression. "Come on in, Mr. McKenna. I'm being a little quiet because my wife is still asleep." Victor beckoned him to sit in the deep-cushioned arm chair just to the right of the door. In their small apartment, the tiny kitchen simply merged into a slightly larger living room. "Please, take a seat. Coffee?"

"I'm good, but go ahead. I know I've caught you off guard," replied McKenna.

"Good answer, Mr. McKenna, because Victor doesn't even know how the coffee maker works," a female's voice called out. Peggy entered the living room area from the bedroom wearing a beige robe over a pair of blue jeans, and slippers.

Just as the federal agent was lowering himself into the chair, he bounced back up, and with a warm smile, responded, "It's really good to see you looking better, Mrs. Drueding. I hope I didn't wake you."

"Nope, I was in there reading, waiting for Victor to finish doing all the grocery work. I was coming out anyway. Nice seeing you, Mr. McKenna." Peg smiled to the young man and, glancing at her husband, gave Victor a wink. "I'm going to make a fresh pot of coffee anyway, and you two gentlemen can figure out if you want some in a few minutes."

McKenna lowered himself once again into the chair, as Victor plopped down on the couch across from him. As Victor descended, the couch let out a squeal, the wood frame obviously strained under the weight of this very large man.

"What's on your mind, Mr. McKenna?"

"First and foremost," the agent said, speaking loud enough for his two hosts to hear, "Please call me Bob from now on. The formality stopped when this sad chapter in your lives ended."

From the kitchen, Peg replied, "No problem, Bob, as long as you call us Victor and Peg. Deal?"

"Deal, Peg," McKenna responded, while nodding to the affirmative. "Now you're probably wondering why I'm here."

The young agent leaned forward, in order not to sink into the deep, ultra-soft cushion of the hefty chair. He assumed this piece of furniture had been purchased with one singular human being in mind. The one he was looking at.

He continued. "I want to thank you both for your efforts over the past many weeks and express the Bureau's apologies for the stress you were forced to experience. The result of your courage and action has undoubtedly saved the lives of many people going forward, on both sides of the border."

Victor and Peg were listening intently but were keenly aware of the agent's body language as well. They both had come to expect the big "but" or "however" that followed flowery language from certain law enforcement officials. Although they liked McKenna, they were instinctively on perpetual alert. It was part of their new normal.

"Victor and Peggy, we at the Bureau have a very unusual situation."

Here it comes, the couple simultaneously thought, and shot hurried looks at one another.

The agent continued, "We seem to have found ourselves with an excessive inventory of helicopters. And with the resolution of the affair we were all just caught up in, we now have even one more craft that we simply do not need nor want. And, as uncomfortable as it is to ask you what I am about to ask, as an obedient soldier of the Bureau, I must do so."

If Victor and Peg were uncertain as to the reason for the agent's visit the moment before he said this, now they were totally mystified. "Mr. McKenna, I mean, Bob," Peg broke in, "you have us totally confused. What are we missing here?"

"You're right, Peg. I'm stretching this thing out too long. I'll wrap it up." The young agent stood up and pulled an envelope out of his

"No shit," Victor replied with a depressed resignation. "I figured we couldn't get out of this mess without one more shoe dropping. What do we owe now that we can't afford?"

"Payment for one Alouette helicopter, to be exact."

"Why, Mr. McKenna, why on earth would we be on the hook for the friggin' helicopter?"

"Victor," Peg's raised voice showing irritation over her husband's rising anger. "Cut it out. We've changed, remember?"

"Yeah, right. Okay, Bob," Victor replied, with the emphasis on "Bob" clearly indicating his irritation. "Why and what do we owe now?"

The agent's tone quieted, almost apologetically. "Sorry, but I've been instructed to give you this." He stretched his hand out toward Victor and presented him the envelope. "If you can swing it, pay this and the helicopter is yours. If you can't swing it, I'll just tell the bureau 'no can do.'"

"I don't need the envelope to tell you 'no can do', Bob." Again, the emphasis on "Bob.'"

"Just take it, Victor, and I'll leave you two to think about it." The agent took a step toward the door, as Peggy grabbed the envelope from Victor.

Both men stopped as Peg began ripping the envelope open and unfolding the invoice within.

She stared at the invoice for a full minute before saying anything. "You're saying if we can 'swing this', then the helicopter is ours, Mr. McKenna?" She handed the bill to her husband, whose mood was souring by the second. "I don't believe it!"

Victor was paralyzed. He could not take his focus off the bill. "Even a damn helicopter could not cost this," he thought.

He studied the invoice up and down:

Seller: San Diego Bureau of Investigation

Buyer: Mr. and Mrs. Victor Drueding

Item: Alouette Helicopter

Price: $1.00

Condition: As Is

"Is this a joke?" Victor asked, with resignation in his voice. Without question, he felt he was being played, and it wasn't settling well with him.

McKenna moved closer to the door, turned and faced the couple. "This is no joke. The helicopter was delivered to Pavilion Air Field last night by two of my best friends in the agency. In fact, they are waiting for me now. We're all heading home together."

He reached into his pocket, "I have the door keys here. That's if you want the chopper." McKenna placed the keys on a nearby end table. "If you don't want the deal, send them back to me. But I'm guessing, you'll want the deal." He smiled at the two most confused-looking people he had seen in a long time.

"Does the government want cash or credit card?" Victor asked, now with the slight appearance of belief and gratitude showing through.

"Send a check, please. Those credit card fees are a killer."

"One more question, Bob...why?"

The federal agent looked down at the floor and answered Peg's question in a solemn tone. "Because you two deserve it. Because you two will utilize it...business, recreational, we don't care. And because you two will appreciate it, like no others we know of."

Peggy walked over to the young agent, threw her arms around him, and, while hugging him, wept.

As they separated, McKenna, damp in the eyes as well, said "One more thing. The aircraft is secure. You have the keys. When you first visit it, I would suggest being by yourselves. The same key will also unlock a customized compartment just behind the back seat on the pilot side. You'll find a briefcase in the compartment. It's yours."

"What's in it?" Victor asked, in a hesitated manner.

McKenna, who had stepped over to the door, looked up at two people he had grown to feel a strong, yet unexpected fondness toward. He had seen their pain, their vulnerability, and, increasingly, their humanity. The agent had been the pivotal influence in the agency's willingness to accept his unprecedented recommendation, regarding the helicopter.

"What's in it?" McKenna repeated Victor's question.

"Let's just say, the seeds to a future."

With that, Robert McKenna somberly nodded to the couple, opened the door, and left them standing there, in silence.

Epilogue

The stunned couple once again sat down at the kitchen table. Peg held a key in her open right hand; mesmerized, as she gazed at it for minutes. Victor, likewise, was transfixed by the simple, yet life-changing invoice reflected on a federal government letterhead.

After a period of time, Victor broke the silence.

"We'll go to the airport in the morning, Peg. I can't handle anymore nervousness today. Also, there will be practically no one around on Sunday morning; maybe one or two people. Not much air traffic over Centerville at that time."

"When exactly is there ever a lot of air traffic over Centerville?"

"Good point." Victor stood back up, his nerves not allowing him to settle. He placed the paper invoice on the kitchen tabletop, continuing to gaze at it. "What do you think is in the briefcase?"

"Exactly what you think is in the briefcase, Sherlock."

Victor lifted his eyes to see his wife, now staring at the apartment door, the door Agent McKenna had just departed from. "What are you doing?" he asked quizzically.

"Waiting for him to come back in and tell us 'April Fools."

"We'd be 'July Fools,' wouldn't we?"

Peg looked up at her husband and smiled. "This is for real, isn't it?"

"Yeah, Peg, we own a helicopter."

"And God knows how much else. So, what do we do for the rest of the day?"

Victor paced back and forth, from the kitchen to the living room, trying to think of something that would occupy their day and take their minds off everything else. Then, it struck him.

He swung around in the direction of his wife, and with a gleam of satisfaction in his eyes, almost hollered, "I've got it."

The big man walked back toward his wife and energetically asked, "Peg, how would you like to go to a baseball game? Centerville plays in the championship game tonight down in Union. Take a nice, leisurely drive. Something different to do. What do you say?"

"My big, rather unathletic husband, your unathletic wife would almost rather be shot again than go to that stupid baseball game. You do know me, don't you? This is Peg you're talking to. You know, your wife?"

Victor wasn't at all fazed by her reaction. "Oh, come on, it'll be a blast. Get some popcorn. We can sit where no one knows us. Act like normal people. How about it?"

Peg continued to sit at the kitchen table. She was still holding the key to the helicopter in her right hand, that for a while had been closed tightly around it. She opened her hand again, stared at it, and thought, "It would be nice to feel like normal people." She couldn't remember what that actually felt like.

Then she looked at her husband and smiled. "Victor, I think going to the game is a good idea. For you. I really wouldn't have the energy to get through the trip to Union, let alone watch a game. And, not incidentally, a game that I think sucks." She winked at her disappointed-looking spouse.

"But I mean it, go. It'll be good for you. I have plenty here to keep me occupied. Mostly the television, which, with you gone, I will control all by my lonesome. That will make me very happy too. And besides, we have a big day tomorrow. I'll need the rest."

Victor sat down again next to his wife. "Okay, I'll go along with that. Although I don't know how anyone can hate the great game of baseball. I'm concerned about you." He leaned over and kissed the top of her head. "By the way, the Johnson boy is supposed to play tonight. You know who I am talking about, right?"

"How could I ever forget? That's good to hear. I hope he's all right. I still can't believe it happened. I'll always feel guilty about it."

Victor whispered, "Me too."

The husband and wife sat quietly for a few moments, as they often did these days, reflecting back to unpleasant memories. Although knowing they could not change the past, that they must move forward, their minds would easily drift back. And in those moments, a sense of sadness and shame would return.

Finally, Peg spoke up. "Victor, would you do me a favor?"

"Sure, what?"

"Would you try to connect with the Johnson boy's parents tonight. At the game?"

"Oh, Peg. I'll try, but I don't know if I can do it. You know?"

"I know. But if you can, just say something, anything, to them. Tell them who you are and they'll just know."

"I'll try."

"By the way, I forget the boy's first name. Do you remember?"

"It's Stan."

Again, they sat quietly, for a while longer this time. Peg finally got up, put her hand on her husband's shoulder, and patted it. "I'm going back to bed for a nap. I don't know if I'm physically or emotionally exhausted right now. I'll see you before you head out for the game. Okay, hon?"

Victor nodded his head, as he simultaneously put his hand over hers. "Sleep well, Peg."

As she walked into the bedroom, Victor thought he heard her say something quietly under her breath. It was a name.

"Stan."

* * *

Many months later...

Without anyone in the town knowing, Victor and Peg Drueding had become two of the wealthiest people in Centerville. They parked their newfound fortune in the bank many towns away, where they were absolute strangers. The couple decided to continue on with their lives as before, and let time dictate their future.

They would not allow themselves to rush into anything. The phrase, "Let's not blow it," was used more than a few times, by both of them. They remained in their small apartment. Victor returned to the airfield and immersed himself in the work he loved. He was able to enhance his income by taxiing passengers, in and around the region, in his newly acquired helicopter. The fact was, he enjoyed flying around so much, he would have flown these people for free. Had his wife found out, however, she would have killed him. So he charged for his service.

Victor kept his ownership of the chopper a secret from the public at large. Only his boss, Teddy Thompson, knew the truth. From all appearances, the Alouette was the property of the airfield, offering an added service to the community.

* * *

Peg joined her mother and continued working in the department store. As before, Peg was employed part-time. She went back to work singularly for something to do. She never did experience the same satisfaction her mother felt in dealing with the public. And Peg never, ever, enjoyed taking orders from younger and, oftentimes, obnoxious managers. It was always difficult for her to hold her tongue.

Now, however, when an overly anxious manager gave her orders at the store, Peg just stared at the irritating little shit and reminded herself she had more than a million dollars in the bank. Knowing she could quit at any time made it easier for her to stay on.

Her mother, Dot, having sold her house to the airfield, was not hurting for funds herself, but Peg overindulged her anyway, by buying her unexpected gifts, for no other reason, than she loved her.

* * *

The younger boys began to thrive in school, both academically and on the athletic front. The sense of love and security they now felt in their home, freed them emotionally, allowing them to enjoy their childhood. As opposed to their older brother, both boys enjoyed academic challenges. And on any sports field, their father's DNA gave them size and strength, the natural advantages that the coaches loved.

Victor and Peg began attending school functions, and slowly were becoming accepted by the other parents. Of course, Peg kiddingly reminded her husband before every school event, he was not to get into a fight.

Dean remained in Garden City, Kansas. He and his best friend, Bucky Lynch, never became great students, but became exceptional helicopter mechanics, on their way to becoming very capable chopper pilots. Dean returned to Centerville frequently to visit his family. It could not have been a better situation, for all concerned.

* * *

Twice, Victor was asked to return to San Diego, to further assist Agent Robert McKenna in the investigation. He gladly complied. Many people were rounded up, from employees of various pharmaceutical companies, to the runners in northern Mexico.

In the end, it became apparent to law enforcement, that the motivation behind the lower-level participants in the criminal network was nothing sinister. In most cases, people were simply fooled into believing, that their actions, although probably wrong, were in many ways serving the greater good. And a few extra bucks in their pocket didn't hurt. To a person, they all pled guilty.

On the American side of the border, the mastermind and his ruthless right-hand man were dead. On the Mexican side, the kingpins of the operation were untouchable, hidden by a complex maze of bureaucracy. McKenna and the Bureau would not actually close the book on this particular case, but in all reality, their job was finished.

* * *

When the active investigation was wrapped up, Victor and Peg visited their friend, Maggie, in Truth or Consequences, New Mexico. They brought with them a business offer.

When they first met, Maggie spoke of the possibility of a helicopter service, not unlike what Victor was doing now. Her idea, however, spoke of delivering urgently needed mechanical parts, on a
"same-day service" basis, to small airfields in and around the Midwest.

When Maggie first mentioned this idea, Victor and Peg were
living in a reality far removed from their present lives. However, everything had now changed.

Over dinner and a few drinks, Victor and Peg reminded Maggie
of her own thinking on this subject and offered her a partnership in a
new venture. The couple would provide the helicopter and fund the
start-up operation; money was no longer an issue of concern. Peg
would manage the office, while Maggie and Victor would do what they
loved to do—fly!

When Maggie accepted the generous proposal, the two women
screamed in excitement, for what Victor thought was a frightening
long period of time. Once the elation subsided, they toasted the cre-
ation of the new entity. Maggie then asked, "What do we call our new
company?"

Peg smiled at her husband, who had already given this issue
much thought. Victor stood up, raised his glass again, and proclaimed,
"We'll call it 'TOC', in honor of your town, Truth or Consequences.
How does that sound, Maggie?"

Maggie stood up as well, raised her glass, and announced,
"Sounds like crap. It doesn't sing. How about 'Tick-Toc', like a clock?
You know, we're going to be 'on the clock' after all, if we're going to run
a 'same-day service.'" Victor looked at this wife and grinned. "It's bad
enough I can't make any final decisions without you second-guessing
me. Now, I'm really screwed."

More hugs and laughter followed.

The next day, corporate papers were drawn up to formalize a new midwestern company; TICK-TOC Helicopter Services, Inc. was born.

* * *

Dot continued to live with her friend. Once her house sold, she could have certainly bought another, but both she and her friend enjoyed the current arrangement. So, she stayed put. "Besides," she thought, "I can see my family whenever I want. And not living with them is probably a little less dangerous."

When Dot found out that Victor was visiting Corporal Charlie Mann's house on a regular basis, doing odd jobs for the old veteran, she offered her baking talents as well. Once every few weeks, she accompanied her son-in-law to Charlie's, and the three of them got on quite well.

Charlie missed seeing Dean but was always happy to see his grandmother. She was a terrific cook, had a good sense of humor, and, not incidentally, was more his vintage than the younger men.

After a period of time, Dot would occasionally drop by the old man's house by herself. Charlie would never admit to it, but when Dot appeared at his door, he felt a youthful boost of energy.

One night, after enjoying a dinner both Dot and Charlie had prepared together, Charlie opened a small box that had been sitting on top of the end table next to the couch. He took an object out of the box and asked Dot to close her eyes.

As she did so, the old soldier placed a ribbon over her head, and she felt the metal clip against the nape of her neck. She opened her eyes, and looking down, saw a military medal. She held the medal in her right hand and immediately recognized it. She knew it was an honor bestowed on soldiers who were willing to put everything at risk.

She was gazing at the simple, yet powerful symbol, when the subdued voice of the older version of one particular soldier, said, "I've never known where to put this, Dot. Never knew where it really belonged. But now I know."

Charlie had placed his most precious medal around her neck and declared, "This is where my Heart belongs, Dot. It belongs with you."

THE END